The Bride's Brother

Iona Rose

Author's Note

Hey there!

Thank you for choosing my book. I sure hope that you love it. I'd hate to part ways once you're done though. So how about we stay in touch?

My newsletter is a great way to discover more about me and my books. Where you'll find frequent exclusive give-aways, sneak previews of new releases and be first to see new cover reveals.

And as a HUGE thank you for joining, you'll receive a FREE book on me!

With love,

Iona

Author's Note

Get Your FREE Book Here:

https://dl.bookfunnel.com/v9yit8b3f7

Chapter One
Evelyn

The high school photos had to be my favorite so far. As I went through the scenes of the couple sitting on the seats where they'd met, by their lockers and where he'd first asked her on a date to the cafeteria, my heart fluttered a little. It was a lovely story, but the way I'd captured every scene in different lighting made me feel very happy. In these pictures, I had told their history, the cracks on the wall, the rust on bars, the chipped paint, broken ceiling corners, and the beaming smiles of the couple themselves. It was fairytale-like and yet it was real.

I was so in love with what I had created.

There was one problem, though. Given that they were my cousin's friends, and they were both blue-collar workers, I hadn't been able to charge them what I normally would.

Not that it was much, but even then, they had trouble paying for my photography.

I looked at the time once again, wondering just how long I'd been in the cafe. I didn't think they had a limit of how long you could stay after buying the cheapest possible drink, which was an iced Americano, but I was ready to pack my things and leave the second any of the staff started heading towards me.

I needed to charge more, and I needed more high-profile clients so I could have something left over after paying my exorbitant, blood-sucking New York rent to repair my broken AC. My inability to call a repairman until I got my next paycheck was once again a wakeup call. I continued on with my edits, anxious to complete it as quickly as possible so that I could post some of them on Instagram and attract some potential new clients.

I had no connections nor did I know any socialites, so this was my only way. This was my fault, though. Rather than spend time during college going to parties and meeting people, I was taking on as many part-time jobs as I could and ignoring the social aspect, which I now realize was the most important aspect of my job.

Sighing, I continued on with my work. When I briefly glanced up to look around the cafe, I met the eyes of someone standing in a corner. She seemed to have purchased some pastries and was sipping on her coffee. However, her attention on me was rapt. It immediately made me self-conscious because this was also sure to draw the attention of the cafe staff.

Annoyed, I looked away from her and continued with my work, but I sent a deep frown her way, hoping that this would immediately put her off showing any interest in me.

I returned to my photos and forgot all about her until I felt someone start to pull out the stool beside me. It was to be expected since I had opted for the window seats rather than an actual table in order to curry more grace for over-staying, so I wasn't bothered, but when I noticed that the person seemed to have their entire focus on me, I looked up and was shocked to see it was the girl that was staring at me before.

She was stunning in a way that made me unable to look away, even though I was unhappy at her intrusion. Her hair was bone straight, shiny, sleek, and jet black, and her eyes were the most beautiful shade of green I had ever seen. Due to my annoyance earlier, I hadn't noticed any of these, but now as I stared straight at her, I couldn't help noticing her beauty.

"Hello?" She smiled.

I nodded in response. "Hi."

"I'm sorry I was a bit nervous to come over." Her glance went to my laptop. "I see you're working, so I know I'm interrupting you." She smiled apologetically, but continued to stare at me. "Sorry," she said. "I've loved your work for so long; I just can't believe I'm actually meeting you in person. You do gorgeous work and I'm just so happy to meet you."

Upon hearing this, all of my annoyance, doubts, and reservations immediately dissipated because she was obviously someone who followed me on social media and loved my work, so how could I in any way be offended or put off by her approach?

Instantly, I gave her a heartfelt smile and offered my hand for a handshake.

I'm sorry," I apologized. "I'm just a bit stressed, so I came off unapproachable. Thank you for coming over regardless. I'm so glad to know you know and like my work; that means so much to me. I mean, I just started so I don't have that many followers."

"You just need time for the right kind of people to find you," she said earnestly. "Because your work is unique... very rustic and special. Most people just go anything pink and glittery."

I nearly laughed out loud at this, liking her even more because she was a hundred percent right. "Thank you so much for saying that; your words mean the world to me because I was just thinking how my style might be affecting my ability to eat." I laughed. "And that maybe, I should start going the way that everybody else is going."

"Oh no!" she exclaimed, nearly startling me. "Don't. You're unique. Please don't change."

I shrugged and laughed. "It's very kind of you to say that, but New York charges even for air, so I might have to start following the crowd soon."

She looked suddenly bright and happy. "You know what, I want to work with you. The style I want is exactly right up your alley. Everyone else in my family didn't seem too taken with it. I'm pregnant and just so exhausted, so I didn't push too hard. But now that I've run into you against all odds, I think it's a sign from the universe."

I stared at her, my mouth nearly open, wondering for a moment if she was playing a trick on me.

"Are you serious?" I asked.

She nodded happily. "I am. We already have a wedding planner and all that, and she's been suggesting photographers to me, but I haven't paid any attention because I hated all her big name photographers. And... I just know you'll love the location. It's a small ancient church. Its stained-glass windows are the most beautiful things you'll ever see, and its domed ceilings are painted with angels."

My mouth nearly fell open. "Are you joking? Where is this?"

"In the Hamptons," she replied.

I thanked my lucky stars that I wouldn't have to travel too far, but still, all of this was sounding too good to be true. I decided to have a little faith, especially since I didn't have much of a choice.

"Sounds wonderful," I replied.

"So you'll do it?" she asked breathlessly

"Of course. I'm just wrapping up the project I was working on, so I'm free and would love to photograph your wedding."

"Wow, this really seems like fate. I'm so excited."

"Me too," I agreed, more relieved than she could imagine.

"There is the small matter of how quickly you can wrap up. Due to my pregnancy it has to be next week, but no biggie, ha ha," she laughed. "So can you start next week."

I nodded. "Okay."

"Great. I want all the little moments captured."

I nodded enthusiastically.

"I'll be picking out a dress next week. Can you be there so you can take photos of the event and you also can meet the wedding planner and anyone else necessary. I haven't really thought about a dress preference, but if I eventually see one that I fall in love with, I want the moment captured."

I completely understood all that she was saying. I was so excited at the concept that I wanted to kiss her.

"I know what you want, and it's just the challenge I need. I'll make it special for you, trust me."

She released a deep sigh of relief, then she rose to her feet.

"I'm so happy right now. You have no idea. Alright, let me get back and make the preparations;

I'll reach out to you next week?"

"Alright," I said and immediately began to fumble through my laptop bag for a business card, but she stopped me with a gentle hand on my arm.

"No need," she said.

"I follow you, remember? Your details are on Instagram, and I can always direct message you."

"You're right," I said, a bit sad that she wasn't giving me her number. I wanted hers in case she forgot about me or changed her mind. I didn't want to sound desperate, but I really needed this follow-up gig.

"Can I have your number now either way?" I asked. "If it isn't any trouble. I won't bug you with any messages, but I'll save your name and look forward to your call."

"Of course." She pulled out her phone, and we exchanged numbers.

"Thank you so much," I said, and truly I wanted to hug her, but I found a way to hold myself back.

"No, thank you for being here," she said, and this made me laugh louder than I should have. It drew some attention, perhaps even that of the staff as well, but I didn't care anymore. I had a new client, and once again, all was well with the world. I would survive the month to come, and it was much more than I could ask for.

I watched her leave, and then with more enthusiasm than before, I continued with my work, and in no time, I was done and out of there. Since I no longer had to worry about money, my mind was free to do my best work, but as usual, that anxiousness that this was too good to be true kept me on edge.

Chapter Two
Drake

"

"Sir?" my secretary called.

"What is it?" I asked, trying to keep my voice neutral. It had been a difficult day, starting with a very disappointing and heartbreaking trip to the hospital.

I felt as if I'd been running for so long, and I had come very far. I was used to this pace and I didn't want to slow down, but circumstances I couldn't control were forcing me to.

I was used to putting out fires and finding solutions. It came with running a billion-dollar conglomerate, but this was different. I could never find a solution even if I went to the ends of the earth, and so far, I already had, but I was not giving up. I was going to carry on trying even if all that remained was a dead end.

"Your sister's here to see you, Sir," my secretary replied, and this brightened me up somewhat. She was always a sight for sore eyes, especially now.

"Let her in," I said, happy for the reprieve.

She nodded and left. The door was pushed open and my smiling baby sister walked in.

"Hey," I said.

"I just ran into my favorite photographer," she said, dropping into the seat in front of me.

I nodded warily. "And you want him to replace the photographers that Victoria has recommended?"

She cocked her head. "Not him. Her," she corrected, then frowned. "But to be honest. I don't understand why you're so involved in my wedding plans." But even as the words left her tongue, she felt remorse, and her gaze dropped to the floor.

"I mean... I didn't mean it that way," she said in a low, contrite tone.

"So, how did you mean it?" I asked gently.

"You've never ever involved yourself in little things like this, and you've never stopped me from doing any of the things I truly wanted. So, I don't know why you're so involved in the organizing of my wedding. What difference does it make to you?"

I wished I could tell her the truth. I wished I didn't have to be the bad guy ruining her most important day, but I couldn't tell her. I'd made a promise. One day she would understand why I had to be this way.

"I told you," I said calmly, opening the document on my desk. "You're the one who chose to get married to someone outside our circle, so the society wedding is needed for his sake. What greater chance is there to improve his standing and associate him with us. It's all for your benefit ultimately."

"Drake," she called softly. "I'm serious about this. I was ready to give in and allow you and Mom to have your way, but after seeing her today, it seems like I've been given a second chance. I don't want a big glitzy wedding; I want it in a small, intimate, gorgeous setting, with a few friends and my immediate family."

I ran out of patience.

"No," I said, and got ready to shut her out and go back to work.

"No? Just no?"

I didn't reply to her anymore.

"What if we just elope?" she asked angrily. "Since you're refusing to listen to me, that's an idea. We don't need a wedding anyway."

"Is the venue that important?" I asked, irritated.

"That's what I'm asking you! If it's not so important, then why don't you just let it be?"

"Because we have contacts and people that we need to take the opportunity to honor, and people need to know that we are ashamed of the choice you have made. That we welcome him into our fold and from that forth they must afford him the same respect they give us."

"You talk as though he runs a street cart," she replied bitterly. "He is a lawyer; he meets plenty of high-profile clients every single day, thank you very much."

"He is a first-year associate," I countered. "He needs another ten years to build his relevance in society."

I looked away because it was clear to both of us now that this conversation was over.

She rose to her feet, snatched her purse off the table and exited the office with an angry expression.

I tried not to be affected by her justified anger, because I knew if she was aware of the true reason why I wanted her to have this ridiculously huge wedding, she would not only understand but embrace it with both arms.

For now, all I could do was hope she would be agreeable and cooperate so that this time could pass as smoothly and peacefully as possible.

Chapter Three
Evelyn

For once, I could breathe a little as I rode the subway over to Anna's place. There was no pressing and unsolvable financial trouble in sight; I had just finished up with my work and sent it over to the client for review.

Things were looking up, so the moment I got off the subway, I went to her favorite Chinese restaurant and got our favorites for lunch and headed over to her apartment.

I had texted beforehand, so I was aware that she was at home; however, she wasn't exactly expecting me. So, when I rang the doorbell and she didn't answer, I wasn't surprised. Soon enough, I could feel someone staring at me through the peephole, and then she pulled the door open. She removed the toothbrush from her mouth, and I couldn't help but be amused at the tiny spiky ponytails that were sticking out from different sections of her hair.

"Were you pretending to see who it was so you wouldn't have to open the door?"

She instead frowned.

"You said you'd be here thirty minutes ago."

"Oh, I had to stop to get food; there was a bit of a late lunch line."

I lifted my hand that held the bag up, and she squealed.

"Welcome, welcome...Oh, shoot, I'm going to get ready."

I knew she meant going to shower and get herself as comfortable as possible so that she could enjoy her meal. So, I smiled and headed over to her kitchen to take the food out the boxes.

Afterwards, I brought up the phone number the girl gave me this morning and wanted to save it but realized that I hadn't even asked for her name.

I wondered if it would be too soon to text her, but ultimately, I sent a quick text to establish our contact. Asking for a name and nothing else was casual enough.

She took longer than I had expected, which made my heart start to sink, but eventually, just as Anna came out from her bedroom, freshly showered and happy, she replied.

"Hey, I'm Aurora," she said. "Nice meeting you again too," I said, and I heaved a deep sigh of relief.

"What is it?" Anna asked as she grabbed a fork and instantly began to dig in.

"The new client I met at the cafe," she said.

"Oh... She's for real?"

"She better be," I said, a bit too fiercely, and Anna raised her brows amused.

"She'll cover your bills for the month?"

"Maybe. Hopefully. I'm just happy I didn't have to go looking for a job to pay for them just yet, plus she told me her wedding was in a church, so I am kind of excited."

"It's a big wedding?"

"No, small," I replied. "Sounded intimate. She said she'd reach out to me next week."

"Nice," she replied, and then we kept eating. I kept staring at her though, especially as she ravaged her food with the utmost enjoyment, but eventually, she set it down to get a drink, and then she gave me a long look.

"What is it?" she asked, and I smiled.

"Mind if I crash here tonight?"

She seemed concerned. "What's wrong?" However, before I could even respond, she produced the answer.

"Your air conditioner broke again? I told you to just get a new one last time."

"Well, I fixed it, and the technician said it would be alright."

"And now, is it?"

"Don't be sarcastic," I said. "Can I or can't I stay?"

"Are you just asking because you want to make conversation, or you really plan on listening to me if I say no, don't stay; let's buy a working air conditioner for you instead?"

"I didn't hear anything you just said," I replied. "But thanks though. You're the best."

Smiling, she shook her head and returned to eating, and then she asked a question that, up until that moment, hadn't really crossed my mind.

"How much is she paying you?" Anna asked. "Is it substantial? Was she cheap about it or was there no negotiation?"

My hand stopped, and as I realized my major blunder, which was the fact that I hadn't even

discussed it with her.

"Let me guess," Anna said dryly as she looked at me.

"You, in your extreme excitement, took a job and didn't even discuss your payment. What if she can't afford it, and you're forced fighting a client for money for months again?"

"Ugh," I groaned. "Well, she hasn't yet booked it officially. She just said she'd reach out to me next week, so I can just wait for that."

"Don't you have her details?" Anna asked. "Why don't you just send her your fee information?"

"Don't jump the gun," I told her. "All will happen in time."

"This has happened before," she said. "Have you forgotten?" she asked. "You getting so excited about a project, only for it to fall through, and then you have no food to eat for the next two weeks."

"It'll be fine," I replied. "I'll look for another gig in the meantime."

"Or..." she said, and judging by the look on her face, I could almost guess what she was going to say, and I didn't like it one bit.

"You could, like I keep mentioning, reach out to Victoria." I instantly fired a glare at her, and instead of her feeling remorse, she was amused.

"I know you don't like her, especially because of that argument that you both had in our freshman year that nobody remembers or cares about, and neither should you, but okay, keep carrying the grudge anyway and allowing it to keep you so proud that you won't reach out for her to connect you with all the high-profile clients that she has been gifted to in the city. No. Don't reach out to her."

"Wow," I said. "You've really been thinking about this one, haven't you?"

"You're too romantic about your work," she said. "And it shouldn't be that way because this is New York. You need to eat and pay rent and thrive, not scramble for cheap-paying clients. One of those clients, I'm sure, guarantees you income for at least six months."

We both stared at each other quietly, and then I gave her a hard blink and looked away.

"You know I'm right," she said, however, I didn't respond.

I kept eating silently. Eventually though, I did respond.

"I'm not contacting Victoria because I'm proud nor because I'm holding onto whatever grudge you think we have."

"You mean you're admitting to having a grudge with her?" she asked, and I sent her another displeased look.

"Anyway, my point is if I had interests in those kinds of weddings, I'd go after them, but I really don't enjoy them as much."

"Have you ever tried, though?" she asked. "You just got started, and you've purposely always gone after the smaller projects which I don't agree with. Start handling the bigger ones, and maybe, just maybe, you can convince them to add that rustic feel that you like with your projects."

All of this talking was beginning to give me a headache. For the most part, she was right, but since I wasn't ready to hear any of it just yet, I decided to simply eat my meal quietly and let the matter go.

Speaking of work," I asked her. "How did it go with your boss and the date you claimed was not a date?"

"It went fine," she said, however, I couldn't miss the fact

that she was suddenly so sullen, and I knew that things had not gone as well as she had planned.

"Let me guess, he was formal throughout the whole thing?"

She was quiet for a while, but actually, she replied.

"He didn't even seem to want to look at me. Meanwhile, on normal days at work, I note the difference between how he treats me and how he treats my coworkers. Even they have noticed the difference, wondering if I was his secret niece or something."

I listened, and then I nodded.

"You really like him, don't you?"

"What do you mean by that?" she asked, narrowing her eyes.

"I mean... he is a bit older than you."

"Fourteen years is not that huge; y'all need to grow up, and you should know that I like older guys. I don't want anything to do with boys."

This amused me; nevertheless, she watched me closely as well.

"And what about you?"

"It's been more than three years now since your breakup with Danny. I know you're absolutely not still hung up on him since you didn't even really like him that much. So, what's the problem? Why have you been avoiding relationships since then?"

I had just the answer for her.

"Oh, excuse me! I was trying to start my business around that time and have worked day and night, through the snow, heat, and rain, to ensure that it takes off so that I don't end up on the street. Oh no, not at all, I should have been dating instead and running around New York looking for a mate."

Once again, we stared at each other, and then after shaking her head at me, she returned to her meal.

I did the same but didn't hold back my giggle. Later on, she did eventually have one more question for me.

"If you met someone now that you liked, would you still be too busy to date them?"

"I don't know," I replied truthfully. "Right now, I'm not interested in connecting with another human being.

"So you've given up on trying?"

"I haven't given up," I replied. I'm just wondering now if being connected to anyone even exists? I mean, I'm up there in adult years, and I still haven't seen what all the stories are about. I mean, was it all just made up?"

This made her burst out laughing.

"Up there in adult years? You twenty-eight-year-old baby."

"Baby?" I cocked my eyebrows; however, this was one comment from her that I had absolutely no problems with.

"Sure," I said. "If you say so."

Chapter Four
Evelyn

"Is it because I'm pregnant?" I heard the voice come from down the hallway. I had only met Aurora once, but I could instantly recognize her voice. It was soft, yet undeniably strong. I really liked her, and I wasn't sure why, but hearing this statement made me instantly concerned. Not for the fact that she was pregnant, but because from the tone of her voice, it was clear that the person she was talking to was not very happy about something. Unconsciously, I slowed my steps and inadvertently heard more.

"It's not Aurora. All of this is for you. Why can't you see that?"

"If it really is for me, then why don't I have a say in it?"

"Because you're not paying for it," came the curt but soft reply, and my brows shot up.

There was a brief silence, and then Aurora replied.

"You want us to go over this again? You want me to explain to you that I can very well afford the wedding that I want, and so can David?"

"You're a part of this family, married or not. I didn't think using your marriage to benefit all of us, including your husband, was too much to ask for. You're getting what every girl dreams of. First of all, we're not even bringing any contention for the fact that you're marrying him and having his child yet—"

"What's wrong with him?" Aurora cut her off.

There was another brief silence, but by now, I had arrived at the closed-off dressing room and was certain that it was best to just wait outside to not intrude on such a charged moment.

Although as I looked around the cordless but classy wedding store hallway, I couldn't help but feel like I was eavesdropping. It was going to be very hard to explain if I got caught, but that awkwardness felt better to me than heading in right now.

"First of all, not every girl wants this... and it deeply upsets me that I can't even have a say at the end of the day in my own wedding. It's been this way ever since I was a child... I never had a say in anything concerning me and my life choices and now even in—"

"You had a say in dating Ronny," the response came. "Which was against all of our approval. And you had a say in getting married or not to him. We didn't interfere. In fact, we haven't interfered in anything you did since you got into college, but on this matter, you'll have to listen to Drake."

"Drake, that betrayer," she scoffed.

"You aren't really saying that about him, are you?" The woman asked. "He's always been on your side more than anyone else."

"If he's always been on my side, then why isn't that the

case now? Why is he deferring to you and what you want? It's strange to me that he's even doing this because Drake answers to no one. He's your puppet; he runs this company, so it just makes me wonder what you are currently holding over him to make him turn against me in this way."

A long tense silence followed, and it gave me the time I needed to mark that name Drake in my head. He sounded like a total domineering and upsetting prick.

On Aurora's behalf, right then, I decided that I didn't like him, but more than anything, as I listened even more, I realized that things weren't as easy for her. So just as I began to hear footsteps approaching from around the corner, I straightened and knocked and started to walk in. I would be on her side and try to support her as much as was needed. I promised myself just as I eventually met the women present in the dressing room.

There were four women present. Two were the staff of the bridal shop, one dressed in a suit as the attendant while the other, who was sifting through the dresses that had just arrived on the rack, seemed much more elderly and almost matronly. But the sleekness of her grey hair back in a bun and the heavy string of pearl beads around her neck, as well as the hard line in the corners of her lips, almost made me think she was in charge of everyone present. She immediately frowned at me upon my entrance, but I turned to meet the two other women seated in the seating area and dressed gorgeously.

Aurora was the last to notice me because she had lowered her gaze to her phone, but the second woman seated, whom I couldn't help but notice had the same sleek shiny jet-black hair as she did, looked quite frail. Though I had expected to see a domineering and unfeeling woman given the responses she had just been giving to Aurora, I couldn't help but notice that my heart moved slightly at seeing her. She seemed sad and exhausted, but as her eyes landed on me, I couldn't decide whether or not she was unkind.

"Is she one of yours, Madelyn?" she asked with a light smile. However, before I could respond, the woman behind spoke up. Her voice was softer than I had expected, but her words were sharper than anything else I'd ever heard.

"Absolutely not. Excuse me, what are you doing here, and what hole did you crawl out of?"

I was just about to introduce myself and say hello to Aurora when I heard her words, and I couldn't help but turn around to gaze at her in shock. She too seemed to realize what she had just said, but as she took in my baggy ripped jeans and the graphic tee I had tucked into them, I almost couldn't blame her. I definitely looked like I had crawled out of some pauper's hole and intruded on some high-class gathering. But I was still irritated at her rudeness and made sure that she understood this.

"Please leave immediately," she said. "This is not the general area. This is a private dressing roo—"

Aurora cut her off.

"Please calm down, Madelyn, you don't have to be rude," Aurora said. "I invited her over to capture this moment or whatever this is now. No offense to you, Evelyn, it's just that I thought this would be a special time, but all my enthusiasm has gone down the drain."

I could understand more than she knew, so I ensured to wear my loveliest smile and then headed over to her. Rather than a handshake, I pulled her into an embrace, and although she remained stiff for a moment as though it was unexpected for her, she eventually relaxed into my arms and hugged me back.

"You heard?" she asked, and although I briefly hesitated since I hadn't exactly planned to hear her, I nodded and admitted the truth. She sighed then, and after a little while, she pulled away.

"I'll not just be your photographer," I told her, low enough that hopefully she was the only one that heard. "I'll also be on your side, so whatever you need help or support for beyond the photographs, I'll be there for you."

Tears slightly misted her eyes at my words, and then she hugged me once again. "Thank you," she said, and a few seconds later her mom's voice filtered through.

"Is this a friend of yours, Rory?" she asked, and Aurora finally released me and turned towards her.

"Yes, she is," she replied.

"She's my photographer, Evelyn. Evelyn, this is my mom."

I held out my hand for a handshake, and although there was a slight delay as her gaze lowered to it, she eventually accepted it. However, her gaze immediately went to her daughter.

"I thought Victoria was going to handle the photographer. Wasn't she working in collaboration with Henry Vaughn from Vogue?"

"I don't know about that, and I don't care either about whatever Victoria has planned. We were just talking about how I have no say whatsoever in my own wedding, but she is non-negotiable. I've followed her work for years, and I want to work with her."

At this, all eyes turned on me, and for the first time in a very long time, I felt very self-conscious, judged, and out of place.

Firstly, I hadn't expected this wedding to be in such an expensive bridal house in the middle of Manhattan. I had some brides tell me that just passing here gave them anxiety due to the

prices, and I wouldn't have pegged Aurora for being from wealth after speaking with her, but now... I could believe it. She had talked about a small church, though, with stained windows, and I started to wonder now if this wasn't the actual ceremony she wanted me to take photos of but just a few prior moments before.

"Sure," her mother finally replied. "Let's just start trying the dresses. We've already been here for half an hour."

With a sullen look, Aurora turned her attention to me, and then she smiled.

"You can get started," she said. "I'm going to try a few dresses on, so please watch me a bit and capture these moments. I'm sure it will be apparent on my face if I find the one I like among the most, and I'll also make sure to be as expressive as possible so that you can also capture all the ones I think are absolutely ridiculous, which will be most of them."

She said the last part louder than was needed, but when I saw her eyes go to the matron behind us, I understood and couldn't help but be amused. I liked her even more.

"Sure," I rolled my eyes. "I'll get started immediately.

Just act as usual and try to forget that I'm here. I'll handle it all."

"Alright," she replied and returned to her seat.

I went to a corner to pull out my equipment and camera, and soon I was set up and ready. I watched as they held the dresses up to her one by one. They debated about the rest, but Aurora didn't actually get to try any one of them, even though the women kept insisting that if she did, she would like it even more. Instead, she kept a frown on her face and kept drinking the non-alcoholic champagne they had delivered to them.

I captured it all—the brooch on the table, her frowned and slight slouch, and the way her mother watched through it all. Then, of course, I didn't miss how Madelyn, the matron, stared at me multiple times as though I was a complete eyesore. As a result, I made sure on a particular shot to turn on my flash with the hope to linger with it. She blinked at the sudden brightness and seemed to be even more annoyed. But when Aurora's mom finally put her foot down and insisted that the dress she was holding on to had to be tried, she turned to her mother and smiled. Aurora turned then to look at me, and I knew that she was asking for my opinion, which made me wonder if she had any true freedom.

I gave a glance at the dress, and although it was a little bit more ballgown than I would have preferred, it was still a gorgeous dress that I thought would be extremely flattering. So, I nodded in support.

"It will give us more pictures to create a story out of," I said, and she smiled and rose to her feet.

"We're not creating a story here or whatever," Madelyn

cut in rudely. "This is serious business. There will be more people than you can even—"

I shut my ears off to her nonsense and lifted the camera to my face to continue on with my work. She was tired out, I was focused, and I enjoyed every minute of my work.

Five minutes in, and I could no longer decide which dress I liked the best. And so, even though Aurora still looked very reluctant, I doubted that it was because of the difficult circumstances surrounding her wedding. Instead, it felt as though she, just like me, was falling in love with every single one and almost not even caring anymore that the direction of the wedding was not according to her wishes.

But these dresses! I couldn't stop pausing in between shots just so I could look at them with my own eyes. Each time she looked at me and I nodded, almost in a trance, and began to even imagine myself in them.

Eventually, though, she took a seat, exhausted, and I smiled and took her photos in this state as well.

"So, what do we think?" her mother asked, looking down at her probably impeccable notes.

"I have no idea," she said. "I like all of them but I don't know yet."

I was in the same predicament as her, but I did have a suggestion.

"I could work on these photos today and send them to you," I said. "I took photos of you wearing each one, so this might help."

"Thank you," she said, her gaze lighting up. I smiled as well, obsessed with my photos as I flipped through the screen.

"We have to choose the menu and desserts in a few

days as well as meet with the event planner in the wedding hall," her mother told me. "Will you be coming along as well?"

I lifted my head then, but before I could even look at Aurora with the question, she nodded and proclaimed her response.

"Of course, she will be," she said. "She will be accompanying me throughout the entire process. So, she'll be there as well."

"You should speak to the event planner about this," her mother said, and this time, I was on her side.

Aurora looked at me and then her mother.

"She's not the one getting married. I'll let her know beforehand so that she doesn't give Evelyn any trouble, but on this one aspect, I'm not budging for any reason."

Sighing, her mom stood to her feet and then grabbed her purse. The attendants, as well as Madam Madelyn, also came over, ready to escort her out of the bridal shop.

"I guess we'll see you then in a few days. Today was successful enough."

We watched her leave, but just before she was no longer within earshot, she thanked her.

"I was happy having you here, Mom," she said. "Thank you."

Her voice was low, but her mother heard her loud and clear. She turned and sent her a brief and small smile. Eventually, we were left alone, and she turned around to give me a smile of her own, this one way more significant.

"Do you have another appointment after this? I'd like us to talk more. My studio is within walking distance from here."

"Your studio?" I asked, wondering if by some strange twist she was a photographer as well.

"Yes, I'm an artist and I paint," she replied, and I nodded. I didn't have anything else planned, so after giving her request a little more consideration, I instantly agreed.

In no time, we were out of the wedding store, mainly because Madelyn didn't seem to want us there anymore, which made me wonder just how rich they were, that Madelyn and seemingly everyone else were more important than the bride and her opinions for her own wedding.

I didn't want to pry, however, so even when we got into the car, I kept my mouth shut and my curiosity to myself and only spoke when I was spoken to.

We had found the sun too scorchingly hot, so the moment we got out onto the street, we decided that taking a taxi would be best.

I had no qualms whatsoever with this, so soon enough, we were riding in the back of the car together. Her studio, surprisingly to me, was in her apartment. But it was so big that it had its own section that it seemed apt. The tall wall-length windows were what took my breath away, and when I realized that this section was the size of my entire apartment, I couldn't help but feel a bit jealous. I had thought her to be just like one of us, the suffering peasants of the city, but it turned out that her family was wealthier than imagined. Or maybe this was all her? Artists made exorbitant amounts of money. I didn't want to pry, though; after all, my job was to support her in the best way I could, like I had promised, and make her moments as memorable as they could be.

So, I decided then to be as completely honest with her as possible.

"I would kill for your apartment," I said, and she smiled in response.

"I understand. I would do the same as well. It used to be about three apartments

including the elevator. I fell in love with the windows and lighting from outside first before anything else, but when I approached the tenants to rent them out of the place, there was a war. One didn't even care about the amount and just wanted to ensure, according to her, 'privileged brats like me don't get their way.'"

"Oh no," I said. "This must have been tough."

"It was," she said, but luckily, that was where my brother came in. His name is Drake Moran.

"He immediately found the actual owners of the apartments and bought them all out. By the following week, renovation had started to turn all three apartments and the elevator in to one apartment, and I couldn't believe it."

"By the way, I felt guilty about kicking them out, but Drake made sure that they were well compensated."

I could see that she felt a little guilty and judged, but I quickly waved this concern away.

"No need to defend your desire," I said. "If I had the means, I'd do the same. That's how life works, and if I really wanted to get back at you, if I were one of the tenants, I mean, I'd work hard and ensure to buy it all back and ensure that you wouldn't have access to it. All is fair in love, war, and hustling for New York apartments."

She laughed at this, and I couldn't help but delight in

her breezy laughter. It was pure and light, such a welcome contrast from how upset she had seemed earlier.

"Alright, let me make us some tea or coffee?"

"Tea," I replied. "I'm trying to cut back on the caffeine."

"Just like my brother," she said and headed over to the kitchen.

Once more, her brother Drake was mentioned, and I couldn't help but be curious about this famous tyrant that was controlling the entire family and not letting anyone get their way.

"He's quite strict with his life and by extension everyone else around him," she said as she filled a kettle with water and set it on the stone.

She continued speaking.

"One day he noticed how dependent he had become on caffeine to perform at full capacity, and he absolutely hated it. He said it was a weakness he couldn't tolerate, and so within the following week, he had immediately switched to tea."

"Wow," I couldn't help but think. He sounded extremely uptight; however, she didn't seem to think so and was even smiling as she narrated, perhaps without realizing it.

"There's a lot of things I love and respect about him, but these days he's being so anal that I can't really think of one. Why am I even talking about him? How did he come up?"

Once again, I was amused by her slightly unhinged personality.

"Anyway, enough about him. Please take a seat. I'll be right there with you."

I sat on a stool at the island counter along the window

that looked like the exact café setting we had met at. She brought over some cheesecake, and I was more than happy to indulge in the late afternoon delicacy.

"So," she said.

"As you've heard, I'm pregnant, so there are a lot of dresses here that I could wear now, but I don't know if I'll be able to that day, and I really don't want to break down."

I didn't have an answer to this, but I did empathize with what she meant.

"When is the wedding?" I asked. I realized that I didn't even know.

"Oh my God!" she exclaimed. "I haven't given you any of the basic information about my ceremony."

"It's okay," I replied as I sipped from the chamomile tea she had made for me. "We can discuss it now and in detail."

"Alright," she said and calmed down. "So, first of all, the wedding is in two weeks," she said, and I was very surprised to hear this.

"Two weeks?" I asked, and she nodded.

"Yeah, but they've been making preparations for the big one for a couple of months now, so don't worry, we're not in panic mode, at least not yet. It's just that after they shut down my church idea the previous time, I haven't bothered bringing it up, but after I saw you, it was revived, and now I can't stop thinking about it."

She truly loved my work, I realized as I watched her eyes sparkle. However, admiration and bills being paid were two different things. So, I pulled out my price sheet and handed it over to her.

She took it heartily, gave it a quick glance before

handing it back. She immediately agreed wholeheartedly, and I wondered if she had seen it properly.

"I'll take the highest package," she said. "I want every special moment covered, and to make Drake and the rest of them pay dearly, I'll even add a little bonus to show my love."

I was more than floored and barely able to contain my excitement, but I managed to control myself until it began to sink in. No one had ever chosen my deluxe package, much less infused it with the promise of a bonus, so I was incredibly excited.

"Alright," she said. "I'll make the deposit for the next two weeks so that you'll be assured for at least the next two weeks. All this has happened so suddenly, so you must be a bit startled and skeptical as well."

I smiled at her kind words.

"More than skeptical, I'm more grateful. Because of how somewhat niche my photographs are and my limited contacts, it can be difficult to get substantial back-to-back work, so it's just wonderful that you reached out to me in the café."

She smiled softly at me and then pulled out her phone.

"The next agenda, like my mom told you, will be to meet with the event planner at the venue. This, though, will be a bit far since it's in the Hamptons. You won't have a problem coming over, will you? If you do, I can arrange a car to come pick you up?"

"Oh no," I instantly replied. "I'll definitely be able to make it there; it'll be no trouble. Just send me the address."

"Alright," she smiled. We chatted a little bit more, and a little while later, I was on my way back to Anna's house.

Chapter Five

Drake

I t had been such a long time since I'd been to the Hamptons, or even been in a car for longer than a few minutes. At first, I hadn't been sure that I would even make it to the event with the wedding planner, since I hadn't heard from Aurora since our last meeting in my office, and her responses to my messages had been few and far between. So, upon the invitation from my mom, I tried my best to find the time.

The drive over was a much-needed, almost three-hour reprieve from the usually bustling flight travel and the office. So much so that by the time I arrived at the vineyard, I was almost reluctant to get out.

So many things weighed heavily on my heart and in my mind, and as I remained in the car watching as people came and went, I could only imagine that things would get even more strained in there.

But it was my responsibility now to lead the family and to be all that I could for every single one of them. And so, after a heavy sigh, I reached for the door; however, just then, a woman hurried into sight, seemingly from out of nowhere. She was obviously running late and scatterbrained, but then she suddenly stopped, and I couldn't help but cock my head curiously, wondering why. She turned around, then took a quick look around, and then she stared straight at me.

I was startled. I knew she couldn't see me since the glass was tinted, but it was almost as though she could, and for some reason, I couldn't look away.

She hurried back to the glass, and in the next moments, as she used the reflection to fix her curly, messy hair and collared, rumpled shirt, I understood that my car was more or less being used as a mirror to help her fix her appearance. I couldn't help staring at her then, from the top of her head to the tips of her toes, and it wasn't hard to realize that she was quite attractive.

Extremely unpolished, but there was something about those eyes of hers that made me unable to look away.

.   .   .

I couldn't quite explain it, but even though she looked stressed in a way, she also looked and felt as light as the wind. Her eyes were clear and bright and seemed to hold no hidden shadows or grief, and it made me want to roll down the window just so that I could stare further into them. Eventually, though, and after glancing at the watch on her wrist, she straightened, and in no time, had dashed away and straight into the lobby of the vineyard.

I couldn't see her any longer, yet I didn't move, perhaps with the hope that she would come out again, but she didn't. A few minutes later, my phone began to ring, and I looked down to see it was my mother. I could no longer delay, so I picked it up, and after giving a look to James through the rearview mirror, he immediately got out of the car and came over to the side to pull the door open for me.

"Are you here yet?" my mom asked as soon as I picked up the phone.

"Just getting in," I replied.

"Oh, that's great news. I didn't think you'd be able to make it."

"Aurora?" I asked, and I could hear the smile in her voice even before she replied.

. . .

"She's here."

"And her mood?"

"She's been sullen as usual, but she keeps staring at the door, so I know that she's expecting you."

This was good to hear, so I ended the call and headed over to the reception desk to ask for directions to the arranged location.

Chapter Six
Evelyn

I had to blame someone for this mess, and for once, it was not going to be me.

Forget being the bigger person because as soon as I got back, I was going to chew Anna to pieces. Not only had she forced me to accompany her for a colleague's birthday the previous evening, so that I could, of course, be her eyes and ears in judging the interactions between her and the guy she had the most ridiculous crush on, she had forced me to drink along with her to calm her nerves and then told me she'd set an alarm for me to be up on time as soon as we got home.

Because she hadn't done any of the above, I'd slept till Aurora's phone call had woken me up, asking me once again if I wanted to ride to the Hamptons along with her since she was on her way.

I'd almost taken it but knowing that I would need a lot of privacy to get ready so as not to seem as scattered and disoriented as I currently did, I'd declined. I didn't regret it, but it now meant that I was later than ever and looked like a complete mess. The plan had been to head back to my apartment to get my already ironed and laid-out change of clothes, which was supposed to be a dress very suitable for the late summer day. Instead, I had grabbed my rumpled black pants from the previous night, found a checkered dress shirt in Anna's closet, and slipped into her gym shoes since I wasn't able to find the decent heels I had worn out with her the previous day.

I looked absolutely hideous, and the reflection in that car had shown just how bad it was. Aurora, until that moment, had left me with two calls and seven messages, less than half of that I had responded to, so I was under immense pressure to hurry up to join her in the hall where everyone was waiting. However, when I saw the sign for the ladies' bathroom, I instantly hurried into it.

In there, I wrapped my hair into a tighter bun, smeared on the red lipstick I had found in my backpack so that I wouldn't look so pale, hungover, and dead, and folded up the sleeves of the shirt I now knew looked quite old and unappealing. Sighing, I stared at myself and couldn't help but feel disappointed because this was not the impression I had hoped to make.

I had connected enough dots by now to know that Aurora's family was not a regular family. Although I still hadn't been curious enough to search for them since I would find out eventually, I couldn't shake the idea that working with her and doing well was the gateway I had been looking for to connect with more elite clients. A few minutes later, I felt a little bit better, but my shoes were lamentable.

In order to appear as put-together and professional as

possible, I pulled my camera out and got ready to walk. I took slow, measured steps as I approached the area that the receptionist had directed me to. However, just as I approached, I was forced to come to a halt.

There was a man standing right by the huge arched entrance door, on the phone, his other hand in his pocket, his eyes trained on whoever was in the room. He was so regal that I couldn't help but stare at him: his broad, tall physique, sharp jawline, and intense glare. He seemed like

a general in the military, impeccably dressed. I was torn between going close enough to smell him or remaining back until he went where he was headed, so he wouldn't see me, and I wouldn't feel even worse about myself.

My hand lifted before I could stop it. I quickly focused my camera and then I clicked. The sound startled me, but as I took the shot, it was as though the moment reverberated through me. And thus, I couldn't stop. He was in a place where the lighting was almost unreal. The area to his left, where I was, was quite shadowed, while from his right was open and filled with sunlight, creating an unreal effect. He straightened and turned his head towards the right, and I took the chance to take yet another shot.

Just before I clicked, however, it was as though he sensed my attention on him, so he turned, and that was how I took the perfect, jaw-dropping but also terrifying picture of his face staring straight at me. From his physique, side profile, and suited appearance, I had been certain that he was attractive, but seeing his face through my lens, I was frozen in place. As I stared at the digital result, I was sure he couldn't look this real. I lifted my gaze and found, to my horror, that he was still watching me. I had been caught red-handed, yet he was every bit as devastatingly handsome as I had seen.

I should have been immediately apologetic or even embarrassed and turned away or continued on my way, but I couldn't. It was as though I was frozen in place, especially when he put the phone away and began to head over to me. I tried to look away, then lowered to put my full attention on my camera as though I hadn't even noticed, but pretty soon, the most intoxicating scent of tobacco and vanilla mixed with lime and something so deliciously exotic and sinful at the same time that I had absolutely no hope of identifying wafted much too close towards me, and then his polished leather shoes came into sight.

"This is my second encounter with you," he said, and my heart thundered against my chest. If someone had told me that there could be anything else remarkable about him, I wouldn't have believed them. But at his voice, as clear and boisterous as the waves smashing against rocks and equally as calm, I was almost struck dumb. I looked up then and had no choice but to summon what was still remaining of my confidence to stare into his gorgeous grey eyes.

"What?" I asked, barely coherent with whatever words I was making.

"You used my car as a mirror earlier," he said, "and now you're outrightly taking pictures of me? Don't you think you're taking too many liberties of my person and property?"

I had absolutely no idea what he was saying or talking about, but he didn't seem to be in a hurry for a response. So, as a result, I was able to put his words together enough to recall that I had indeed stopped before a dark sleek car by the curb and quickly checked my appearance in the tinted window at the back. My hand immediately slapped over my mouth.

"Holy shit!" I swore.

He cocked his head at the fact that I was swearing while my entire frame began to burn in embarrassment. I was flushed red and warm from the heat and shame and self-consciousness until I understood then that I could no longer remain in his presence.

"I'm sorry," I apologized, and without waiting for his response or reaction, I hurriedly made my way over to meet Aurora.

I was sweating even more by the time that it took me reach her, but the good news was I was still so startled from my meeting with the man that when I took in the women seated and conversing as they waited, and of course noted that Victoria was also among them, I couldn't even muster up the energy or zeal to be taken aback.

It was a day of surprises and annoyances, and all I could do was approach it calmly for my own peace of mind. She, however, seemed hell-bent on being dramatic about the whole process, and I ensured to indulge her.

"Oh wow," she said, just as I shared a smile with Aurora and her mother. "You're - you're the photographer?" she asked, almost as though this was some joke solely orches-trated for her amusement.

I nearly rolled my eyes but managed to hold myself in check. Plus, I wasn't exactly scoring any brownie points for showing up the way I did. I mean, I didn't think I looked bad, but as I took in the women before me and the fact that they were all staring at me with distaste that I was sure they tried to hide but I couldn't help but cower just a little.

"You two have worked together before?" Aurora's mother asked.

"Oh no," she laughed a little too loudly. I couldn't, however, get over how slick and shiny her blonde hair looked. It had always looked this way, straight, primed, perfect... and she was dressed just like the other women. Only Aurora looked a bit more down to earth with jeans and a jacket, while the others donned pearls, gold jewelry, and invisible makeup.

"So how do you know her then?" Aurora's mom asked. "Or you don't?" The way she asked the question rubbed me the wrong way, almost as though she was hoping that she truly didn't know me, and her daughter was just making an unacceptable and misguided decision as usual by involving me in all of this. I didn't blame her because if things had gone according to plan today, I would have been more confident and able to retreat.

"We met in college," she replied. "We were in the same dormitory, but that's about it."

Aurora gave her a look then, but she didn't seem to care about the curt and distasteful way she had delivered her response. I didn't have any response, but none was needed because just then, the faces of all the women at the table seemed to light up. Victoria especially stood up, seemingly like the perfect hostess, and before I could blink, she was striding across the room, her heels clicking against the polished wooden floors, and going over to the man.

I turned as well because it would just be weird if I ignored him when no one else seemed to be able to. What I saw, however, was that even though Victoria was right in front of his face, being all teeth and overly courteous, his gaze lingered on me.

He was so bold and unapologetic with it that I had to look away. And as soon as I did, I saw that Aurora and her mom were looking at me curiously. There was no way for me to explain this, so I simply sent them a smile and went over to Aurora's side.

"I'll get started," I told her, and she nodded. Then she looked towards the man who now had his attention on Victoria and was nodding quietly as she rattled off.

"That's my brother," she said, and my brows raised. I wasn't surprised because I had suspected as much. It wasn't that they looked together; more like I didn't think a man this gorgeous could just be randomly walking around here and in the vicinity. I mean, it was an extremely luxurious location, but somehow, he just seemed like he was beyond it, so he had to be here for a very specific and almost obligatory purpose.

He eventually walked away from Victoria and then he headed over. He kissed his mom, and even though I tried, I found that I couldn't look away. He seemed so affectionate with her, so careful that even though I had told myself that I was for whatever reason going to ignore his existence, I found myself unable to look away.

Afterward, he came over to Aurora, and she still had her guard up because she turned away.

He, however, kissed her on the forehead, and even though she didn't smile or react, I could see her posture instantly soften. Her shoulders relaxed, as well as her scowl, but she still didn't look at him. Instead, she started scrolling through her phone, which meant that his attention had nowhere else to land but on me.

I wasn't exactly pleased about this, but I wasn't able to cover either, so I sent him a brief and polite smile and then began to walk away so I could get to work. However, at the last moment, he grabbed my arm, and I was stunned. His grip was hard, but it was too audacious for me. I looked at it, frowning, and then looked up at him.

"Who are you?" he asked. However, before I could respond, his mother explained, once again as though my presence was an apology.

"Aurora hired her to handle some of the photos."

"Yes," Victoria suddenly added out of nowhere, and I was taken aback to hear her voice. I had almost even forgotten about her presence.

"She was hired, but I don't think that was necessary. Aurora?" she called.

"I have already hired the photographer that will be taking all your shots. He's worked for Vogue for years, and he will be more than capable of handling this project in the best possible way."

"No offense, Evelyn," she said, and I nearly rolled my eyes.

I pulled my hand out of the man's grip, and thankfully, he let me go quite easily.

"Well, that's all well and good, but I don't need only the ceremony photographed. I need all the moments leading up to it. So can you get your Vogue photographer to come over right now and do his job?"

"Um…" she seemed stumped as she looked between Aurora's brother and mother.

"He's not a roadside photographer, Aurora," she said. "I've already scheduled him in advance for the big day, so –"

"Well, since he can't be here since he's too big to capture my most precious moments, then please stay out of this. At the end of the day, this is my wedding and not yours."

Her smile at this was almost painful to watch, but she managed to gather herself together to give some sort of excuse about going to the kitchen to arrange the menu for the day. I couldn't help but like Aurora even more. Her brother took his seat beside her while I moved away and began to take my pictures.

It upset me to focus on Victoria, but she was busy with the staff, and so when I had taken enough photographs of the family conversing from a distance and against the backdrop of the vineyard beyond, I headed over to the kitchen to find her. I especially kept my distance here, but I was eventually able to take some pretty nice pictures. Just before I left, however, she noticed me and then she turned and came over.

"It's nice to see you here," she smiled, and I nodded in response before placing my camera to my eyes once again to peer through. I had no interest in her fake niceties, but then again, as I continued with my pictures, I wondered exactly why our relationship was so sour. I mean, it was expected since I had now been given the freshest reminder of her personality, but I tried to recall the exact details of how we had fallen out from being roommates to being mortal enemies, seemingly now for life.

She came over to me once again as I worked, and I sighed as I felt the tap on my back. I put my camera away then and turned around to face her.

"Can I give you some advice?" she asked.

I took another sigh and then I nodded. Because I was curious and because for some reason, I needed someone to fuel my already sour mood so that I'd be angry enough perhaps not to get distracted or affected by anyone else. An image of glistening leather shoes flashed into my mind in that moment, but I ignored it.

"Go ahead," I said, and she smiled. Which was way too genuine. But when I glanced back and realized that the said object of her attention and my distraction was watching us, I understood.

I couldn't believe her. I also couldn't believe the next words that she said to me.

"I didn't think this is... your scene," she said. "Don't take this the wrong way, but I'm just concerned that doing work that is not... best suited for you might hurt your small business more than help it."

I stared at her and decided then that I truly needed to test whether she had a mental glitch in her brain.

"Do you actually think you're being helpful and respectful to me right now? Or are you fully aware that everything you've just said to me is a backhanded insult?"

"I would never insult you," she smiled. "There's no reason to. It's just that high-profile clientele has been my circle for the longest time, and I can tell you all that you need to know and what you can't bother about. Plus, right now you're obviously helping Aurora do nothing more than rebel against her family, so what good exactly do you think is going to come from it? You'll just leave a sour taste in their mouth, and whatever recommendation you think is going to come for your next job as a result will be nothing but a pipe dream; rather, cooperate with her mother and leave. Instead of a sour taste in their mouth, the people with the actual money and influence, which is her brother and not Aurora, will think of you fondly."

"Hm," I nodded. "You know what? This is solid advice. I'll make sure to repeat it word for word to Aurora so that she can understand my stance as well and won't feel too bad about letting me go."

"What?" she asked, but before she could say another word, I went past her and made sure to bump into her shoulder on my way. She staggered a few steps backward, but no doubt and as usual, she was able to quickly right herself before anyone noticed.

Chapter Seven
Drake

I saw it all. There was no way for me to know what their interaction was about and why it had been so charged, but I had to admit, as I watched her seemingly grow even colder as the meeting progressed, I became even more curious.

Eventually, as I caught her during the tour of the vineyard heading over to the bar, I followed and ended up beside her.

She was seated, staring out at the gorgeous landscape as she sipped from her wine. However, it was as though she became aware of my presence because the second I spoke, she didn't seem to have a reaction at all.

"How do you know the wedding planner?"

·   ·   ·

She took a sip of her drink and then turned around just in time to watch me order my tumbler of whiskey.

"Um... college," she replied. "Years ago."

"I take it you two weren't friends?" I asked, and she seemed taken aback by my interest.

I, however, was just as surprised as it was very unusual for me to strike up a conversation of this sort with a female, which made me realize then, in something akin to shock, that it had been forever since I had been properly attracted to a female this way.

In terms of my needs as they came up, for as I was aroused, there was always an endless availability of women, and I only required a few attributes and a few minutes to get the release I wanted.

This time around, however, I was truly unable to look away from her gorgeous hazel eyes. They were every bit as pure and bright as I had predicted earlier, and it made me truly wonder about her. Her appearance wasn't exciting in any way, and I had almost lost interest truly after I sighted her gold and dirty sneakers, but then, at her blatant annoyance at the wedding planner, which I had also felt as well due to her jumping at every chance to pester me, I couldn't help but be somewhat entertained.

.   .   .

"What's the story there?" I asked, and she turned to me almost as though in disbelief that I was asking her.

She cocked a brow.

"You really want to know?" she asked, completely surprised, and I nodded.

"Sure."

"Um... I don't remember," she said. "She was my dorm roommate freshman year, things didn't go smoothly for some reason or the other. We parted ways, and it isn't exactly the best of sights to see or run into her."

I watched her after this, and for a few seconds, she managed to hold my eye contact, but then she turned her face away and continued on with her drink.

"What are you going to do with the picture you took of me?" I asked, and this time around, I couldn't physically see her stiffen. It made the corners of my lips slightly lift in amusement.

.   .   .

"Um... uh," she stuttered. "I'm supposed to take photographs of all her moments."

"You knew I was her brother when you first saw me?" I asked, and once again, she seemed stumped. But perhaps it was the alcohol and the liquid courage it gave; she didn't seem to give a fuck because she responded.

"I didn't know. I just thought you ... looked interesting."

She held my gaze then, and I scoffed silently.

"You thought I looked interesting?"

She turned around then, and I shook my head as I lifted my glass for another sip. The rest of my family was outside on the terrace talking as they reviewed different options for the dessert. At this point, I was ready to leave and sure that Aurora was just rejecting everything because she purposely wanted to make everyone's life involved difficult.

I knew her and was almost completely certain that she had made her decision even before this entire meeting started.

. . .

When I was somewhat certain that they weren't looking, I looked at this member of her party and asked the question I needed a very direct answer to.

"You find me interesting enough to kiss me?" I asked, and this time around she nearly choked on her wine. Or perhaps she did because after this question and for the next two minutes after, she didn't seem able to control herself and recover.

I watched and waited patiently, and eventually, she found the courage to turn around to look at me.

"Excuse me?" she asked in a little more than a whisper.

"I want to test out this attraction I have to you."

After this, I said nothing more, and her entire skin began to flush. Her cheeks grew puffier, her chest heaved harder, and I could understand that her entire system was now going into overdrive wondering how to respond to my offer. Unluckily for the both of us, we ran out of time, and then I was forced to go as soon as I heard my mother call out to us.

. . .

"Think about it and let me know," I said. However, before I could leave, she held onto my wrist.

My heart seemed to skip a beat as she did this. Her grip was stronger, much stronger than any woman's I had ever seen, but there was also something so warm and soft about it. Her nails weren't manicured like the women I was used to, but as I watched those hands, I suddenly wanted more than anything to see just how my cock would fit in them.

She stared at me, and I stared back, yet it seemed as though she still had nothing to say.

And then, eventually, I saw her eyes move to decide when she realized that we probably had an audience even though they were at a distance away.

And then she let me go. She went back to her drink without saying a word, and I smiled as I returned to the table.

Chapter Eight
Evelyn

I was still and had my phone against my ear, but it was either I called Anna now, or I came certified mentally incoherent. The second he left to return to his party, like I should have done but was not able to due to the shock that still permeated my system at his request, I texted her the explanation of what had just happened. And now, ten minutes later, I was calling her and walking out of the area preparing to scream.

To my surprise, she picked up as soon as I called, and I couldn't even be as mad because it was perfect timing.

"What's wrong with you?" I asked through gritted teeth. "You've seemed quite dedicated to messing me up through the day."

It took a while for her to compute anything I was saying, but eventually, she yawned and replied.

"Stop blaming me for this morning. I told you I set the alarm. And what's this about meeting some guy and kissing him? Did you do it? You should. You need to be kissed or even more. You've becoming so uptight."

"I didn't call you to scold me," I shot back.

"So why do you call then?"

I stopped, then realized it was a very valid question. Thankfully, though, I didn't have to search for a reply because she had one for me.

"Ah, you want to do it but it makes no sense to you because he's a stranger, so you want me to give you permission?"

This was it; however, there was no point in being humble and admitting it out loud, so I just remained silent.

I heard her amusement but ignored it.

"Just go for it," she said. "What do you have to lose?"

"Just like you did yesterday?" I couldn't help but tease her, and she sighed.

"If he wasn't my direct boss, I would have thrown all caution to the wind. This Drake dude is not your boss, and from what you've said, he's hot, so why the hell not?"

"Well, he's not my direct boss, but he is my client's brother."

"I'm going to bed," she replied. "Do whatever you want."

She ended the call before I could say a word, and I was left to my own devices.

I turned around then to watch their table and brought out my camera. The framing of the wooden beams from this position and the display of cakes and desserts that they had across their table was incredibly interesting to see, so I couldn't help taking a picture of it.

I took a few shots, went around to the corner before any of them could notice me, until eventually, Drake looked up, and our eyes met.

Once again, I pressed down on the shutter and took his shot, and it was disconcerting to say the least. I looked at the result on the screen, but when I looked up once again, he had turned away and was listening to Victoria. Her arms were flailing all about as she explained whatever she was, and it all just made me wonder if the previous ten minutes had even happened. I no longer wanted to join them, but I needed close-up shots that I couldn't get from afar, so I went just close enough and got my shots.

Afterward, they were heading over to check on accommodations in the venues, and I was more than grateful for the stroll. The weather was cooling down, the views were breathtaking, and it was just what I needed to clear my head.

Aurora came over to me then and held my arm.

"Are you alright?" she asked. "You've been awfully quiet."

Her brother was in front of us with his mother, so I couldn't help but feel awfully self-conscious.

"I'm fine," I replied.

"And the photos?"

"They'll be gorgeous," I replied with a smile and was more than happy to see the happiness it brought to her face.

Soon enough, we arrived at the accommodations, and I followed them through the rooms. It was a bit rustic but in such an elegant way that I was blown away. The emerald green draperies, the dark patterned wallpapers, the golden accents, and white calla lilies were beautiful. It made me wonder just how rich they were because no expense seemed to be spared. Thankfully, all of this was able to capture my attention, and in no time, it seemed like we were done.

There was one more shot, though, and this was of the whole family and unfortunately Victoria as well as they conversed about this final stage. I took the photos; however, just as I was perusing through them, I heard him call out to me.

It was startling because, up until then, he had managed to ignore my existence, but it didn't seem to be the case anymore. And I wasn't sure how I felt about it.

"Evelyn, come over here," he said, and I looked up. All eyes turned to me, and I was about to decline when I saw the scowl on Victoria's face, and I could no longer resist.

It was worth it if it made her this pissed.

I went over aiming to stand by Aurora and her alone.

"We need to see the pictures you've taken so far," Victoria said. "I contacted my photographer, Ethan, and he's willing to do the kind of shots you're doing right now. As you know, the client comes first, so I'm trying to ensure that they get the very best."

"Are you trying to say that she's not the best?" Aurora asked, to my surprise.

I smiled then, however, just before I could respond, she kept going.

"You know what, you're pretty annoying, and I don't want you as my wedding planner. Don't bother changing the photographer; you can just drop the project altogether."

Victoria stared at her, mouth wide open, and so did everyone else. It took everything inside of me not to laugh out loud.

"I think it's high time we called it a day," her brother said, "It's way past time for me to get back to the office, so I'll leave whatever is left here for you all to handle."

With this, he turned around but after taking only a few steps, he stopped and glanced back at me.

"Send me a few of the pictures you've taken so far. I want to understand Aurora's insistence on having you."

He pulled out a business card then and held it out.

I hated that I had to go over to receive it, but he was the boss, so I did as asked, and he handed it over. I tried as much as possible to avoid our hands touching during the exchange, but in the end, it wasn't entirely possible.

Sparks flared through me at the touch, so much so that I couldn't quite look him in the eyes.

"My personal email is attached as well as my phone number," he replied.

I nodded in response, and he went on his way.

Chapter Nine
Drake

T he more I thought of her, the harder I became. And this inconvenient and highly annoying fact became quite aggravating as the day wore on. It made me realize just how stressed I was because my mind was defaulting to her as an escape.

One image in particular kept coming to mind, and it was when she had squatted down for a shot in the vineyard. The sight of her full ass and hips straining against the fabric had instantly turned me rock hard, and it had taken a very upsetting phone call afterwards to bring me back to my senses.

I wanted her, briefly, but since she was still working for Aurora, I couldn't help but wonder if this would interfere negatively with the wedding. We were already taking a lot of control away from her, and I didn't want to mess up the relationship between her and the photographer she liked to be added to our list of offenses, or else her grudge might truly become immovable.

Still, I couldn't help but inform my assistant to be on the

lookout for her email and to ask for her phone number. Afterwards, I waited as I sat through meeting after meeting until eventually and quite unexpectedly, at a few minutes past ten that night, it came in.

I was already on my way out, but my assistant forwarded it to me, and I opened the link to peruse the pictures.

I flipped slowly through them and nodded. They were alright, good actually. Perhaps Aurora would love them and find whatever she was looking for in them, but I didn't have anything else to compare it to. The lighting was good; it was clear moments were captured. I logged out of the link and checked the email that it was sent from. I instantly replied to it. "

What's your phone number?" I asked and waited.

I had given her my business card, and like most women usually did when they had access to me, they usually didn't waste any time in contacting me, but she didn't seem interested whatsoever. Or perhaps she had just been busy with her work. I gave her another half hour, and when she still didn't respond, I threw the phone aside and forgot about her.

When I arrived at home, I had a guest waiting for me. She was in my living room and had the television on, eating through a tub of ice cream. I had no idea where it came from.

I was exhausted and didn't really want to entertain any guests, but I was always happy to see her.

"Thought you were going to ignore me forever?" I said as I headed over to the kitchen. After taking my jacket off, I grabbed a bottle of water and drained more than half of it in one go.

"I am, and I'm not here because I want to talk to you. I hate to even be doing this, but I just came to tell you that I don't care what you all think about my photographer. She's going to be with me until this wedding is over."

I watched from across the apartment, and then I went over to take a seat. She pretended to ignore me, but I knew that she was paying rapt attention and waiting for what I would say.

"Why couldn't David make it today?" I asked. "You didn't invite him?"

"Why do you think?" she asked.

"You told him I was coming."

"He's not scared of you," she said. "He just doesn't want things to be more difficult than it should be for me."

I nodded then. "I appreciate him for that." However, she was far from happy.

"Why can't you just let him be?"

"I didn't interact with—what do you mean?"

"Exactly. He feels like he's not good enough, and as a result, he keeps working like a dog as though he's trying to gain the respect of the whole family."

I sighed then and hated just how tormented she was.

"Rory, let me make something very clear," I told her. "I don't have any problem with David. His credentials aren't the most prestigious, but he has a lifetime to make his name. And if he doesn't, you'll be taken care of regardless. So, as long as he doesn't hurt you, I'm fine. The only place where I want to be involved is the wedding because of your status as a member of our family. This is an opportunity, as I told you, for us to honor business contacts. The owner of the vineyard we're using is a partner we've had an exclusive contract to export their wines for the past fifteen years. We're not even paying for the venue or much concerning your wedding. No one's trying to restrict you; we're just trying to take advantage of the situation, amongst other things. I don't think we're asking for too much."

I stared at her and then she sighed and looked away.

"Someday you'll understand a bit better," I said, and she frowned even more deeply.

"And as for your photographer, I saw her work. She's alright. She doesn't have to leave."

"What about the event planner, Victoria?" she asked. "She's annoyed me from the first moment I met her and she opened her mouth."

"That's another one of the business partners we cannot offend. Her father is on the board of Qattara and you know what that means and what that does to our partnerships with their hotels all over the world. There's no way that suddenly firing his daughter when she's already months into planning the wedding will bode well for either of our families. So please tolerate her till this is over, and if that gets too hard, then you can put your attention on Evelyn instead. She seems to have a beef as well with her so it might make you feel even better."

Afterwards, without a word of response, she got up and returned the half-eaten tub to the freezer.

"I'm sleeping here," she said and went on her way. I couldn't help my amazement but once again Evelyn popped into my mind, and I instantly got up and headed straight to the shower.

Chapter Ten
Evelyn

"Is that him?"

I was instantly startled at the sudden voice overhead.

I instantly shut my laptop, and at the shock on Anna's face, I knew that I had done something very unnecessary and very shameful.

Sighing, I shut my eyes knowing the mockery that was coming, but instead, all I heard was silence. Until I reopened my eyes and saw that she was quietly eating her diced cubes of watermelon, all while trying to control her smile.

"I was working. I was editing his photos."

"Right, you mean the shots you've been working on for the past six hours and have already sent off and have no business looking at again?"

My gaze darkened at her.

"Why do you act like this?"

She laughed then and continued eating.

"It's a relief to be able to laugh at you because I've hated being the only dumb one for so long."

"I'm not dumb," I told her. "I have no business with him."

"Why?" she asked, and her question somewhat startled me.

"Why should I?"

"You're not attracted to him? I mean, you've been staring at him, and you did call me in a panic earlier."

"It wasn't in a panic, and I haven't been star-" I stopped then because who was I kidding. I hadn't been able to stop thinking about him from the second we parted from the vineyard. To an extent, it almost felt as though I was losing my mind because the more I stared at him, the more aroused I felt, and it had been forever since I had felt this way about someone. I was excited about it and truly couldn't understand why I was so hesitant. Man, was there really any risk here besides me having a good time?

Just then Anna set her bowl and fork down and started to open up my laptop once again.

"Don't fight it," she said. "Just let me see."

Sighing, I allowed her, and once again his face came into view.

She was silent for a few moments but eventually even she gave her comment.

"Damn, I thought you were kidding," she said, and I smiled.

"He's attractive. Look at those thighs... look at his shoulders... Oomph, that hair. He will never go bald!"

This made me smile now and made me equally as

relieved since it was confirmed that I wasn't crazy. He was actually all that.

"Did you kiss him?" she asked, and my heart literally sank because I had to admit to myself, for now, that was a damn shame.

"You messed up there," she said. "You should have. How often are two people equally attracted to each other in this way?"

"He just wanted to test out if it was a fluke or something," I said. "Or at least that's what it sounded like."

"And the problem is?" she asked.

"That makes me like him even more because it shows that he's straightforward and doesn't see you as some damsel. He's assertive, knows what he wants, and asks for it. There will be no troubles with this one, so please tell me why you're hesitating?"

I sighed.

"I'm not anymore, but it might be too late, so I guess... the next time we meet or if he approaches me again?"

"He's not going to approach you again," she said, and I didn't even need to ask to know that she was right.

He probably already has another girl on his arm right now.

"Do you know about their family? Do you know what they do? Why are they so wealthy?" she asked, and I realized that I hadn't even checked.

"He told me to send him my phone number," I said as I pulled out his business card and searched their surname on Google.

"Have you?" she asked as we waited for the search results.

"Not yet," I replied, and I could feel her shake her head above me.

Soon enough, the results came out, and then my brows raised.

"They're new money millionaires," she said, and I nodded, amazed.

"Wait, so... health and fitness. Explains his ridiculous body. His father started several gyms... he came in during college and turned their business model into a licensing division... made almost 200 million."

Holy crap!

"Oh!" she said.

"He's more than capable. I was already irritated with him, thinking he was a nepo baby that was, of course, controlling everyone around him for no reason."

"There's more," she said. "Now he's into business acquisition... Well, not full acquisition, partnership. They help companies grow and take a percentage. Hmm..." she said.

"Oh wow. He's impressive. And you said no to him again because?"

I wanted to bang my head against the table.

"I didn't say no to him," I replied. "I just ..."

"You just what?" she asked.

"I just haven't responded yet.

"Because?"

I didn't respond to her. Instead, tired of defending myself, I slammed the laptop closed and rose to my feet.

"Time for bed," I announced. "And time as well for you to stop hounding me."

She smiled and went back to her couch to resume her lounging. I, on the other hand, took my phone with me and, although I tried to ignore it as I brushed my teeth and took a shower getting ready for bed, I eventually couldn't hold myself back as I sat down on the toilet. So, I pulled up the email he had sent me, and instantly I sent a reply.

This time, however, and a bit nervous at the fact that Anna had mentioned that he wouldn't contact me, again I decided to extend an olive branch which he was free to respond to, but at least it would convey the fact that I hadn't rejected him because I wasn't interested but because it had been all too much to process too soon. But of course, I said this with as much class as I could muster.

"Hello," I wrote. "Mr. Moran. This is Evelyn. Here's my phone number as requested."

I started to send the message but then I recalled the stress that Aurora was going through because of his domineering nature. He was basically forcing her to endure the wedding that he wanted, so why was I even giving such a narcissist the time of day? Previously, I had thought it to be a unilateral old money unavoidable decision, but now that I knew that he was more or less at the helm of everything and should know better, the light I had previously painted around him began to dim.

And so, I reconsidered sending the message. Eventually, though, and with the conclusion that it was best not to be rude, I sent him my phone number and tried my very best to ignore my phone. There was no additional note, no suggestive or flirtatious comment like I had earlier planned on including to resurrect his invitation earlier. It had been cold and informative, and that was all I had to give to him until I knew him enough to decide whether to push him even further away or to dip my toe into whatever this was that was between us.

I headed straight to the bedroom, caught up on some emails and settled in for the night. However, just before I shut my eyes and drifted off to sleep, I received another message from him that nearly made my jaw drop down to the floor.

Chapter Eleven
Drake

"I want to see you. Where are you?"

This was what I had written straight to her phone, and my only hope was that she would honor this and give a response. I was already pissed off that I was trying too hard, but I was now lying in bed with a hard on that refused to go away, and I just knew that the only solution was for me to taste her.

Even if it was just her lips, at this point, I didn't really care because all I wanted to do was indulge for once.

She, however, was being quite difficult to get to, and it was truly beginning to irritate the hell out of me.

"Brooklyn," she replied, and I sighed. She truly was testing my patience.

"I'll send a car over. Get in it. I want to see you."

I sent the message, and it was a while later before she finally responded.

"No thank you, it's already too late. I'll see you the next time I meet up with Aurora," she replied. "Or whenever the family meets for wedding preparations."

Her response made me frown, but I also felt the rejection all the way to my core as it twitched, and it only made me more insistent.

"I'm not a man people refuse, Miss Snow," I replied to her. "I don't care to see you then and perhaps even after tonight."

This time around, she responded on time.

"You are quite straightforward," she said. "And blunt. And maybe a tad bit rude?"

This was an amusing surprise.

"You feel disrespected?" I asked. "Because I want to fuck you? It's just a midnight craving. You know how those go."

I sent this as well and threw the phone aside. It was time to go to bed, but still, and as expected, I waited for her response.

"Wow," she said. "You don't think this is inappropriate. Especially since we literally just met?"

I'm clearly stating my intentions and if you were completely uninterested, then you wouldn't have held my arm before we parted at the vineyard. You didn't want to leave, but you didn't quite know what to say just yet. I'm assuming you've had some more time to think, and this is why you have sent me your number?"

Another five minutes passed once again before she responded.

"You're making a lot of assumptions, Mr. Moran," she said, and I smiled.

"Alright, goodnight then," I said, and threw the phone aside. A few minutes later, it lit up once again, and I picked it up. There were no words, only the link to a map. And then an address that followed.

Smiling, I called my driver, Andrew, and immediately sent him over to Brooklyn.

Chapter Twelve
Evelyn

I had now officially lost my mind. It was basically the middle of the night and not only had I just accepted a booty call, I was also sneaking out of the house so that Anna wouldn't wake up and catch me about to make what would probably end up being the dumbest decision of my life. I didn't make it, she heard me and got up.

Still, my sex was throbbing so hard from all those filthy words he had said to me that I couldn't stop leaking.

I had touched myself over and over, and yet nothing had satisfied me. I was restless, horny, frustrated, and excited. So, here I was throwing every ounce of reason to the wind. He was bound to have a huge cock, at least hopefully he did, and where I wanted it to reach, no one else or thing right now could. I wanted to be fucked so hard that I forgot myself. It had been my wish for the longest time, and it had never come true, but given his arrogant self, I was once again quite motivated to take a chance.

The car arrived faster than I had expected, and even though I couldn't quite look the driver in the eye, I had no qualms about staring at the man's picture on my phone. He was motherfuckingly breathtaking and the more I stared at him, the more I was convinced that yes, this was indeed a stupid and impulsive decision, but yet I couldn't wait.

My excitement was further reinforced when the car pulled up to Billionaires' Row and then stopped in front of 220 Central Park South. I knew he was wealthy, but this was a level of wealth that I couldn't help but appreciate. And coupled with the silence of the night, it all seemed like a dream. There were no distractions, I was fully engaged in my mind and heart, and in a way, it felt like an out-of-body experience.

Instructions had already been given to the doorman to allow me in, and by the elevators, another uniformed man was waiting to escort me up this floor. Everything looked so polished, clean, and wealthy that, once again, as I quickly stared at my reflection in the mirror behind, I was glad that I had taken a bit more time with my appearance this time around.

I barely had on any makeup but was clean with a light blush and a peach tint to my lips. I looked fresh, rosy, suckable, with my hair freshly washed and my entire body scenting like blackberries.

And then my outfit...It was an elegant, checkered skirt, a white button-down lace shirt, and a pair of brown designer sandals that I had fought with Anna to lend me. I looked casual but sheer, and even though my outfit was considerably less rosy than what I had worn earlier in the day, I still felt much more confident, attractive, and presentable.

I was so incredibly nervous to see him. Much more nervous than I had ever been, and as I thought on why, I realized that it was because things were becoming more real than I could

have ever imagined. Another very good reason was the dirty talk. A complete stranger had sworn to eat me out and me, a complete horny idiot, had jumped up immediately and gone over.

My head still couldn't wrap itself around it, but it was too late to go back, and I had no regrets.

Anna had been filled with concern before I left, asking me if it was dangerous. And all I had said in response was, what is the worst he could do? Fuck me? That was the exact reason I was going in the first place, and so she had sat back and forced me to bring back the details about everything to her. I couldn't wait myself to gather them, and hopefully, it would be a memory that I could cherish.

. . .

He met me at the door. He didn't have a shirt on but instead, he had long cotton pajama pants on, and his hair seemed tousled. It was as though he had just rolled out of bed and for a moment, I couldn't speak or move. This was a different version of him that I was seeing, and I just loved it so much. He looked more relaxed, more approachable, and so goddamn sexy. I didn't miss the bulge straining against his pants, but somehow, I was able to discipline myself enough to look away from it.

"Hello," he said, and all I could do was smile.

I walked in and was met with the most beautiful arrangement of flowers on a console by the side. It caught my attention for several minutes and then I turned to see him walking away. The muscles in his broad back shifted as he moved, and my mouth watered at the sight of him. He was so smooth and strong, so virile, and the way the warm light of the apartment shone on his skin made him look like molten gold.

The apartment, to say the least, was gorgeous. It was befitting of a man as wealthy as he was, but what I loved the most was just how cozy it felt. Perhaps it was because most of the lights were turned off and only warmth flooded the space, or perhaps it was due to the dark green and monochrome decor.

. . .

It smelled, though, far from a home and more like a scent store. There were no scents of food or pastries, but instead, it was smooth of sophistication and luxury. It smelled like him as well, I realized.

Tobacco, vanilla, lime...

I stood in place then, just completely overwhelmed because he didn't seem real. None of this seemed real, and it was becoming quite a lot to take in.

"Are you alright?" His voice suddenly reverberated through the entire room, and I looked up to see him behind the huge kitchen island.

"Yeah, I'm fine," I said, dragging my full attention to him. Once again, my gaze went down his gorgeous body, and truly, it was hard to breathe. His torso was built into well-defined slabs of
muscle that I wanted to run my tongue down or eat off. My breath instantly became short, and the troublesome bud between my thighs was ready for him to take me however he wanted.

This attraction was dangerous. I had never felt this way about anyone before and so quickly. The rush...the admiration...the arousal...

It felt like I was on a cloud. My heart was warm, my skin tingling, my breathing short.

"Do you want something to eat or drink?" he asked, and I shook my head in refusal.

I wanted to say yes to spend some time getting to know him, but I deeply suspected that this would be dangerous. I didn't want to like him, and the more I knew of his existence, the more I realized that the possibility of this was increasing with every moment, and it was dangerous.

There most likely couldn't be anything or a future between us, and with the way he was treating Aurora, I was pretty sure I wouldn't be able to stand all aspects of him.

These, however, were just what I wanted to keep me here tonight and excited.

"You sure?" he asked. "Cranberry juice? Wine? Fruits? Champagne?"

"Cranberry juice is fine," I said, wanting the sweetness and tang. Alcohol, though I was staying away from it, maybe until later. I just wanted to kiss him more than anything else. It was the one thing I had been unable to get out of my head all day long, and I truly couldn't take it any longer.

So, I headed over and retrieved the glass from him. I came around to where he was standing and leaned against the counter and took a small sip.

He was watching me closely, and as a result, my stupid heart kept tumbling out of place and falling into my stomach.

It was all very disconcerting, and so I looked away and stared out towards the dim living room where the windows overlooking the city were. They covered the entire wall, and the view was so panoramic that they were the perfect anti-dote to my current anxiety and nervousness. The stars were shining brightly in the darkness and never more than at this moment, did they seem so beautiful to me, even though I had a slight fear of heights.

"How did Aurora come to know about you?" he suddenly asked, and I returned my attention to him. I took one more sip of the juice and then held onto the huge tumbler. He had poured me a generous amount, which I most definitely couldn't finish at the moment but definitely, as the night wore on, I would definitely need it and as a result be able to.

. . .

"We met at a coffee shop," I replied. "She came up to me because she recognized me from my posts on social media, and that was how we connected."

"Oh," he said. "So you were a recommendation?"

"No," I replied, and as usual with him, I truly couldn't decipher through his tone what was a compliment or an insult. It didn't matter anyway because I wasn't here seeking anyone's approval. I was just here to get fucked and then to be let go so I could move on with my life.

So, I set the glass down and looked up at him.

He leaned forward then, and as his big warm hand wrapped around my neck, I felt myself begin to melt.

I felt so fragile in his arms, so delicate, so wanted, and so, when he slightly lifted my chin and moved to kiss me, I was ready with my whole heart. His lips connected with mine, and it had to be the sweetest thing I had ever tasted.

He smelled so clean and so exotic that I lost myself in his taste. My eyes tightened shut, and before I could stop myself, I was holding onto his thick biceps. He was so sexy, so strong, so big...my knees could no longer hold me up. I moved even closer, just so that I could press my body against him.

Knowing what I was coming for, I had foregone a bra altogether, and I was now being very well rewarded for it because my hardened nipples grazed so hungrily against the hardness of his chest. His arms went around my waist, seeming to encapsulate me and bend me like a doll.

It was the perfect move, however, because it ensured that he could lean down even further and deepen the kiss.

I had expected something of a hard and rough kiss given how charged and tense our attraction was to each other, but perhaps it was because of the calm night, but this was soft, sweet, intense. It was as though it could go on forever, as though we both intended it to go on forever.

Eventually, he pulled away to suck on my lips, and it was a fight before either of us let go. That slight pull at the end floored me, and so I held on even tighter to him just so that it wouldn't be revealed just how much of a puddle I had been turned into. I looked up then into his eyes, and he did the same, and then to my disappointment, he let me go. I quickly held onto the counter for my stability while he reached for my half-filled glass of juice and took a healthy drink from it.

. . .

"Afterwards," he set it down, and although I didn't want to keep staring at him, I had to look away. I couldn't read his expression at all, I realized. It was as though he was contemplating the kiss we just had and whether it was worth the trouble of even going further with me and as a result, I became instantly defensive.

I had just had the best kiss, so why did he seem to be contemplating if he had made the biggest mistake of his life? I truly didn't know how to process this.

"Let's go upstairs," he suddenly said, but I found myself reluctant to move even though he did. I watched him leave as he was already heading towards the stairs before he realized that I wasn't
following behind. He stopped then and turned to me, and the glow of the night on him made him look surreal. I knew then that I hadn't been dumbfounded all day and practically from the very moment I laid eyes on him because he was interesting to look at, and that I hadn't thrown my brain into the gutter and jumped into his car to come all the way here on a whim.

I was so attracted to him that it was terrifying, and this kind of attraction, the only way I could see it ending, was with my obsession and a heartbreak so extreme that I would probably not be able to recover from it.

· · ·

Unless he turned out to truly be the absolute dickhead that he appeared to be with his dealings with Aurora.

"Um...," I swallowed, wondering how I could stall to give myself one last chance to make a better and wiser decision.

"Aurora," I said. "Why don't you want her to have the wedding that she wants?" I asked. "I mean, it's her once special day. I don't understand why you're fighting her so much about the things she wants, the size, and just everything in general. It's making her very unhappy and miserable."

As my words left my lips, I could very clearly read his expression because suddenly and right before my eyes, he turned from a neutral expression to something so menacing that I felt chills run down my spine.

"Why are you asking me about Aurora?" he asked, a very deep and dark scowl forming between his brows.

"Well, uh..." I felt myself instantly begin to stutter. But I wasn't going to back down because this was probably now more for me than for him. Perhaps if he was angry enough, he'd throw me out before we even got started, and I'd be able to dodge whatever incoming bullet this entire night felt like.

"I...," I began, not exactly sure what I was going to say, but soon enough, and as the very heavy seconds passed between us, words formed.

"It's her day, and I believe she has the right to spend it however she wants. Understand that—"

"Get out," he said, and the entire room came to a halt.

At first, I was sure that I was mistaken, that he hadn't just said what he had, but then as I saw the anger in his eyes, I grew afraid.

He looked furious. So furious that I was truly terrified.

I wanted to argue, to shout back at him and hurl off some insults of my own as well because he had no right to talk to me that way, but the redder his eyes became, the more I understood that I

had hit a very, very sore nerve.

. . .

I expected him then to lunge for me and attack, and so without saying a single word, I went around the counter and began to head towards the foyer. I tried not to run, but the moment I got to the door, I couldn't help it. I could feel the daggers from his eyes piercing into my back and at any point almost expected to feel actual pain from his attack. Eventually, I got out and shut the door behind me, but I couldn't explain or understand what had just happened.

It took me a while to calm down. I walked slowly back to the lobby, and of course, there was no driver and car waiting to take me back to my apartment, so I had to hail down a taxi by myself.

All the way through, I went through a myriad of emotions. Sure, that was basically what I had been trying to achieve when I had brought up Aurora, but I could never have imagined he would act that way. This proved a point that he was a narcissist.

So, I was right. Yet as I rode home, his eyes never left my mind. I had a narcissistic father, and his reaction and eyes in that moment hadn't exactly seemed as though he was one. Instead, it had seemed that more than anything, he was hurt, and I couldn't understand why. Nothing made any sense anymore, and I was so filled with shame at how he had kicked me out that I didn't want to care. However, later that night and just before I finally drifted off to sleep after chugging down half a bottle of wine, I truly wondered if there was more to his authoritative control over Aurora's wedding.

And just like that, all of a sudden, rather than hate him so easily, I wanted to find out even more about him.

Chapter Thirteen

Drake

"I don't understand this itinerary," Aurora said as she finally put down her fork for the first time that morning, caring enough about the events planned for her wedding.

"A week? An entire week?" she asked. Victoria immediately looked away from her glare, turning to me for help, but I was not in the mood to engage in any of this, so I returned my attention to my phone and continued working.

"Drake," Aurora called, but I ignored her.

"Mom?"

"It's not a week because we want it to be exorbitant," my mom replied. "It's a week because—"

Aurora cut her off. "Let me guess, it's some sort of business gathering."

My mom gazed at her exhaustedly, and then she finally nodded. "Yes, it's a business gathering."

"Ah, I'm spared once again, your royal highnesses," I forgot that this has absolutely nothing to do with me. My bad."

She flung the itinerary card aside.

"In fact, why do any of you even need me here? The way things are looking, I'm pretty sure you can have the wedding without me."

She rose to her feet, and without bothering to finish her breakfast, she stormed off the patio and returned to the house. I was very aware of the entire episode; however, I kept my gaze on my phone, acting for all the world as if I hadn't even heard a single thing. Even at Aurora's departure, I could now see everyone's eyes on me, as usual, looking for guidance and a conclusion.

I didn't intend to say a word, but then I didn't even have to because a few seconds later, Aurora returned still fuming.

"If this were reversed and this was Drake's wedding, would you all disregard his wishes and treat him so blatantly disrespectfully in this way?"

I replied to this one without missing a beat.

"If this were my wedding, I would be more understanding and patient with my family and

understand their desire to use this avenue to strengthen their business ties and relationships."

I looked up then and glared at her.

"No one stopped you when you decided not to work for the company, and that you would go your own way. But now you can't even be slightly inconvenienced for us?"

At my admonition, she kept silent, but there had already been an underlying tenor of annoyance that had been plaguing me. I rose to my feet, ready to leave. On my way, however, just as she had done, I paused at the door.

"What's bad about a vacation, by the way?" I asked her. "In as much as you didn't care that this will be an appreciated provision and a much-needed break for the caliber of guests we are inviting, then what about me? I haven't taken a vacation in at least the last five years. Given the chance now to do so because of your wedding, isn't it a good thing?"

At my words, and just as I knew she would because she cared about me, she quieted down and then she stormed off.

My mom's soft comment followed her departure.

"When did she get so impatient and disagreeable?" she asked, and I ignored this comment. I heard, though, Victoria's laugh and something about it irritated me enough to look up.

It was polite and all, but it sounded so insincere I wondered if she was truly aware of it.

I understood that it was part of her job, like Aurora, to be agreeable, but to be this artificial. I rose to my feet then, unwilling to stomach any of this. It had been a bright and slightly cold morning, and so, as per the itinerary, we had met here for a beginning breakfast to discuss the week, any precautions to be taken, and any notes to be noted.

My father wasn't present yet, so it felt a bit demotivating, but now that Aurora had turned it into a fight, it all seemed even more stressful.

"I really want to rest this week," I told my mom. And then I glanced at Victoria.

"Is there a way to make this hassle-free?" I asked her. "And I don't want to be involved in the planning whatsoever. Instead, I want to arrive when the guests are arriving. In fact, you should only contact me if needed and after you've reached out to my parents and assistants first."

She looked at me, and I couldn't help but notice the hurt in her eyes.

It was quite easy for me to read people, so this was impossible to miss. But what I couldn't tell was if her distress was simply because of the resistance from Aurora or from the fact that I had just clearly told her not to reach out to me.

Besides the actual reasons I had listed in front of everyone else, I hoped that she understood

that it was also because of her constant attempts through my assistant to see me in the office or run into me in restaurants under the guise of discussing urgent issues pertaining to the wedding. Each time I had refused, reminding her that my sister and mother were present to handle this; however, she had remained persistent.

Throughout all, though I had been civil and patient, but then the last instance before we'd all arrived at the Hamptons for the ceremony, she had insisted, despite my receptionist's rejection, to see me.

Under the guise of being very concerned and diligent about her work, she had waited nearly all day just to see me to discuss something urgent and crucial to the wedding. Only to mention, when she had finally cajoled me into giving her an audience, that she wanted Evelyn fired.

Her reasons were built on logic, seemingly, as she showed me different pictures taken by the magazine professional she wanted to hire for Aurora.

"He's more refined," she said. "More sophisticated. I want Aurora to have the best, but you know she's already a bit attached to Evelyn, so I don't know how to get through to her to make this happen."

I stared at her quietly and sighed, truly wondering now

if this was all out of concern or because, and for some reason, she just wanted Evelyn gone.

I wish I could tell her that Evelyn more or less felt the same about her, but I had instead given some sort of curt response or the other, and then I had continued on with the rest of the day.

Now, I had been hoping that she would take this cue as what to expect with our interaction but seeing her at the family breakfast as though she belonged here was quite disconcerting to me.

It had meant to be a private affair, but here she was again encroaching under the guise of doing her job.

Sighing, I headed straight to the library, which had always been my favorite place in the house. It was huge, sleek, and modern, with concrete walls and mahogany cabinets. I rarely ever read physical books anymore since I was always on the move and barely had the time. But coming here, I could ditch the audio I slipped into my ear when I wanted to discourage people from approaching me for whatever reason and browsed through a few of the titles I was interested in. It truly was a place I had my earliest memories along with Aurora, but while I had been drawn towards the books, she, on the other hand, had been drawn towards the art.

Recently, all I'd been involved in and learning about was medical research, but now with this current week, I decided to relax. However, and had been happening the second I sat down, yet another pesky woman came to mind. This one was the opposite of Victoria, and I couldn't really understand why. It would be easy to chalk her large disinterest in me up to the fact that I had all but kicked her out of my apartment, but I was very used to dismissing women at will, and them being willing to come back and ensuring to act that whatever previous tiff we had had been erased and forgotten.

With Evelyn, however, I was almost sure that I had made a mortal enemy. And it excited me. I wasn't sorry about the way I had kicked her out. It wasn't entirely her fault because, unbeknownst to her, she had hit a very, very sore nerve, and I couldn't help but react the way I had. But now, knowing that she was still working with Aurora, I was quite curious to see how she would take it and how she would behave around me. I sighed then and called for a bottle of rare wine delivered to me from the vineyard. I hadn't really cared much about this week, seeing it as business as usual, but as I relaxed in the quiet, a part of me, waiting for her arrival, knew that it was going to be one of the most thrilling times I had had recently.

Chapter Fourteen
Evelyn

Coming here felt as though a leash had been put around my neck, and I had been dragged here like a dog. I was so reluctant I couldn't believe it. So much so that I had refused to pack and purposely missed my bus to the Hamptons. And thus, I was arriving late and ready to apologize, but I didn't care how this made me look because I had already decided earlier that morning that I was going to call Aurora and inform her that it was truly best that Victoria's photographer handled her ceremony.

However, and whether it was because I was attracted to fire and embarrassment all of a sudden, I had decided against this in the end and went to work anyway. It wasn't that I was embarrassed, I corrected myself. It was just that I couldn't picture a way in which our interactions after the last time we had met wouldn't be awkward and painful to bear, at least on my part. He, on the other hand, would probably act like I didn't exist since I didn't think he was one to gloat; however, it was still all nerve-wracking. This was why you didn't ever mix business with pleasure, no matter the justification you gave for it, even extreme stupid horniness.

Sighing, I looked up at the gorgeous mansion and shook my head. I had become somewhat used to wealth after moving to New York—wealth from a distance, that is. Seeing it, being envious of it, recognizing it, admiring it... but theirs seemed to be of a different kind. Everything they had and did was extravagant in a way that they didn't even seem to notice, and I couldn't help but feel severely uncomfortable and out of place.

Which had made me realize earlier that I would be reluctant as well in the future to go after clients like these, so it was best to take advantage now of being associated with someone as down-to-earth as Aurora. I had business cards ready and had an idea of how I could distribute them without being annoying, but for that, I would have to, of course, ask Aurora's permission. And... I sighed as some attendants came over, asked me my name, and immediately took my luggage; I would probably have to also ask Victoria since she was the event planner.

None of this made me excited, but still, I sucked it up and headed in. I asked instantly to be taken to Aurora and was led to the red room. In there, and unfortunately, I met a bunch of people. One was Victoria, of course, and two assistants with her, as well as a house attendant. In the corner was an assortment of food, while standing before Aurora was a rack of clothes.

"Evelyn," her face immediately brightened the moment she saw me.

In that moment and at the very warm reception, it became difficult for me to regret coming. I was always so floored at how she appreciated my work, so once again, I convinced myself that this was more than enough reason for me to be here despite her brother and Victoria. After giving me a hug, she pulled me over with her, and I was almost amused at how her expression changed towards Victoria. In that moment, I felt a bit sorry for Victoria because this truly wasn't her fault. She was taking her instructions from Drake, that asshole, and she couldn't help but be out in the crosshairs between both siblings.

"I have to choose dresses for the entire week," she said. "Well, all sorts of outfits and accessories."

At this, she gave Victoria a sour look, and it was a feat for me to control my smile. Unfortunately, Victoria saw this, and I could tell that in that moment and especially with my presence, she couldn't stand the disrespect anymore, and so she excused herself and left the room. Aurora took a break as well and took me with her into an adjoining room which looked like a lounge. It had a chaise lounge, velvet tapestry, and just the most intricate of textures and colors. It was so absolutely breathtaking that I immediately wanted to go get my camera.

"Just a moment," she said and handed me a drink with a pineapple.

"It's so gorgeous here," I told her. "And the lighting."

She smiled and nodded.

"I know. Right, go get it; I'll wait for you, and then we can talk."

I looked towards the gorgeous open windows and was so worried the light would be leaving that I nearly whipped out my iPhone. Just before I left, though, as I looked back once again to see the way the sun hit her at just the perfect angle, I whipped the phone out much to her amusement. I took a few pictures and could see the genuine joy in her eyes, and it was so incredibly beautiful. Afterwards, I left my phone with her to peruse through, and then I hurried away as per her directions. She said that my room would be on the last floor, which I wasn't averse to since it was always an opportunity to exercise. However, after climbing three floors of the grand staircase and nearly collapsing on the way, I stopped by the rung and tried to catch my breath.

"Absolutely motherfucking not," I swore, with my gaze on the floor and sweat beading across my forehead. There had to be an elevator because this was motherfucking ridiculous. Just as I got up, however, my heart nearly left my chest. To be honest, I smelled him before I even saw him, coming up to a room and heading my way. He was dressed impeccably in a light blue dress shirt and tailored slacks but in sleek house slippers that, although giving him a casual look, still couldn't hide his wealth and sophistication. Instantly, it was as though I was attacked in the stomach by butterflies. Vicious, horny, shameless, cruel butterflies. All I could do was stare as though I was trying to convince myself that he wasn't real and that he wasn't here, which made absolutely no sense because this was his fucking house.

He gave me a peculiar look but of course acted like I didn't exist. A few steps down, however, he stopped and turned back to me. My heart briefly stopped in my chest since it seemed as though he was about to say something to me. But then he seemed to take me in, and I had never felt more insignificant. He continued on his way, and I almost threw myself at him just so that he would roll down the stairs and perhaps break his neck. I didn't even care if I died in the process as long as he did as well or broke several limbs and ended up in a wheelchair, best with a blind eye and half of his face scraped off. After this, I paused for a moment and shut my eyes to calm my temper, and by the time I reopened them, he was out of sight.

How fucking annoying he was, I couldn't help but lament, but then I was even more bothered by how immensely his mere presence could affect me. I continued down to my room then, a bit more calmly and with the conclusion that I couldn't give less of a fuck about his presence.

Rather, it's because of the way he had looked at me with his gaze running down my body. It didn't seem sexual; rather, it made me feel as though I wasn't up to par in appearance even though I had shelled out $300 fucking dollars for my week here. That was the most I had ever spent on clothes, ever, and he wasn't even the least bit appreciative. Well, I didn't do it for him, but I didn't need him undermining my confidence anyway.

I sat on the bed then, fuming, and nearly forgot what I had come up here for and even why I was in this fucking gorgeous room. The moment I recalled; however, I gave the room the appreciation it deserved, grabbed my camera, and was returning to Aurora's room. She was on the phone when I arrived and wanted to end the call to give me her attention, but I shook my head and refused.

"I'm not here," I mouthed to her, and she smiled, her eyes sparkling because I was most definitely there. It warmed my heart as I truly wondered why she liked me so much. Either way, I lost myself in the following moments, capturing the little moments in the room. The way the light filtered in and illuminated the gorgeous bouquet of flowers on the coffee table that looked like it was carved out of painted chalk. The statues, the textures, her eyes so filled with love as she spoke to her fiancé on the phone. Soon enough, she was done, and I waited for the melancholy that I was sure would set in at missing him. She didn't realize this, but eventually, she put the phone away and looked up at me, and then she smiled, realizing.

"You captured that?" she asked, and I nodded.

"Yes, I did. I'll make a personal album for you."

"Really?" she asked.

"Yes," I replied. "At no cost."

Her gaze softened even further, but I was more than happy to do it. She had been absolutely lovely to me so far, plus I was going out of my mind with just how many photographs I could take of this location, so I didn't mind at all. I was going to have too many anyway. She handed my phone back to me, and together we walked back out of her bedroom. She continued trying on clothes, and even though she rejected some, I immediately knew my next idea for her because they were extravagant enough to look absolutely breathtaking with some of the landscapes of the beach and vineyard around. So far, it seemed as though all would go well, and so I admonished myself that if I could just keep her brother out of mind and hopefully out of sight, I would be able to have one of the best weekends ever.

Chapter Fifteen
Drake

Seeing her had been a serious trip, I realized. As I returned to the library to continue with my serene time alone for once, I couldn't help but think about her. I had noticed her long before she had noticed me as I emerged from the room. Her struggle up the staircase had been absolutely amusing to see, from the sweat that dripped down the sides of her face to her very dramatic gasping for air every chance she'd gotten. I'd instantly wanted to speak to her but held myself back, and then in the last moment, thought of mentioning to her that there was an elevator and that she didn't have to go through this, but then she'd given me the cruelest, darkest scowl, and I decided that she didn't deserve the information.

I truly thought she would have brushed away what had happened between us, at the very least for the fact that I was basically her boss, even though she listened only to Aurora. At the end of the day, I would be the one paying for all of this, but instead, she had looked at me like the enemy. I didn't care, and at seeing the gorgeous sundress she'd had on and how it'd cupped her full, gorgeous breasts, my struggle heading down the stairs had been most of the blood rushing down from my head and straight down to my dick. By the time I arrived on the ground floor, I was fully hard and had nearly forgotten what I had headed down the stairs to do in the first place.

I stopped then and couldn't believe how distracted I was being. It was so rare that I was this way. However, as I turned to glance back at the girl that had now hurried to her room, I shut my eyes and took a deep breath. I had been headed to the library, which was on the second floor, but now that I had missed it altogether, I decided to just head outside. I had some administrative things to handle anyway, and so I headed out to the patio. It was already evening, and the sun was already setting. The air was cool, the pool was glistening, and it was generally a nice time out.

One of the kitchen staff came over then, and after placing an order for some whiskey, she left while I crossed my legs and tried to distract myself from my fucking hard-on. I wondered truly then if I wanted to take things all the way with her because, if I didn't want to, then for my peace of mind, it was best that she went to a different house. Perhaps one of the accommodations close to the vineyard that we had arranged for our guests. However, I was aware that Aurora might object to this since she wanted her around at all times to help her with photographs.

Sighing, I decided to just put her out of my mind and concentrate on my work. Nearly an hour later, however, I heard soft laughter emerging from the house. More than anything, I was annoyed by the interruption, but all of that quickly dissipated as I looked towards the pool and saw the two girls taking off the cover-ups they had worn over their bathing suits. I immediately made out Aurora as she revealed the pink one-piece swimsuit she had underneath. I could see the slight bulge of her belly for her pregnancy and couldn't help but worry that it wasn't entirely safe for her to be swimming. However, when I turned to the woman that was also stripping by her side, all thoughts and concerns for my lovely sister immediately dissipated.

She had on a black bikini and although it was supposed to be covered, I imagined. It didn't

seem to be her size. And thus, it was so skimpy that the panties disappeared into her fucking ass. The bra barely covered her breasts, and she was so self-conscious about this that she immediately dove into the pool, hiding all of this from sight. I could hear Aurora shouting words of encouragement to her; however, she didn't seem convinced.

Getting out of the pool, she dried off then grabbed the camera bag she had brought along, retrieved the DSLR, and started taking pictures. She stood at the edge, moving slowly, but the tiny bra strap made her quite uncomfortable.

I knew that it was only a matter of time before they noticed my presence; however, I found myself unable to look away. My dick definitely wouldn't let me, and so eventually, as she took her pictures, her lens turned towards me, and she took the shot.

She seemed shocked for a moment as our eyes met through the lens, and then she lowered it down to stare in my direction. Aurora had been diligently swimming, but the second she noticed that Evelyn had more or less frozen, she turned and smiled when she finally realized what had caught her attention.

"Drake!" she called out; however, it was a struggle for me to take my eyes off Evelyn. I fucking couldn't understand what it was about this woman that turned me on so much. In a moment, she turned around as though she hadn't seen me and continued with her work.

"Come join us," Aurora shouted, and I shook my head at her.

It was my cue to leave then because I was now so uncomfortable that it was nearly unbearable to remain seated. So, I got up and immediately left. The library was better, plus I was in the midst of resolving something crucial plus she was too much of a distraction for me to stomach.

. . .

The time quickly passed by, and it was especially enjoyable because, unlike in the office, I didn't have phones ringing or anyone knocking and demanding an audience every five minutes. Suddenly, about an hour later, I heard a small knock on the door. At first, I was sure I had misheard it because I wondered how anyone could possibly be looking for me. Frowning, I lifted my gaze, wondering if it was one of the housekeepers, but then, instead, whom I saw coming in cautiously and carefully was the current object of my attraction.

Chapter Sixteen
Evelyn

Aurora had told me about him. Even if this was supposed to be a vacation, he would, of course, be working, and thus he would be in the library. She also explained to me when I worried about him leaving that I shouldn't bother about that because he hated being distracted.

"But he can't complain because this is literally a family space," she said, so I didn't worry about it; he's in the library so he can focus. I, however, couldn't help wondering if it was because of me. Every time I had run into him so far, he had barely spared me a glance, and then he had gone out of his way to not be in the same space I was.

Sure, he had offended me immensely when we had met up. But now, according to my suspicion from back then, that perhaps he had gotten angry because I had said something that had hurt him, I couldn't help thinking that this was the reason why he couldn't even stand the sight of me. I didn't care, and I shouldn't have cared; however, it was making me very uncomfortable. Plus, with the bikini that Aurora had forced me to wear since I hadn't brought any along, I was sure that the show I had put on for anyone who had eyes wasn't exactly the most decent. I was much more endowed than Aurora, I now knew for a fact since I had imagined from the beginning that we were the same frame and size. But as her new bikini could barely fit my ass, breasts, and hips, I understood now that I was much thicker than I had earlier judged.

Anyway, I wanted to clear the air for my peace of mind because I couldn't imagine going through the rest of this week this on edge. For one, all this anxiety was making me so fucking horny that I could barely think straight. It wasn't because I wanted to do anything with him; it was just because something about my nerves being so raw and frayed was making me so sensitive that I had even forgone wearing underwear because even the rub of the fabric against my clit was torture. I couldn't understand it, but I was pretty sure that getting back on somewhat good and platonic terms with Drake would increase my chances of returning back to normal.

I had already rehearsed what to say; I had my camera in hand and would, of course, act as though I had just been scouting locations in the mansion. I would then mistakenly wander into the library and after explaining myself and, of course, apologizing, I would head out and move on with my life, and most importantly, be able to wear panties again. Determined for this to be the outcome and conclusion of my evening, I knocked again even though the previous time had yielded no response, and then I received the call from him or whoever was to come in. His tone was gruff and slightly annoyed at the intrusion, but I admonished myself and my shaky knees that all I had to do was say what I wanted to and be on my way. It was up to him to accept it or not. I had no possible say over that.

Hence, I pushed the door open, and my heart jumped into my throat. I didn't want to be nervous because if I acted nervous, then of course, I would feel too vulnerable, and it was the last thing I wanted. So, I took my time in shutting the door behind me and then paused for a few seconds to breathe.

Thankfully, he remained silent and wasn't too brash and impatient, ready to throw me out the moment we made eye contact. Instead, he waited until I turned around, and then he met my gaze. Truthfully, I was a bit surprised at his state. I had expected that he would be sulking in a corner; instead, he was at his desk with a book open before him and a bottle of scotch. He didn't seem angry or stressed. Instead, it was as though he was having a chill evening and enjoying himself. I expected this, though, to change at any moment, and so I quickly said what I wanted to.

"Um, sorry," I apologized. "I was just going around scouting locations." I had stuttered on that one and not sounded nearly as nervous as I had practiced, but it was acceptable, I guessed, since he hadn't kicked me out yet.

"Um... " I stared at his gorgeous face then and completely forgot what I wanted to say. And so, to my horror, my body reacted before my mind could even step in to bail myself out. I turned around and started to walk away, but then at the last moment, I stopped myself.

"You want to take pictures here?" he asked, and I let out a deep sigh of relief because even that question was enough to make me think. I turned around then to meet his gaze and nodded.

"Not now, though," I said, "I'm just trying to familiarize myself with the house to see if there are any particular shots that would... I mean spectacular locations that would come out particularly well."

"Okay," he said, obviously far from interested, and then he returned his attention to his book. I was able to think then. I probably had a few seconds, and thus tried to put my sentences together. However, when I realized that this would be absolutely fruitless, I decided to just say what came to my mind.

"Um.. I wanted to apologize," I said, and although my voice was low and croaky, he heard me loud and clear. He raised his head to look at me, and even though his face was expressionless, I still continued speaking before I could completely lose my confidence.

"About last time," I said. "I hadn't meant to be rude; I wouldn't have asked the question I asked if I had known you would react that way."

At my words, he watched me, and even though I wasn't expecting us to kiss and make up, I still hadn't anticipated him just staring at me either.

And then, once again, he surprised me.

"Is that true?" he asked, however, I didn't understand what he was asking me.

"What do you mean?"

"Is it true that if you knew I was going to react that way, you wouldn't have still asked the question you did?"

And just like that and once again, I was severely perplexed by him and his questions.

"Are you insinuating that I deliberately set out to annoy you?" I asked in disbelief; however, he shook his head.

"The subject matter," he said, "You're friendly with Aurora, so of course you care that she wasn't exactly getting the wedding she wants."

"Oh," I replied and nodded. He was right, again. Shaking my head, I had to deeply fight the urge to slap my hand against my face.

Sighing, I looked up at him.

"I'm still…" I tried my best to tread carefully. "I'm still not very happy, of course, that she wasn't able to get the wedding she wants. But what I am apologizing for is stepping out of line and criticizing you for this. I mean, I'm just someone employed, and I shouldn't have asked you that. It's not my business. I just, as you said, appreciate Aurora's treatment of me and how much she likes my work, and so I couldn't help but empathize with her."

He pushed the book aside and crossed his arms across his chest, as though I now fully had his attention. I truly tried my best not to notice how the muscles shifted underneath his clothing and just how broad his shoulders were. Truly, I had to shift then from one leg to the other because my clit was throbbing so hard that I nearly couldn't speak. It was so frustrating and upsetting, and multiple times, as well, I had to look down to be sure that I wasn't dripping onto the carpet because my thighs were now wet as fuck.

"Empathetic?" he asks. "Have you been married before?"

This was an unexpected question.

"No," I replied.

"So, in what way exactly were you empathetic?" he

asked. This was a difficult one, but as I watched him, my brain geared back up into action and began to work.

"Well... I am a wedding photographer, so even if I am not married, I have photographed a lot of weddings, so I have intuition and experience with these things."

"Which are?" he asks, and I frowned deeply because I didn't know how to answer this goddamn question.

"Let's just say I know that a bride being upset that her once special day is not going to happen the way she envisioned it is very, very upsetting indeed."

He continued to watch me.

"Is this something that would upset you as well?"

Truly, his questions were getting out of hand because how the hell was I supposed to respond to this?

"This is not about me," I reminded him, and a sliver of a smile appeared on the corner of his lips, making me wonder if he was just taunting me.

"So, you don't have an answer?" he asked, and I sighed again.

"Yes, if it was me, if I was in Aurora's shoes, I would be absolutely fucking pissed."

His eyebrows raised.

"So, you're not sorry?" he asked, and I frowned.

"That's what I just said," I replied. "I'm not sorry that I asked; I'm just sorry that perhaps the fact that I had asked may have upset you. I didn't want it to cause any discomfort or take away from the focus of Aurora and her ceremony this week. Since I'll be constantly taking pictures and thus be everywhere, it is unavoidable that we'll run into each other, and I didn't want things to be awkward."

At my words, he continued to stare at me, and then he

rose to his feet. My instincts automatically took a step back, but I managed to catch myself just in time before I totally submitted, like a complete buffoon. Slipping his hands into his pocket, he began to walk toward me, and all I could do was stare at him.

"I accept your apology," he said. "However, I can't guarantee that it won't keep hanging over our heads."

At his words, I wondered if he was joking. I studied him, however, it couldn't possibly be because he seemed too serious, so I couldn't really understand what was happening.

"Um... okay," I said, and he smiled.

"Okay? So, you don't care to wipe the slate clean?"

At these words, I understood then what was happening. He needed his pound of flesh before he would completely accept my apology, and instantly, I was wary. However, I couldn't truly help but be curious about what he was going to ask for.

And so, I sighed and decided to play along.

"Okay," I said and lifted my chin, returning the strength and will to my backbone. I had apologized; he was now being opportunistic; I had nothing to be afraid of anymore.

"What do you want?" I asked. "I mean, what would be acceptable for you as a token of a proper apology."

He watched me, and then he passed by me and headed over to the couch by the huge floor-to-ceiling windows. The grounds of the mansion could be seen from this window, and as I looked out toward it, it took my breath away. As far as I could see was the beach and rolling hills and the gorgeous sunset in the sky. The hues were pink and magenta and a burnt orange, and they all brought an excitement in me that was difficult to contain.

He took his seat on the couch, lounging on one end, and then he casually crossed one ankle over his knees. I watched him, and my hands began to twitch. What I wanted more than anything else was to lift my camera and capture this gorgeous moment.

"I only want one thing," he said, and I barely heard him. I wanted to take this photo of him. I lifted my camera eventually and, before he could turn away and protest, I took the shot. I looked at it afterward, my heart racing in my chest, and it instantly took my breath away. This was what was commonly referred to as picture-perfect, and I didn't think so far, I had had a shot even remotely beautiful as this. Our eyes once again met through the lens, and as I stared down at it, I knew that I was also trying to remove myself.

"You just took a photo of me?" he asked, and I was so grateful that we were talking about a less intense topic because I needed it to get my bearings together.

"I did," I replied as confidently as I could manage. "It's my job."

I found the courage then to look up to see if he was annoyed and if it was reflected on his face. However, I found that he was none of the above. His expression was neutral, but his attention was so focused on me that for the seconds afterward, I was almost scared to breathe.

"Have you ever sucked cock before?" he asked, and this time around, I truly froze in place. He kept staring while it took me quite a while to recover, and then I processed the question and didn't truly know whether to be offended at all. I mean, this should classify as sexual harassment;

however, I had had the intention of being intimate with him before, so would that accusation and avenue for offense hold?

These were the very reasonable and logical questions that my head was asking. My sex, however, was throbbing so painfully that I wanted to grab myself, just so that I could reduce the ache. So that I could put myself out of the misery that this uncontrollable arousal was causing to my body. Still, I didn't want to seem naive or shy or unprofessional, and so I managed a smile and responded to him.

"No," I replied. "Have you?"

He smiled then, knowing I was genuinely being defiant.

"Come here," he called, and I was once again presented with a different dilemma.

Would I do as he had asked? However, if I did, then my reason for coming in here in the first place would be completely useless.

"What's the worst-case scenario?" I asked myself. I truly thought about this and agreed that the worst was that somehow, by answering his call, he would actually get me at the end of the day to suck his cock. The problem now was, did I mind? Just the thought of it was making my heart race with need and anticipation because, wasn't this what I wanted? Despite how angry I had claimed to be with him over the past several days, it was more or less all that I had been able to think about. I had imagined it, fantasized about it, rubbed my clit to the thought of it. I was nearly hyperventilating now just at the thought of it, but of course, I didn't want to appear too eager to or easily manipulated by him. I wanted to go over to him and curse him at the same time, and the inner turmoil at these two conflicting needs was pure torture.

I watched him then, waiting and decided that I could try a way to hold an element of control.

"I could," I replied. "But first of all, I'd have to see what you're working with. It would be terribly annoying if I went through the trouble of getting on my knees and then realized that it's a waste of time."

At my words, his brow raised, and even though my blood was now roaring through my ears at my audacity, which certainly didn't match my guts, I couldn't help but be impressed. This was surely a way to keep him in check; my only hope was that it would actually work.

He watched me, and I waited with bated breath for how he would react. Then, to my surprise, he gave me a command.

"Shut the door," he said, and my heart jumped into my throat.

This was the moment of truth. This was the moment where I had to decide if I was going to do this or if I was going to literally tuck my head between my legs and run for my life. However, the more I looked at him, the more my knees literally weakened.

Now I had captured the moment, and I truly, beyond all else, wanted to live in it. So, I turned and did as he had asked. I headed over to the door and turned the lock. I couldn't turn around yet, though, but he didn't force me. He waited until I was ready, and then I turned around.

"You can come over," he said, "to see what you want to."

I almost couldn't breathe, but I was ready and more than eager. So, I headed over to him. When I arrived, I loved that I could stare at him from the top to the bottom. Eventually, I had to lower down. However, I squatted and went down to my knees.

He straightened, then uncrossing his legs, his legs were wide open before me.

"Do you need help?" he asked, and I nodded.

"You should handle that yourself."

He studied me, and then he smiled.

"I don't want to. You're not going to insist I do, are you?"

I glared at him, not at all surprised that he was going to do this. Regardless, I didn't mind, despite the fact that I was nervous. Something about that intoxicating scent of his made me want to remain in his presence for as long as possible.

I placed a hand on his knee and tried to catch my breath.

There was something about him that made me too nervous, too needy. I could barely even meet his eyes, and I knew he was enjoying every bit of watching me squirm and tremble.

I took in deep breaths and eventually looked up to gaze into his eyes. They were sparkling, excited perhaps, or unreadable? I wasn't sure. But when my gaze lowered once again to his crotch, I, for once, received a very accurate judgment of how he currently felt.

His bulge was pressing against the fabric of his slacks, and it was impressive. Without the ability or reason to delay any further, my hands went to his buckle. He shifted without me needing to ask, giving me all the access I needed. In no time, the buckle was undone, and I was staring down at his button.

It was getting harder, and my heartbeat was raging, but it was too late to turn back. I reached out and grabbed the button. This one was a little harder to take out of its hole, and I knew he was enjoying every minute of it. Eventually, when my gaze connected with his, I couldn't miss the smile curving the corner of his lips.

I nearly rolled my eyes but looked out at the setting sun. I knew that sooner or later, someone somewhere would be searching for me, so I had to get this over with. Hopefully, I wouldn't regret it. As he lifted suddenly and pulled his zipper down, and I glimpsed the dark briefs beneath, I didn't give a care about regret.

It was unusual for me to be so lust-driven, but this man was a once-in-a-lifetime delicacy that I had to have, even if it would solely be for telling the story afterward. So, boldly, I reached into his briefs and felt his cock.

It was satiny smooth, heated, and the light dusting of hair across his crotch tickled my hand. My lips parted then to support my breathing, and I couldn't help but glance back at the door to ensure that no one would come in, as I, for sure, would never be able to live beyond the shame.

I wished I could go back once again to check, but when I turned back and saw that he had pulled his cock out and it was staring gloriously back at me, any subsequent thoughts were wiped out of my head.

I had never given much thought to cocks in general and had nothing interesting to say about

them, especially given I had seen only two in my life-time. But this one, I nearly gasped out in wonder.

It was fucking gorgeous.

Thick, long, pink, clean... my mouth instantly began to water.

I looked up at the man, then, wondering what it was exactly about him that made me so attracted to him.

Before I could think too much, however, and possibly talk myself out of this, I reached for the root and circled my hand around it. It filled my grip in the most gorgeous, sexy way, and for a moment, I wanted to take a picture. I looked to my side, then, glimpsing where I had absentmindedly set my camera and wondered if I could indeed do so.

Suddenly, his frame began to shake, and when I looked up, I realized that it was in amusement.

"What is it?" I asked, his smile nearly taking my breath away.

"You're not seriously considering taking a picture, are you?" he said, and I couldn't help but be amused as well, although thankfully, I had the good sense enough to hide it.

I did go on to ask, though, because why not?

"Can I?" I asked, and his brows furrowed in surprise.

He went completely silent, and I instantly knew what the response would be. So, before he could have one of his sudden bursts of anger once again like the last time, I lowered my head and covered the head with my mouth.

His scent was the first thing that overwhelmed me. He smelled clean and wealthy, just the way his body was, and it instantly removed any hesitation whatsoever I would have held in going further, thanks to one of my prior two experiences being absolutely traumatizing.

But this time around, I was nearly frantic with excitement.

Shutting my eyes, I ran my tongue across the slightly

damp head and loved the little twitch of his cock. The reaction spurred me on, and so in the next breath, I covered him even more fully and hollowed my cheeks to suck as hard as I possibly could.

"Hm," he shuddered slightly at the resulting sensation, and I was rewarded with a small but sweet burst of precum. The moment I tasted it, I didn't want a single drop of it to go to waste, and so I lapped it all up immediately and then sucked him even harder for more.

He kept leaking, and slowly growing wild for him, I began to stroke his length as well. I loved his girth even more than the length, which was quite intimidating, but the more my enjoyment of him increased, the more audacious I became.

As soon as I had gotten my feel of the head, I lifted myself up slightly just so I could take him deep. As deeply as he could possibly go, all the way to the back of my throat.

It was a lot to handle at first, but his slight gasps and restless movements on the couch, though little, encouraged me to keep moving. On the way up, I tightened my lips as hard as I could and sucked him all the way back to the tip.

"Hm," he said. "Hm. Doing good."

The last thing I wanted to do was acknowledge his appreciation of me, but I had to admit to myself that it made my heart feel warm and my sex pulse, leaking arousal even further down my inner thighs.

Angling my head, I continued to rub and jack him, amazed at every passing moment as he leaked even further and became even slicker. With the pad of my tongue, I licked him from tip to root and then back up again, and he leaned back into the chair with a ragged sound of delight.

I wanted to take my time, but at the same time, I was too nervous to prolong it. No doubt this was going to end somehow, and I needed to be able to get away with this unscathed since I had confirmed now that there was no way in hell that I was going to stop.

And so, my fervency increased in the way I milked him, my grip hard and relentless.

"Suck!" he rasped out the harsh command, interrupting my enjoyment of simply watching the gorgeous pink cock pulse and ooze out cum from the tip. He was so turned on, so virile, so I couldn't even protest against this command. I lowered my head once again and returned to bliss.

Relaxing my throat, I took him all the way back once again and then back up before my mouth finally closed around the head. Working in tandem with both hands at the root, I settled on a starting rhythm, and soon I was lost in the motions and in the taste of him.

I couldn't help but moan as my pace increased, fueled by his very vocal enjoyment of what I was doing to him.

"Fuck," he called over and over again, his hand eventually finding its way to my hair. He held me in place as he thrust his hips into my mouth, and I allowed him to take the pleasure he wanted. Hearing what it did to him was immense compensation until I needed to take charge again.

He let me, and soon my thighs were trembling in delight.

"Your mouth..." he moaned. "You're good at this. Fuck."

I went even faster, sucked even harder, and I could soon feel his thighs bunching as his pleasure raced towards the edge.

I couldn't help but look up then to watch him, and I was

struck for a moment at the sight of him so unraveled. Ever since I had met him, he had always seemed so put together, so unflustered, but in this moment and as his hand threaded through his hair and tugged almost viciously, I knew that I had him in my grasp.

It was an indescribable thrill, and it spurred me on much further than I thought I could go. My eyes were burning, my throat sore, yet I refused to stop, not until his hand moved to my hair and I felt the hard grip of the strands by the roots.

"Evelyn," he roared out as his body tensed up for a long moment, and then he was bursting into my mouth. I nearly choked from the flood and had to pull away to some extent when I couldn't take it any longer. Still, I only needed a short moment to recover, but before long, the head of his cock was back in my mouth, and I was lapping him all up.

The moment was obscene, and I reveled in it in a way that I couldn't comprehend. He kept thrusting his hips, restless and so shaken that I couldn't look away. His eyes, which were at first wide open, completely focused on the ceiling and seemed dazed in wonder. His chest was heaving, his pants stained, and it seemed like he still couldn't process what had just happened.

Soon though, and as I wiped the moisture off the corners of my lips and stared up at him, I wanted to get up because being on my knees in this way wasn't exactly the most empowering position, especially now that the haze and pleasure of the moment had passed, and reality was creeping in cold and cruel.

However, I found myself unable to move as his gaze finally lowered and caught mine. He stared at me as though he was seeing me for the first time, and then he leaned forward and caught the back of my neck. Before I could decipher what he was going to do, he had tilted his head and was taking my lips in his.

This was a filthy kiss, and I melted into it like wax. He didn't hold back in expressing his appreciation of me through it as he licked into my mouth with lush, heated strokes. He sucked on my tongue, and I responded heartily to the intoxicating dance. I moaned then, unable to contain the pleasure this was eliciting through me, especially at the taste of release mixing with the kiss.

It was so intimate that by the time he pulled away, I was the one left dazed and questioning almost everything I had thought about life up until that moment because I couldn't understand why that had been so sweet and almost special.

I looked up then and could see the smile on his face, making me certain then, without a shadow of a doubt, that he had felt it too. There was something special here, and although I tried to screw my head back on, my heart was racing too hard to listen to me.

"I knew you were going to be special," he said, and I nearly forgot how to breathe.

"It's your turn," he said, then reached forward, and in the next moment, I was being pulled into his lap. I had no clue what he meant, but when he cupped my face and pulled me in for yet

another kiss, I had no complaints whatsoever. He kissed me long enough for me to lose myself in him, for me to forget where we were and how inappropriate this was. However, his kisses told me over and over again, as he sucked on my lips and breathed into my mouth, that nothing else mattered beyond this moment. And I believed him.

Eventually, we broke apart, and he stared deeply into my eyes. There was something indeed different about the way he looked at me. It almost seemed affectionate. I no longer felt like he was a complete stranger, especially as he lifted his hand and gently brushed my hair out of my face.

"You're beautiful, Evelyn," he said. "You know this, don't you?"

I didn't respond; however, alarms began blaring through me, especially as I looked around and saw that the library was gradually getting dark. It was a massive space and was so gorgeous that I couldn't get over how all of this seemed like a dream. To think that barely a week ago, I was escaping to coffee shops just for the air conditioner and wondering how I was going to pay my rent. None of these problems had been significantly solved, but in the midst of the constant horror, a breathtaking fantasy had been added. As a result, this had turned into a fairytale that I didn't quite want to wake up from just yet.

"Are you on birth control?" he asked, and I nodded.

However, at the feel of his cock beneath me, I couldn't help but begin to churn my hips. At first, he was solely focused on our conversation, but soon enough, he noticed what was happening and looked down slightly in confusion. Then he returned his gaze to me and cocked his head.

"You're not wearing any underwear?" he asked, and I nodded.

"Why?" he inquired, his expression unreadable at first, but pretty soon he brightened up.

"You were expecting this? Thinking ahead?"

"No," I replied, leaning forward once again to kiss him because it felt as though I was losing my mind without his taste in my mouth.

He, however, held on to this story just as though it was any normal day, and we were having a simple conversation. It felt too good, too real. In order to remind him of what this was, I positioned his semi-hardened cock along the crevice of my sex and began to rock my hips.

"Hm," he groaned, that hoarse, gorgeous sound of his.

"I just ..." I tried to string words together in my head. "I was going to take a shower, I think. I wanted to apologize first."

"Without underwear?"

"It was becoming quite uncomfortable to have on."

"Why?" he asked, and I rocked into him even harder. It weakened me, my thighs trembling at the pleasure that wreaked through my system. I was overtaken in that moment by my need to fuck and be fucked, and it was all I could think about.

"I'm on birth control, I'm clean, but I didn't have a recent test. You can go check if you want, just let me know."

I leaned forward because I needed to kiss him, and he submitted. I didn't know how long the kiss lasted, but when we parted once again, I couldn't think of anything at all.

"We'll use a condom too," he said. "I'll arrange for a medical person to come over to test you before the day is over. We'll get your test tomorrow."

"Okay," I breathed into his mouth, nibbling on his lips. He caught my neck once again and slid his tongue into my mouth. Eventually, he guided me off his lap, and even though I was reluctant, I eventually didn't have the choice but to move away so that he could get up.

I was dazed as I tried to make myself decent, but I couldn't. Instead, I waited for him until he returned and took his seat once again. I wanted to watch as he slipped the condom on, but all I could do was stare, ambushed and drained of strength, up at the gorgeous ceiling.

Eventually, though, he caught me by the arms and pulled me, and I was once again back on his lap.

"Ready?" he asked, and I managed to nod.

Throwing my arms around him, I held on tight, and soon the gorgeous head of his cock was positioned at my entrance. He stroked me, loving the small gasps that escaped my lips at the tease.

"We're going to have a wonderful week together, Evelyn," he said, and I truly didn't know how to respond. My hope was that after this, after he had hopefully fucked my brains out, I would be able to come to my senses. I would no longer think of this as madly and obsessively as I had since I met him, and I would be able to control myself. With this plan in mind, I gave myself the permission to enjoy myself to the fullest right now because I was going to do everything I possibly could to ensure that it never happened again.

"Ready?" he asked, his arm going around my waist. It wasn't an affectionate act; rather, it was operational, ensuring that I didn't slip off. It was unnecessary, though, because I held onto the armrest beside him, and then I was truly ready.

He watched me, and I didn't understand why. It was such an intimate act. I didn't know what he'd see if he stared so closely into my eyes. I didn't want to know what I'd see in his. So, I

simply shut my eyes as I felt the nudge of his head at my entrance, trying to calm my heart. Pleasure had turned my stomach to mush. Excitement and anticipation were stinging up my spine; anxiety and fear of being caught were causing sweat to mist across my skin. I was feeling too much all at once.

I didn't quite want this to end because it felt too good, but truly I couldn't wait until I got back to normal. Till things got back to normal. I held on as his cock pushed into me. He was deliciously girthy; however, just as I had expected, it was incredibly difficult to accommodate him.

"Fuck," his heated breath brushed over me. "You're so tight."

I took it as the compliment that it was but relished the fullness that came with his size. He was more careful than I would have expected, given that we were just having sex and he really didn't need to be. However, he took his time, watching my every expression until he was eventually and fully sheathed inside of me.

I froze in place for a moment, then my eyes tightened even further shut as I inhaled deeply and exhaled. I felt exquisitely stretched, more than I had ever been, and it was unreal.

"You okay?" he asked, and it took me a moment to decode. Soon enough, as pleasure began to tingle up my spine, I nodded.

"Please move," I told him, and to my surprise, he leaned forward and kissed me. I could taste the smile on his lips, the ease, the enjoyment. He was so intense in everything that he did, but in this instance, I was surprised at how fully and easily he seemed to be enjoying himself.

"Let me know if you need me to pause at any moment," he said, and I nodded.

"I will."

He grabbed my hips then; his strong hands digging into my skin and lifted me gradually off his cock. He was so strong, his biceps flexing hard at the strength he was expending in lifting my weight. I wasn't a huge girl, but I wasn't dainty and petite either, but he controlled my dance on his cock.

Once again, he leaned forward to kiss me, and I melted into it. There was something about his kisses that seemed to stop my entire being the moment we connected. It was warm, wet, and so sweet that in these moments, I forgot everything else beyond the heat and weight of his tongue. His slides in my mouth were expert, with just the right pressure and at just the right pace to keep me restless.

The orgasm was building all over my body, making my hair stand on end, unraveling me.

I was trembling from the inside out, and I couldn't contain it.

"Want me to go faster?" I heard his voice in my ears, and I nodded.

I hoped he could hear me, but just in case he couldn't, I managed to relay my response.

"Yes," I shuddered, and he obliged my request. Once again, he thrust into me, his pace controlled and measured, and I almost cried out then at the sweetness of it. Lust was taking over my whole heart, mind, and senses, and I was completely powerless to stop it. He went faster, then, unable to control himself as his own primal, urgent need took over.

He let go of me, but I knew how to position myself so I could ride him the way I wanted to, and this worked out in my favor. He grabbed my ass, and the aggressiveness of it turned me even more wildly on.

At this point, I didn't even think it was possible, but then his lips connected with the swell of my breasts, and my head fell back with a gasp. I was so sensitive and tender, and he knew just how to work my nipples through the fabric. With his hands, he cupped the weight of my mounds, and then with one sharp pull, my breasts were released and completely exposed to him.

"Fuck," his hips pumped even faster into my core.

"You're fucking perfect."

He leaned forward then, his breath on my breasts one after the other, and I couldn't hold back my moan. His lips covered my nipples and sucked, hard, his tongue flicking over the engorged tip, and it made me leak even harder. I was stimulated from every part of my body, and it was too much to take.

I could feel my sex pulsing and trembling around his cock, rocking my hips on him, going as hard and fast as my trembling thighs would allow me. It was impossible for me to last or him for that matter. We were too in tune, too frenzied, too aroused. Lust hung heavily in the air as we fucked each other without pause, my hips tilted at just the right angle to drive us both wild. I could feel the head of his cock as it hit the end of me, relentlessly, making me whimper and cry out.

I lost all sense of shame and caution as I rocked into

him, the fierce pants of his breathing burning across my cheeks and against my neck. He was close, I could feel it, and so was I, and so we held on to each other even tighter.

I loved the way he gripped me, so hard. It revealed a moment of vulnerability that, even though I knew was involuntary, still felt nice. Incredibly nice. Maybe too nice because I returned it and couldn't stop myself from kissing him. There was very little lust involved as I tasted his skin— the underside of his jaw, the ticking vein in his forehead, and down his neck. He was so strong, so virile, so gorgeous... I couldn't get enough of him.

"Come for me," he said, just as his hand moved between us and began to stroke my clit.

"Ah," I cried out at the added stimulation, and I was sure then that we had been heard. I couldn't stop myself, and he didn't seem to care as he went even faster and harder. My hips lost control. I rocked into him like someone crazed, and in no time, my hand was slapping over my mouth to muffle my scream.

It was barely effective, but I needed more to keep me somewhat grounded to reality because as the orgasm hit and wreaked through my body, I felt myself go slightly unconscious. For the few seconds after, I felt formless, nothing registered as red-hot pleasure overtook my mind and senses. In the midst of it all and at last, I could feel him clenching hard as well around me like a vice as he too got his release.

His groan was fierce against me, his grip so hard I felt as though he was going to snap me in two. I relished every moment of it, feeling him so shaken and affected as he continued to spurt. He seemed to come forever while I couldn't stop myself from rocking on him, squeezing every bit of pleasure left from our joining.

Eventually, we were both able to catch our breath, and slowly, life around us and beyond this moment began to register. The sun had set, though there was still a little light out; the air had gotten much cooler, and it was such a relief as it filtered in from the porch and brushed against our heated skin. Our heartbeats weren't heaving like mad anymore; our hips weren't churning, and our minds weren't racing.

We were calming down, yet he still held onto me as tightly as possible. His face was buried in my neck as though he never wanted to move, while I had to fight the urge with all of my heart to keep from kissing his head.

Suddenly, though, there was a knock on the door. A hard, curious one, and this did the trick.

It jolted us both immediately to our senses, and I sprang off his lap so fast that I stumbled backward. He tried to hold onto me, to stop me from falling, but it was fruitless. I landed on my ass, butt naked, with my legs spread out before him; however, his face was full of concern.

"Are you alright?" he asked, and I nodded.

"I am."

Immediately, I scrambled up, but of course, I wasn't quick enough. His eyes lowered down, and my soaking sex was completely open to his perusal.

Now, shame was eager and quick, striking me like a boulder, and as soon as I got back up to my feet, I turned away from him. His following words, however, startled me.

"Come here," he said as I started to pull my dress back over my breasts and down. However, I didn't reason.

"Your cunt," he said. "I need it in my mouth."

Pleasure struck me then so painfully in my core, a gasp tore from my lips. At his words, my clit once again began to throb, hungry, greedy, and it took every ounce of me not to turn to look at

him because I knew that the moment I did, I would be lost, my brain would cease to work, and lust would drive me like a crazed woman.

"There's someone at the door," I reminded him, and my gaze went to it. I was nervous because I couldn't even begin to imagine who was there. They had probably heard us, and I would probably be fired because this was sure to get to Aurora.

Sighing, I looked down at myself, and regret was the last thing I felt. I should have controlled myself better, just as I had all these years. How could I have given in this way when, for once, I had such a huge opportunity within my grasp? The contacts I formed here could establish me the way I wanted to. I wouldn't have to run to coffee shops to escape the heat because I couldn't afford to fix the air conditioner in my apartment. Yet here I was, unusually letting lust run me, and I didn't know how to explain it.

"Regret coming in?" he asked, and I was jolted out of my rapidly darkening thoughts. This was his fault, I decided, so I turned around once again to face his gorgeous face.

"I need to head back," I told him, trying my very best to ignore the fact that his cock was still hanging out of his pants and still somewhat hard. He was sated. I could see it in his eyes and the gorgeous glisten of his release and mine on the satiny smooth skin. He had disposed of the condom and no doubt would rapidly be able to get another one if needed.

I found the courage to look into his eyes then, knowing that this wouldn't happen again.

"This was good," I told him. "But let's, um... hopefully it won't happen again. I mean, it definitely shouldn't happen again. It's extremely unprofessional on my part. You're basically my employer."

At my words, he didn't respond. Instead, he seemed to go very still, and I couldn't help the shiver that crept up my spine.

I loved it when he got this way, and at the same time, I couldn't help but feel somewhat intimidated.

He continued to watch me while I used the time not to wait but to convince myself that it was alright to just turn around and leave. However, it was as though his gaze had me frozen, unable to move or even speak, and it terrified me that he had this kind of hold over me.

"It's because he's technically my employer," I tried to convince myself. "That's why I'm hesitant... that's why I give a fuck."

Thankfully and fortunately for me, and as the knock came once again followed by the handle being pulled down curiously, he responded.

While I was panicked with my heart about to leap out of my chest, he appeared calmer than ever before.

"Sure," he said. "You can leave."

It was what I wanted to hear, but I couldn't help feeling dismissed, which just made me feel worse altogether. Unwilling to waste any more time, I grabbed my camera, headed over to the door, and unlocked it. I hoped with all my heart that whoever was there wasn't still waiting. This, however, was a very far-fetched dream, and so I prepared myself to meet whomever it was with a bold face and to accept whatever consequences would arise from this, after all, I couldn't take it back.

My hope was that it would be one of the countless servants in the house. Dressed in pristine uniforms, they seemed to be everywhere and ever busy, moving food, toiletries, and bedding from one floor to the other. Now, however, none of them were in sight. Instead, a man was before me dressed impeccably in loose slacks and a dress shirt.

He was obviously quite elderly, but his build was amazing, as though he had lived in the gym for most of his years.

I didn't have a choice then but to meet his gaze, and although it took me a while simply because I wasn't expecting it, I soon understood that this had to be some relative of Drake and Aurora.

He took his time in regarding me, and I was sure that he had heard most of what had happened. He had probably even been the one to send whomever else had been around away.

"Hello," I greeted, and immediately started to hurry away, but he turned around and calmly stopped me.

"Who are you, Miss?" he asked, and I was forced to a halt. Releasing a deep, heavy breath, I turned around and just then recalled the weight of the camera in my arms.

"Photographer," I replied, not even sure if I was saying the truth because how in the hell could I guarantee myself a job after this.

"You take some great pictures in there?" he asked, a

smile playing at the corners of his lips. I was sure that I was going to die of shame. There was simply no other way out.

"Great location," I somehow managed to reply, and before he could ask any further questions, I turned around and scampered away.

Chapter Seventeen
Drake

I was in the midst of putting myself together when the door was pushed open. Whomever came in was quite cautious, as if they weren't sure if they should just barge in, yet they were important enough not to really need to call out to me and ask for my permission either. I knew whom it was before his face even appeared.

The older version of me, or what I hoped would be, came in and stopped at the open door. He narrowed his eyes, giving me a peculiar look, and then his attention returned to my pants. I was pulling up the zipper and buttoning myself up, and at this, he shook his head.

"The wedding photographer?" he asked as he came in and shut the door behind him.

I didn't acknowledge this question. Instead, I watched him with a smile and took care to inspect his frame for any health concerns.

"I thought you were going to come earlier," was my response.

He stopped in front of me, his gaze perusing me as well, and then he slid his hands into his pockets.

"I came just in time to ride. But I see you got started before me."

This made me laugh out loud, and then I stood to my feet and couldn't stop myself from reaching out for a hug. He, however, refused and started to take several steps backward, but I caught him and forced him to accept the embrace.

"It's been too long," I said, and he finally sighed in defeat. He eventually returned the hug, and we were silent for several moments. It had been a tough couple of months for our family, and we were all still in the thick of it, so we needed and treasured each other more than ever before.

We pulled apart then and stared at each other, and then his eyes went behind me. I knew exactly what he was looking at, and it was a bit shameful, given that he was my father. I couldn't help but lower my head.

"Good thing you bought this house with your own money," he said, and I smiled.

He looked around the space.

"In the library though? This was going to be my sanctuary."

"It still is," I replied. "And how loud were we?"

"Enough for me to hear you down the hallway."

"Anyone else hear?" I asked, and he shook his head.

"Lucky for you, they're all out by the stable. The new mare is putting on a show."

" Oh," I was immediately excited. "I was waiting for that all day. They brought her in?"

"She's beautiful to watch now. I've been there the past half-hour. I can't wait to ride her."

My gaze lowered then, and I could see the cowboy hat attached to his side.

"You really came prepared."

"It's my daughter's wedding," he said. "Why shouldn't I? You, on the other hand, came to properly enjoy yourself for once, I see. I'm not even mad. I'm happy you're letting loose a bit. You've been so frigid these past few years."

"I haven't been," I replied as I returned to the desk to pick up my phone.

"Yes, you have. When was the last time you were with a woman or even had the time or patience to think of or accommodate one? You've been locked up in your office for years."

"For a good reason, no?" I asked. "Look at where we live."

At this, he laughed and then he shook his head.

"Go clean up. I'll meet you there. I heard from the wedding planner that there's an opening tonight, something of an opening down by the restaurant by the beach."

"Yes, there is," I replied. "I was given the breakdown earlier today at breakfast. You were supposed to be there."

"Well, I'm here now. Stop complaining," he said. "And your mom is waiting for me. Want me to wait for you?"

"No," I replied and saw him to the door, and then we parted ways. "See you soon."

Afterwards, I headed over to my room. At first, I thought to just clean myself up and head out, but when I thought about the evening gathering that was coming up, I decided to just hop in the shower altogether.

Plus, and I hated to admit this to myself, but I needed a couple of moments of reprieve. To think and reflect because even though nearly half an hour had passed since I had come harder than I could ever remember coming, I still felt slightly hazy and destabilized. The entire experience with her had been unreal, and I found myself now, and just as I had expected, replaying it over and over in my mind.

I wanted more, but as she had clearly informed me before she left, she wasn't interested in such. Especially due to the current circumstances and stipulations of our daylight interactions with the others. Sure, I could have any female staff I wanted and whoever was interested in return, but I was known for keeping things private and for not acting so sloppily around my work or family.

Yet, I had lost my head there with her from the start to the finish, and I truly didn't know who I could blame this on. Until I sighted Evelyn, I didn't realize how little attention I had paid to females in recent years. Granted, a lot of changes had happened, huge, monumental milestones had been reached, and also a lot of very unpleasant surprises. I had been so busy through it all, and no one had caught my attention. This made perfect sense to me, so I couldn't help but be further curious as to why she then had so wholly caught my eyes.

Stepping into the shower, I turned the cascade warm and lifted my face up to it. And then I tried it back to cold because I realized just how heated I still was. I needed to calm my body and mind down, but as I shut my eyes, all I could see and think about was her. The way she had held me so tightly and rode me on that chair. I would have expected her to be a bit tamer when it came to fucking and being fucked, but she had surprised me immensely.

She had completely let loose, and now I understood that it was probably because she had decided, as she had informed me, that it would never happen again. However, was I ready to accept this? I looked down at my cock, which had been half hard after we had finished but was now fully erect and pulsing, needing to be sheathed once again in her warmth. I could still smell her all around me, could taste her skin on my tongue, and it was becoming quite frustrating, to say the least.

I had just had her, yet it wasn't enough, and while it made me excited, I didn't like feeling so unhinged and unsure of my complete control over myself. However, for instance, this shower was supposed to be a quick one, but then here I was, stroking myself and thinking of her.

I wanted to stop right then, willed myself to stop; however, the pleasure felt unreal. I could almost feel once again the tight grip of her walls around me, and it pulled a ragged groan from my throat. My grip tightened then, and quicker, as I fantasized about her, my eyes closed, imagining her in front of me. She was so gorgeous and beautiful, very apparent, not wealthy, but there was a grace about her that couldn't be replicated or explained in any way.

"Focus," the hoarse cry followed as I quickly reached the brink, and then I was spurting out onto my hands and the glistening tiled wall before me.

It took me a while to recover from this, mostly because I couldn't stop imagining what it had felt like to kiss her the moment I came. There were very few moments in my lifetime thus far that I had labeled as perfect, but that one with her had made the list. So, as I washed myself up, I had to admit to myself that I couldn't wait to see her again.

In short, I was buzzing with excitement for it, and since, for once, I had time, my next game plan was to ensure that she found it impossible to deny herself and refuse me once again.

Chapter Eighteen
Evelyn

"I think I'm going to leave tonight," I told Anna as I sifted through the clothes that I had hung in the closet.

"What? So soon? Why?" she asked.

I sighed, contemplating her question as I listened to the clanging of pots and her chopping things in the kitchen. I couldn't help but wish I was there with her, in this moment, safe and clear-headed, not tormented by anxiety and regret.

I didn't regret my time with him. How could I? It was amazing. However, I regretted that I han't controlled myself better. I felt as though I had lost something, suspecting that I might never find out what it was, was troubling to say the least.

"I spent money on clothes," I told Anna, opting for the politically correct answer. "Yet I still don't think I fit in. Every time I meet someone new, I feel as though they're looking down at me, wondering about what the hell I am wearing."

"Oh my God," she said. "That can't be right. Maybe you're reading too much into it?"

I was definitely reading too much into it. Under normal circumstances, none of this would have bothered me. I was there to do a job I was grateful for, caring deeply for it, so who the hell cared what anyone thought about me? The truth was that I was running... from what I had started, from myself.

I had boldly told Drake that I didn't want anything to happen again, yet I couldn't get him off my mind for even a moment. I should have been worried about us being caught for being too passionate in the library, yet I was concerned about how I would keep myself from jumping him the next time I saw him.

"I'm not reading too much into it," I told her. "I just... I was right to stick to smaller weddings."

"You mean a lower circle?" she said, and I immediately began to take offense. I didn't respond, hoping she would move on to other topics, but she wouldn't let me.

"I would never have pegged you for this kind of person, Anna," I said, and my heart dropped into my stomach.

"Let's talk about something else," I said, but she refused.

"Evelyn," she said. "Are you trying to self-sabotage yourself? Is this what's happening here?"

I sighed and pulled out three outfits for the dinner ahead, still considering whether to attend or not. I laid them down on the bed, momentarily considering ending the call. However, I knew she would haunt me until I picked up again, or she wouldn't care and not bother to call back, leaving me in a state of confusion and fear.

"I've always been sure that passion and interest are what keep you playing small, but now—"

"I wasn't playing small," I complained, but she wasn't buying it.

"If you weren't playing small, then what are you doing now, trying to run away from the first big thing you've been involved in since you started? Come to think of it, you've always said you didn't like big projects, but why? Because they were too polished? Too fancy? That makes no sense. I mean, you could have made it as rustic as you wanted. Rustic doesn't mean poor or small; it—"

"I slept with Drake," I said, interrupting her, needing her barrage of comments to come to an end.

Whether it was because I didn't want to hear what she was saying or because they were true and I needed an immediate solution, I couldn't tell. What I did get, though, was a long minute of silence, which we both needed and appreciated.

"That's, um..." she eventually found her voice. "You just got there, didn't you? A few hours ago?"

"That's your strategy? To slut-shame me?"

She was amused.

"What's yours? I mean, when did this even happen? How? I thought you two were mortal enemies. You did that within just a few minutes of seeing him again?"

"It wasn't a few minutes," I grumbled.

"But you hate each other!" Her interest grew. "He kicked you out of his apartment for asking about his sister."

"Wow, I didn't know any of these," I said dryly as I placed the phone on speaker and set it down on the dresser.

Then I stood before the bed and spread out all three dresses so I could look at them properly.

"Stop being sarcastic and explain yourself," she said, and I sighed.

"It happened."

"It happened?" she asked. "That's your defense?"

I sighed again. I knew I didn't need to tell her the details, but everything was so fuzzy in my head, almost a blur, and I needed to make sense of it. Somehow.

"I wanted to apologize," I told her. "It seemed as though he was extremely upset about my presence here because wherever I went, he would seem to get irritated and leave. I didn't want things to be uncomfortable, so I decided to be the bigger person."

She went silent again, and in that time, I decided on the outfit for the evening. It was white and a romper, quite ironic given how very black and red I was feeling, but I was hoping it would give me a sense of safety and confidence. I turned around and started to get ready. Since I had chosen what I would wear, I put my hair up in a half-up, half-down style.

When choosing between jewelry, my eyes automatically reached for my daily gold necklace, but another layered beaded pearly ensemble caught my eye.

"Do pearls scream 'makes bad sexual decisions'?" I asked, and she laughed.

I was surprised she was still on the phone, though, but I could hear her moving around, busy and deep in thought as well.

"Sleeping with your boss the moment you meet him is generally not a good decision, yet you can't just judge this to be a bad one. Plus, your work dynamics are not usual. Anyway, pearls are good. What's important, though, is how you're going to handle this. Are you really going to leave? It doesn't sound like you want to leave."

"Of course, I don't want to," I complained. "I don't want to disappoint Aurora, and I want to see this thing to the end. And, of course, give out my cute business cards."

"The business card idea as Amex business cards is so cute," she said. "And their guests are super rich, so they will appreciate it even more."

I sighed and then unzipped my makeup bag to begin the process of smoothing out my skin and bringing life to my cheeks.

"I say, act like nothing out of the ordinary happened."

"Um, we were loud," I said. "Something definitely happened, and the world has probably heard by now."

"You don't know that, and it might not have been you. No one has evidence that you were the one in that library."

"A man saw," I replied. "An older man. I think he was his father or at the very least an uncle. He is shorter and smaller in stature than Drake, but their facial features are immensely similar."

"Well, fathers don't speak carelessly about their son's private business," she said. "So, you have nothing to worry about."

I stared at myself in the mirror as I lightly filled in the strokes of my eyebrows.

" You really think I should stay, don't you?"

"No, I know you want to stay," she said. "If you leave now based only on assumption alone and not with a real reason like being kicked out or treated badly, then I feel you'll always wonder what if and you might, in the end, come to regret it. You know how much I hate that; it currently haunts me."

"I know," I replied as I dabbed blush on my cheeks and patted it in.

I gave her words some thought, searched my heart, and in the end, decided that she was absolutely right.

"Alright," I agreed, loving the way I was feeling and looking, even though I was concerned I'd feel too down and afraid to attend tonight.

"I'm ready," I said. "I'll go. I mean, I'll stay until there's a real reason to leave."

"Alright," she replied.

"Send me a picture and videos," she said. "I have nothing interesting to do this week, so I want full updates on your daily shenanigans."

"Sure," I smiled and thanked her. Then the call came to an end.

Chapter Nineteen
Drake

"She has got to go!"

Startled at the sudden command whispered in my ear, I turned around, and it was just in time to see my mother arrive in shorts and cowboy boots. For a few seconds, as I lowered to kiss her, I was concerned about what she was talking about. But when she gave me a narrowed look and then glanced at my father who was busy riding the horse and having the time of his life, I understood that he had tattled.

Sighing, I shook my head and returned my attention to the show. As parents, they had never been particularly close. He had worked a lot, and she had been dragged around states she hated for him to expand his gyms. There had been a lot of tension. But now, given the difficulty we had endured over the past few months, they had become closer than ever.

This was great. I was happy for them, but it was now clear that it meant as well that I would be a victim of their renewed camaraderie.

Sighing, I tried my best to discourage any further inquisition.

"I don't know what you're talking about," I replied, and she bumped my shoulder with hers.

"Want me to refresh your memory?" she asked, and once again I turned to meet her gaze.

Still, I remained defiant and hopeful.

"Who are we talking about? Victoria? Because that's what Aurora wants as well. Her gone; I mean."

My mom observed me, a ghost of a smile playing on her lips, then she returned her attention to my dad. I pondered on the best way to address the situation at hand. Should I ignore the fact that she, as well as my dad and perhaps even more people, were aware of what had transpired between me and Evelyn? Or should I insist that she keeps it to herself? This had nothing to do with preserving Evelyn's honor; instead, I didn't want to further divert attention from Aurora for the week.

So, I sighed and turned to my mom; she glanced at me, that smile still tugging at the corners of her lips.

"What do you want to say?" she asked, but I redirected the question back to her because I knew her well.

She laughed, and the sound made me quite happy. It had been a while since I had seen her laugh this way, and a part of me had wondered if I would ever get to see her laugh like this again. So now, all I could do was stop to appreciate the beautiful sound. I wished I could pull out my phone then to record it, but there were a few people around, and I didn't want to draw unnecessary attention.

"What do you want to say?" I asked, and she leaned her head against my shoulder.

"He's enjoying himself, isn't he?" she asked as she watched my dad, and I nodded.

"Yeah, it's been a while."

"For all of us," she said and sighed. "I want the same for you. I mean, I don't know what this is between you and Evelyn, but—"

"Mom, I've only met her twice," I said, deliberately omitting the time she came to my apartment, but no one besides the both of us needed to know that.

"So... I mean, your dad didn't make it seem that way."

"You know how he is," I said, and she nodded.

"I do. So... it's just a fling then?"

"I'm not in high school, Mom," I said. "You shouldn't be asking me about this."

"I know," she laughed. "It's just that more than alarmed, I was just excited. I don't think I've seen you with a woman in a long time. Romantically, I mean."

"I've been busy."

"Of course, and that's my point. You've been busy and troubled, thanks to me especially, so I'm glad that this week seems to be doing you some good. Plus, we've had several events in the past where it was required for you to bring a date, and you never bothered. But now, you meet a woman, and on the second date, your dad is hurrying over to me with gossip?"

I stopped then and scowled at him.

"He was excited," she rubbed my arm.

"Nothing to be excited about."

"Alright," she said. "If you say so. I guess I don't have to insist that she leaves anytime soon, but you have to be careful. Only your dad is aware now, but I really didn't want Aurora to find out. It might upset her, and Evelyn seems to be the only one Aurora likes these days."

"She probably is," I replied as I curved my arm around her. She leaned into me until eventually, my phone began to ring. I pulled it out of my pocket, and when I saw that it was Victoria, I couldn't help but be somewhat upset.

"I told her not to call me directly," I said, and my mother smiled.

"She wouldn't listen to that. Unlike Evelyn, she hasn't been able to gain your attention."

I turned to her, surprised.

"Why does she want it?"

My mom sucked in her breath, and then she shook her head.

"You really don't know how much of a catch you are?" she said, and I smiled.

"I'm well aware, but I've also expressed my disinterest to her several times, so why hasn't she caught on to this?"

"Because you're still very publicly single," she said. I turned away in thought and couldn't help but think of what Evelyn had said to me before she'd left the library. She'd basically vowed to never let our rendezvous repeat itself, and truly, it intrigued me now more than ever.

"Most women wouldn't reject me, right?" I asked, and my mother turned to me.

"Who would?"

I smiled.

"I barely note attention, but—"

"But what?" she asked.

"Rejection is very easy to take note of. Maybe that's what Victoria should have done to gain my attention."

"Someone rejected you?" She was shocked; however, my phone began to ring again, thankfully diverting our attention.

"Victoria again," I said and picked up. "Yeah?" I answered.

"Are you all at the stables?" she asked. "I'm sorry for calling, but I couldn't reach your mom. The cars are ready, and we're ready to leave for the restaurant soon. Aurora is ready as well."

I turned to my mom then, knowing fully well her phone was with her. We had mandated that she always be with it so that we could reach her in case of an emergency.

"We're ready," I replied. "Check on Evelyn?" I asked.

She went quiet for a few moments; however, I didn't notice. I needed to end the call and turned to see my mom's widened eyes on me.

"Check on Evelyn?"

I wondered what I had done wrong, but slowly and eventually, it dawned on me.

"Oh," I said and sighed again. "I didn't mean anything by it. I just didn't want her to leave anyone behind. She's the event planner."

Shaking her head, my mom leaned away from me and began to head towards my dad.

"Let me go and get him, and you, mister, have to learn to read the room."

I was amused.

"Your phone is with you, right?" I asked, and she pulled it out of the purse she had in her hand.

"Of course, always."

"Victoria said she couldn't reach you," I said, and she turned the screen towards me.

"Not true. No missed calls."

"Of course," I said, and she continued on her way.

Chapter Twenty
Evelyn

I had never felt so out of place. All the guests who had arrived so far were standing outside of the mansion, waiting for the chauffeured cars to drive us to the restaurant. And there I was, in kitten heels with my camera. I didn't particularly need any bells and whistles for tonight, so this was a relief. But this, I was beginning to see, might be the only comfort I would receive.

More guests had arrived, important people probably that I didn't know, and they all chatted in clusters. Aurora wasn't out yet, and neither was Drake, so I was forced to scroll through my phone and social media to distract myself.

"We're ready to leave," one of Victoria's assistants finally announced, and one by one sleek dark cars began to fill up. All in all, we seemed to be about fifteen people, which wasn't too much of a crowd, I guessed, for an opening dinner. I wondered for a moment as I watched the cars.

I wondered if it would be best to go with them. However, when I thought of Aurora, I decided against it. I would have waited by her room, at least to capture some photos, but I had only been able to do that in the beginning, and when her dress had still been on the rack before she had politely asked me to leave. Her fiancé had called her, and I could see that something was making her upset that they needed to talk about, so I had immediately excused myself. I looked towards the entrance to the home once again and hoped that she would be out soon.

"Oh, you're here," I heard Victoria's voice seemingly out of nowhere, and I sighed. I considered ignoring her; however, this would probably set the tone for the rest of the night and be the last thing I wanted, so I worked up a smile and turned to her.

"Yes, I am," I replied. However, I was forced to stop for a moment because she looked absolutely stunning.

My eyebrows raised at the sight of her, and of course, she didn't miss this.

"Great dress, right?" she asked, and I gave her a look.

"It's a bit much, don't you think?" I asked as my eyes ran down the actual bells and whistles on the fabric. It was a dramatic flare from the waist with intricate beading and flowers. It was a nice dress, but as I looked at her again, I couldn't help but point out a very important fact.

"You're not the bride; you do know this, don't you?" I asked, and she frowned. "Aurora's wearing a very simple pink dress. You're more dressed up than she is."

"That's not my problem," she replied. "I arranged a brilliant selection of outfits for her for the week as well as several stylists so that she would outshine everyone. If she decided to ignore all of that and wear something simple instead, then again, that's not my problem."

With that, she turned around to leave, and I was glad to be left alone.

Just then, there was movement from the entrance, and I turned. Aurora appeared; however, she wasn't alone. She had her brother by her side, and she had her arm in his.

My heart skipped a beat as I took him in, dressed impeccably in a velvet blazer with a crisp white shirt. I was suddenly parched because it had to be illegal the way he filled his clothes up so sinfully. He was all muscle and breath and so heartrendingly handsome that I had to look away to regain my sanity.

"Fuck," I sighed under my breath and could do nothing but turn to my camera for some element of focus. After all, I was supposed to be working. And after turning it on, I headed towards them and took the shots I needed for both him and Aurora and, of course, of her getting into the car. The moment she noticed me, she waved heartily, and I felt a profane sense of relief.

"Let's ride together, Evelyn," she said, and I nodded. I was a bit surprised, though, because I was expecting that she would do so with either her brother or fiancé, but this was apparently not the case. What I found out soon enough, though, was that this was going to be the case because instead of riding beside her, I was sitting in the front seat while the two of them rode in the back.

I had to work through it all, so of course, I kept taking pictures. The sight of them in the back, and every time I turned round to take a shot of them speaking to each other, all I could think about was what his cock tasted like. I had really shot myself in the foot with this one because I couldn't imagine how I was going to survive the car ride to the restaurant, much less the night.

"Evelyn, did you bring comfortable shoes?" she suddenly asked just as I took a shot. Her brother turned right at that moment, and even though it was through the lens, our eyes met. I immediately looked away and faced forward.

"My heels are low, so I didn't need to," I replied.

"We're going to go out to the beach afterward," she said, "but I'm sure there will be provisions for the shoes. Victoria should have made arrangements."

"It's okay; I can walk barefoot as well," I said, however, I soon came to instantly regret that because of what her brother said in response.

"There could be broken bottles or other dangerous things in the sand. You should absolutely not walk barefoot."

At his words and the harshness of it, a slight chill seemed to permeate the car. Even the chauffeur turned for a moment to glance at me and then up at him through the rearview mirror.

"Um, sure," I replied before recalling that Aurora was in the car with us.

"Um, I mean, definitely," I replied with a smile. "I'll be careful."

Aurora's giggling was the next thing that filled the space.

"Don't mind him, Evelyn," she said. "He's just being a big meanie."

"Right," I replied and tried my very best to avoid looking at him through the mirror. I did wonder, though, why they had become so close because I could have sworn they were at the most extreme of odds. Frowning, I slightly turned back to look at her, and I could see that her eyes were even shinier than usual.

"She's been crying," Drake explained, and it finally made sense.

"I'm fine," she said not realizing just how wide her smile was.

"You have to keep an eye on her for the rest of the night," Drake admonished me, and I instantly nodded.

"Of course."

"No need," she, however, drawled. "I was just a little bit upset. Evelyn, I thought my fiancé wouldn't be able to make it. Can you imagine it?"

I had no choice then but to look at her in the mirror, and so I couldn't miss Drake as he turned away.

"He tried his best to leave work early but couldn't. Thankfully, Drake saved the day and hired a helicopter, so he'll be here soon. Thank you so much," she grabbed onto her brother's arm and held him tight.

I couldn't help but smile because she was just so adorable, especially when she was giddy. As a result, my eyes met Drake's, and for the longest moment, I couldn't look away. My smile immediately deflated not because I was unhappy to see him; it was just... uncomfortable. He had seen parts of me just a little while earlier that made it incredibly difficult for me to even look at him now, not to mention acting normally around him, and so I couldn't help but look awkwardly away.

Chapter Twenty-One
Drake

She looked so beautiful. I wasn't surprised that she could clean up this nicely but given that she hadn't exactly been dressed to the nines every other instance I had seen her, this was a very welcome change.

She, however, couldn't look me in the eyes for too long. It was almost amusing to watch, but I was in a sour mood, so I couldn't appreciate the moment fully. I didn't, however, share in her shyness, so I took my fill of her appearance before I looked away. She had on a nice-looking set, white romper and delicate pearls on her slender neck, seemed to pull it all together. She looked casual yet elegant, and it just made me appreciate just how gorgeous she was even more.

And then on her lips, she had the darkest shade of red, and all it made me think about was kissing her and once again drinking in her taste.

"Do you have siblings?" I asked. She knew I was talking to her; however, she pretended not to hear me, and that annoyed me.

I didn't ask the question again, but pretty soon she

looked up and confirmed that Aurora was now asleep, resting against the window.

Then she met my gaze.

"Uh... no, I don't," she replied. "I'm an only child."

I nodded in response, and she returned to staring at the road.

"Would you have wanted one?" I asked a bit surprised at my behavior because usually, I didn't like to speak much in the car. However, as I watched her, I couldn't help but ask. I was curious about her, I realized, which was in itself a rarity, so I didn't want to just blatantly ignore or push it away. Plus, none of these were intrusive questions, at least not yet, so I didn't expect her to have any difficulty whatsoever in responding.

She thought about my questions, and I watched as she lifted her gaze to think. And then she looked at me.

"I don't know," she said. "I mean, if they were kind and loving and caring, then yes. But if they were toxic and uncaring and forceful, then, of course, no."

I was almost amused at her words because it was so obviously a dig at my relationship with Aurora.

My gaze lowered to my dear sister Aurora, and I couldn't help but sigh. If only she knew what she was supposed to, none of these would be an issue. She wouldn't feel so sad and as though nobody was on her side.

However, if she did know, then this week would be even worse for her, and so I had no choice but to stand by our unilateral decisions to keep things as they were until her wedding was over.

Turning, I stared out of the window, deep in thought and with my mother on my mind, I loved seeing her smile.

Over the past few years, she hadn't quite been that way, but now she seemed to have shed so much emotional weight. She had obviously accepted what was to come and was literally living out every single moment with all of her heart, and I couldn't help but be happy about this. It also made me feel quite sad, but I couldn't help but smile once again.

"I'm sorry," I suddenly heard the voice in the car, so I turned and met Evelyn's gaze through the rearview mirror.

"What?" I asked.

"I did it again," she replied. "Assumed. I didn't mean that."

At first, I wasn't sure what she was talking about, but when I recalled what she had said about having a sibling, I understood.

I watched her then, and my mother's words filtered through my head. She was right, I realized. I had taken a liking to her more than any other woman I had met in recent years, and now I wanted to know why.

She was gorgeous for sure, but that was the least criteria that could inexplicably draw me to anyone in this way. Even now when she had stepped out of line again, I wasn't even mad. At least not as I had been the previous time. Now I was almost beginning to accept that she couldn't help it and that she wasn't trying to be judgmental. She just couldn't help but put herself in Aurora's shoes, and I completely understood. I sighed and sent her a smile so she wouldn't feel uncomfortable once again around me.

"I know you've put yourself in Aurora's shoes, so you can't help but feel bad for her, that she is not getting the wedding she wants, but I hope you can consider that things are never that simple. And life is never that simple. You've put yourself in her shoes, so you can empathize, but remember that she's only one side of the story. There are others as well, and I'm sure that if you saw my side as well, you'd understand."

At my words, I could see her gaze soften in contriteness, and then she nodded.

"I know," she said, in a low voice. "That's why I'm apologizing because I meant that simply as a tease. It wasn't that I was trying to judge or chastise you. I only realized what it sounded like after I had said it."

I didn't respond to this because I didn't want to give her the whole satisfaction that this interaction had been fruitful. I simply wanted her to not feel too tormented by it as this was already severely affecting the degree and extent to which I could get to know her much better.

Chapter Twenty-Two
Drake

I had followed her out.

At first, it was simply to check if she was alright since I had seen the way she had angrily left the bar thanks to Victoria. This was the second time this had happened and truly I didn't blame her for being absolutely disgusted with her. I was curious, though, what Victoria had said this time that had made her so annoyed. I doubted I would ever know, but at the time, I was trying to avoid stale conversations with my own parents, so I had excused myself and just headed towards her direction.

The garden was gorgeous but given that only sections of it were fully lit, most people remained indoors and only a few littered around. Still, it wasn't difficult to find her because only a few minutes later, I saw someone sitting alert in a corner and watching the entrance like a hawk. If I didn't know she was there, I would have for sure been startled because her eyes looked crazy.

"What are you doing?" I asked; however, the shock still

remained on her face. This time I supposed it was because she hadn't quite been expecting to see me.

"Um… " she tried to straighten, but it was as though her arms weakened and she instead almost fell off the bench.

I jumped forward to catch her, but just as my hand closed around her arm, she righted herself. Then she stared at me once again, wide-eyed.

"Sorry, uh," she said as she moved away, and then she rose to her feet.

"Are you okay?" I asked, and she nodded. "

Just a bit lightheaded from the alcohol."

I took a seat then because this was a good place to relax. It was away from people and the bustle but still airy and pleasant to look at. Plus, I had to admit to myself that she would take the initiative to join me so that we could have at least one conversation. As the wedding party grew, I was certain that it was going to get more and more difficult for us to be alone.

"I'll head in," she said, and I nodded. Disappointed, however, before she could go out of reach, my hand caught hers. I was just as startled as she was, and it took me a while to come up with what I wanted to say.

"Sit," I told her. "Let's talk."

"I, uh, I have to work," she said.

I stared into her eyes, wondering if this was true. And then I saw the danger because I wanted this so badly not to be true, and so I let her go. I couldn't handle the complication anyway, especially since dark days were coming for the family. I'd already been preparing my mind and could only imagine going through it alone. Adding another person to the mix? Or maybe I was thinking too far ahead? This was the problem because with her, I just couldn't help but think far ahead.

"Enjoy your night," she said, so awkwardly that I was almost amused. I watched her scurry away, and then took a deep breath.

It was a nice quiet space to be in, so I leaned my head back and stared up at the stars. It was as though the heavens knew it was a very special evening for my family because the sky was glittering. However, and despite how gorgeous they were, I felt so inexplicably sad that it was nearly overwhelming. I had truly driven myself into the ground the past few months with work so that I could get moments like this. Moments when I recalled, moments where I thought about anything but work.

So instantly, I got ready to leave, but then, to my surprise, someone came into the area, and I as well was startled.

"Evelyn?" I called when I saw who it was.

"Uh," she said, staring at me, and I understood then. She wanted to return but didn't know how not to be awkward around me.

"We fucked," I told her. "Not a big deal. Just sit down and talk. Surely that can't be more difficult or more intimate."

I said it so nonchalantly that it amused me, and when I lifted my head to hers, I found that she as well was nearly doubling over.

We shared a smile, and then a small laugh, and then she came over and sat by my side. For the first few moments after, we were quiet, and I realized just how comfortable I felt. There was something about her that was so comfortable and reassuring. There was no pressure to speak, at least on my part, but soon enough she did and, to my delight, noted the sky the exact way I had.

"Striking," she said. "The stars, I mean. I don't know why, though, but it makes me feel a bit lonely?"

My gaze lowered to hers then, and she seemed to panic.

"I mean, I'm not saying I'm lonely, it's just that it's so vast and it just makes the world seem so impossibly big, though it's beautiful. But not everything that's beautiful is completely great, I guess."

She kept rambling, and I kept listening, and it was highly entertaining, to say the least. Then she eventually noticed how nervous she sounded and just stopped. This amused me even more.

My gaze lowered to her lips then, and the biggest urge to kiss her hit. However, I restrained myself.

"Sorry," she said. "I'm not nervous, but I tend to just talk when I feel awkward."

"You feel awkward around me?" I asked, and she smiled.

"How could I not."

"Yeah," I replied and looked away, my attention lowering to my feet.

"Have you been enjoying the party so far?" she asked.

I nodded in response. "

Things are going smoothly, at least from my end. It must be chaos from Victoria's."

At this, she went silent, and I wondered why till I realized that I had just once again mentioned the person she was probably the least fond of. I turned to her then, and although she was looking away from me, I didn't miss the disgusted look on her face. It was quite amusing, to say the least.

"She irks you that much?" I asked, and she sighed.

"She does, true. I don't even think about her, but she keeps wanting me to think about her, and I cannot understand why. Or does it just give her joy to see me annoyed?"

"What did she come over to trouble you with this time around?" I asked. However, she went silent again. She looked at me, and then she smiled.

"Unimportant. Uh, Aurora seems happy."

"She is whenever her fiancé is around. They're really good together."

"Yeah," I replied. "The way he looks at her is magical. I managed to capture some of that. She'll love it."

"There's a magical way to look at someone?" I asked, and she turned to me. She met my eyes then, and for the few seconds afterward, I, for some reason, found it extremely hard to breathe. And in that moment, I knew the answer to the question that I had just asked, and I looked away.

"Yes," she said. "You might not even notice when you're doing it, but other people might."

"Okay," I replied and wished to God that I had something to drink right then.

It was time to leave, I was sure, however, I didn't want to just yet. I wanted to know a bit more

about her. But then, at the end of the day, I decided that there was no benefit to this. Only trouble. So, I asked something else instead.

"Are you still sticking by your resolution from earlier this evening?"

Just as I expected, she went silent. I was expecting her to say no. However, she let out a sigh.

"I want to," she said and met my gaze. "I don't even know why I'm being honest now, but..."

"It's the alcohol," I said, and she smiled.

"I want to, but there are a lot of risks."

I listened.

"Aurora's wedding, I don't want anything to take away from that."

"That's easy to fix," I replied. "We can have our fun and keep matters between us."

"Yes," she said. "That's the next issue. I don't know how much fun this can be. I mean, the first time was good, but... maybe we should leave it at that. I mean..."

I waited; however, she didn't go any further.

"I don't think we should delve any deeper," she said.

I frowned, then, wondering what she was trying to say because so far, she seemed just too elusively to be talking around in circles.

Chapter Twenty-Three
Evelyn

I was making absolutely no sense. I was literally talking to what had to be the most gorgeous man I had ever been in the presence of, and I was babbling away like I didn't have a lick of sense. I couldn't believe it, but at the same time, I didn't think I could stop. I knew what I was trying to say ... what I was trying to ask, but it didn't seem as though it would come out. He watched me, and I would have given anything in that moment to know what he was thinking because I was sure it would be along the lines of what a train wreck I was. However, I didn't want to sound or appear this way. I stopped and straightened my shoulders. Then I said exactly what I wanted to.

"Do you have a girlfriend?" I asked, and the moment it came out, all the anxiety seemed to drain out of me. There was no longer any need to dance around the bush because I needed to know. I also knew what the natural assumption for me asking this question would be, so I immediately countered this and explained myself.

"I'm not asking because... I mean, it has absolutely

nothing to do with me. I just don't want to cross any boundaries. I wouldn't want to do to someone what I would absolutely hate if it were done to me."

He watched me, and then he smiled.

"Isnt it too late for such concerns?" he asked, and I sighed.

"It is indeed too late, but I have to still salvage this the best way I can. I was carried away the first time, but it doesn't mean I have to be again."

We both went silent, and in the passing moments, I couldn't believe how worked up I was. It felt good, but it also felt dizzying. There was no doubt in my mind now that I was completely and totally infatuated with him, and it just made me happier that I was addressing the hard matters now. Hopefully, he would tell me that Victoria was right and that he had a girlfriend so that all of this unnecessary inner turmoil would come to an end.

"No," he replied. "I do not."

I heard him; however, only when the words came out, did I realize that I hadn't quite been expecting him to tell the truth. I mean, what man did. However, as I stared into his eyes, I

realized that this wasn't true. I was expecting him to tell me the truth because why would he lie. He was gorgeous, handsome, unbelievably wealthy, and he was at a freaking wedding party. He could line up all the women here with married and unmarried and take to his bed, and no one would resist or bat an eyelash. Including myself.

But still, and for common sense, I had to ask outright at least once.

"You're telling the truth, right?" I asked, and he smiled.

"Why would I lie?"

"Yeah, right. I mean, you can sleep with anyone here that you want to probably, so I guess there isn't really any reason to lie. I just, I just heard that you had one and it made me feel a bit ill. Because I never want to cheat with someone else's partner. I would absolutely hate it if someone did that to me."

"You would?" he asked, and I was surprised at his question.

"Of course, I would. You wouldn't?"

He didn't respond.

"A lot of women and men, I guess... our generation - they don't seem to think that way. If someone isn't married, then no chains are on, apparently."

"Absolutely motherfucking not," I refuted this, quite incensed at the fucking ridiculous logic. "If you can't even fucking respect something as simple as a relationship, then how the fuck do they expect to respect a marriage?" His brows slightly raised at my outburst, making me realize that perhaps I was overreacting.

"Sorry," I apologized and lowered my head, but he smiled instead.

"You seem to be quite passionate about this topic. I don't think I pictured you as the cursing type."

"I only curse when I'm pissed," I said.

"Oh? Do you have personal experience with this then? Is this why you're pissed? Do you have a boyfriend? Have you been cheated on before?"

"No, I haven't," I replied. "I mean, I don't know if I have, which is exactly my point. But you know if I was ...I would be fucking pissed."

He smiled again, and it was just so beautiful that I couldn't stop myself from smiling as well.

"A drink would be great right about now," he said, and I let out a deep sigh in agreement.

"Exactly. Exactly."

I expected him then to get up and go on his way, but he didn't. Instead, he remained seated, and so I was forced to look away.

"You didn't answer my question," he said, and I wondered which he was talking about. He repeated it.

"Do you have a boyfriend?" he asked.

"No, I do not."

"I should believe you, right?" he asked.

"Of course, you should. I mean, I believe you and... the only reason why I even doubted you was because Victo—" I stopped instantly.

He, however, was more than smart enough to catch onto what I had been about to say.

"Victoria?" he asked. "Why is she coming up again?"

I sighed because I had to accept now that I was part of the problem.

For a long moment, I contemplated telling him about what she had said and decided in the end that there was no point in holding back. The more things were in the open, the better I would be able to navigate whatever this was between us.

"You asked me earlier what she said to me when she came up to me at the bar," she said, and I nodded.

"Yes."

"Well, what she came to tell me was that you had a girlfriend. And that basically I should stop building castles in the sky."

He stared at me, and then he smiled.

"You were building castles in the sky?"

"Absolutely not," I replied. "I was simply minding my own business, and there she came yet again to bother me. She insisted that I was always seated alone at bars to wait for you to come speak to me and-"

"She's not wrong."

"And I was just so irritated by her that-"

His words struck like a gong.

"What?" I asked, and his smile widened even further, literally setting off a colony of butterflies in my stomach. I hated this; I hated this so much.

"She's not wrong," he repeated. "I get bored after a while with all the socializing, so naturally, my eyes strayed to the bar. Since you don't know a lot of people here or anyone for that matter, it's expected that you would go to the bar to sit in peace."

"Thank you!" I explained, wondering how he could understand this, but she couldn't.

"I didn't have anything to do with you. I mean ... no offense, but I just wanted to relax and drink when I went there, yet she was insinuating that I did it to get your attention."

"She is right as well about that," he said, and I stopped.

Something about my sullen expression made him laugh out, and the sound was so electric to listen to.

"She's right?" I asked, nearly out of breath.

"It's very hard for a man to resist approaching a gorgeous woman sitting alone at the bar. That is the ultimate attention grabber." Listening to him, I realized he was right, and so I sighed and gave up.

"I'm exhausted," I said, and he smiled again.

"That's why I came out here," he said, his voice lowering even more dangerously. It sounded husky just like it had earlier that evening but was rapidly bringing memories to mind that hit painfully against my stomach.

The flashbacks... fuck! These damned flashbacks.

I couldn't look away from him or breathe for that matter.

"I didn't sit there to get your attention," I said, and he nodded.

"Noted. I'm glad you did, though, because it made you easier to find."

My gaze couldn't help then but flutter down to his lips.

"Would setting some ground rules make you consider spending your week with me?" he asked, and my heart dropped into my stomach.

No! I screamed internally because this was exactly what I wanted, yet I knew it was wrong. Or maybe it wasn't? My head was conflicted, but my heart... my fucking heart as I stared at him.

I looked away then, knowing that I needed to think straight.

"I need time," I replied.

"Sure," he said, "You can take as long as you need."

He rose to his feet then, and I was a bit startled, so I rose as well with him.

He gave me a questioning look, but I couldn't sit back down because it would feel even more awkward.

"I uh... I'll be heading in soon as well, but of course, I'll wait till you're in. I have work to do."

"You'll wait till I go in first because you have work to do?" he asked, and I heard just absolutely how nuts I sounded. I soon decided, though, upon seeing his smirk, that he was for the most part to blame because he was the one intentionally misinterpreting my words. Of course, he knew what I meant. I wanted to hit him, but I simply just shook my head.

"I'll go in first," I said and started to leave, but then, before I could get out of reach, he caught my arm once again.

Chapter Twenty-Four
Drake

I couldn't let her leave. I needed to touch her, but still, she was still trying to make her decisions, and I didn't want to push her either. And so, for the first time in my life, I did something that I never could have imagined that I would ever do, I sought permission.

"Can I kiss you?" I asked.

She seemed quite stunned at my words, and it was understandable. I was surprised as well, but in the moment, it felt like the right thing to do, and I had learned over the years to trust my own instinct. She didn't respond. Instead, she seemed to falter slightly, so my hold tightened around her, and then she nodded.

She seemed a bit dazed, and in a way, I understood because as I slanted my head to kiss her, I felt the same way as well.

Her taste felt like coming home and being set on fire all at once. It was sweet and warm yet so fucking sensational that my heart raced.

It had been a long time since I had felt this all-consuming feeling with someone... this being drawn like a moth to a flame.

Once again, I was struck in wonder because what the fuck was it about her. She kissed me as well as though she understood. As though she felt the exact same way I did and couldn't get enough, and I loved it. We were in a public place. Anyone could walk by at any moment, especially from our party, and this would no doubt immediately ruin our resolution to keep things hidden for the moment. However, I couldn't care less. I held her tight as my tongue sleeved deeper, drinking her in, sucking on her tongue. It felt so sweetly intimate, and I loved that. That's the thing about her; I didn't have to be on my guard. There was something so refreshingly simple and honest about her that I deeply loved and appreciated.

I couldn't say any of this verbally to her, so of course, I showed her with the way that I kissed her.

Suddenly and unfortunately though, I heard voices. It was upsetting because it startled her. Still, she was reluctant to pull away, but eventually, and as they drew nearer, we had to.

I broke the kiss, but it was much, much harder to catch my breath. And even when I could open my eyes, I couldn't stop looking at her; there was something here. I felt it with all of my heart, and even though I wanted to ignore it, I don't know that I could. Perhaps it was a fluke, and if it was, then I at least wanted to find out.

"Tomorrow evening enough time for you to make up your mind and get back to me?" I asked, and she nodded. However, she seemed so dazed that I was sure then if I had asked her where she wanted to fly on brooms, she would have nodded as well. I was amused and felt my heart

throb with affection for how much of a dork she was. So even though I tried to, I couldn't resist leaning forward and pressing a kiss to her cheek.

Her eyes fluttered shut at it, and when I pulled away, I noticed that she was a bit more clear-headed.

"Tomorrow night?" I asked again, and she nodded. Since it had been agreed upon, I let my hands move down her gorgeous figure, and then I continued on my way.

Chapter Twenty-Five
Evelyn

I t took a while before I was able to remember how to walk again. Yet it was barely enough for me to get my legs to work enough to guide me back to the bench. Afterward, I literally sat in a daze until once again, another pair of footsteps and laughter walked past.

It was time to return. I needed to get back to work. And so, the second my heart somewhat settled down, I rose to my feet and returned to the restaurant.

He had given me until the following night; however, the moment I walked in, my eyes searched for him. He was across the room, a tumbler of golden liquor in hand, surrounded by a group of people he conversed with.

I watched him, quite embarrassingly mesmerized, and it was as though he felt it because a few seconds later, he turned his head and met my gaze.

It lingered. He stared for a total count of three very long seconds, and my heart nearly thundered out of my chest.

Sighing, I walked myself back to the table where I had left my camera and plopped down onto my seat.

This was trouble. I was in trouble, but my question to myself was if it was something I could tolerate and manage for the next few days.

This would be over by the weekend, I told myself, and just then, Aurora came to mind.

I looked around the hall and realized that I couldn't see her. So, I rose back to my feet and took my phone along with me.

I called her, and at first, she didn't pick up, but eventually, she did.

"Hello," she answered, and I was incredibly glad to hear from her. I also couldn't help but feel a tad bit guilty.

"Where are you?" I asked. "It seems more people have arrived. The restaurant is fuller than when it started."

"I know," she said and then she went quiet.

"Aurora?" called.

"I'm in the car, with my fiancé," she replied. "I told him I wasn't feeling well, so he came out here with me."

"Oh," I said and felt even more racked with guilt. I was here to work, to capture her moments, yet I had literally been frolicking in the gardens with her brother that she wasn't currently on the best of terms with.

Sighing, I lowered my voice and my tone.

"Are you going to go home to rest?" I asked. "Maybe you should."

"I can't," she said sounding even sadder. "He wants to stay. He has to stay but... he feels so uncomfortable. He wouldn't tell me, though, but I'm sensitive towards things like this."

I nodded.

"I completely understand"

"I'll be back in soon," she said, however, I wanted to go to her.

"Please tell me where you are?" I asked. "Do you want me to come to you? I'd love to."

She went quiet again as she contemplated this request and, to my disappointment, she refused.

"I'll head back now. I'll meet you at the entrance."

"Alright," I said, put the phone away and waited.

She soon returned, and I watched her walk side by side with her fiancé as they returned. He sent me a huge smile as we met at the door, and then she urged him to head in alone so that she could talk to me.

I watched her and instantly leaned forward to give her a hug, and when I pulled away, she was incredibly surprised and somewhat amused.

"What's that for?" she asked, and I smiled, however, her face seemed to freeze in dark suspicion.

"You were not thinking of quitting right? Why does this feel like a goodbye?"

"I'm not quitting," I told her, "and it's not goodbye. We both needed it, I think."

"You're right," she beamed, her eyes sparkling.

We started to head in then, but she stopped me.

"Wait, why did you need a hug? Is anything wrong? Is Victoria bothering you again?"

I smiled, wondering how someone could be so sweet.

"No," I replied, "At least it's something I can handle. Everything is fine. I'm having a blast."

"I know that's not true," she smiled. "My fiancé said the

same thing. But it'll be over soon, so please bear it a little while longer."

I nodded, and we looked out across the crowd.

I saw her watch them, and immediately, I pulled out my camera to take a photo. She turned to me then, and a gorgeous smile spread across her face.

"Drake really wasn't kidding when he said that even though it's my wedding, it has very little to do with me. I guess I shouldn't be complaining because I don't really care for the attention, but it's just … it's taking away the magic and excitement I'd expect to feel when I was getting married. My fiancé hates the crowd as well. We're very similar in this regard."

She looked at me.

"Am I whining again?"

"No," I replied. "I completely understand what you're saying."

She nodded then and smiled at me.

"Thank you for being here. My furry son only gets in Friday, so till then, I'm going to lean completely on you. Please don't refuse."

This made me laugh.

"I won't. I'll lean completely on you as well."

Her fiancé came over then with a flute of sparkling grape juice for her, and after sending a nod in greeting to me, they once again disappeared into the crowd.

Once again, I was left alone with my thoughts, and they were brutal. Everyone truly was making this about themselves, including me now. Instead of doing my job and keeping my focus on the couple, I was allowing myself to get unnecessarily distracted with other trivial matters, and it wasn't right.

It made me upset, and so in that moment, I made my decision. I didn't want to run into Drake again, and so I stayed out of sight, and thankfully, I didn't see him afterward as he became immensely busy.

Later that night when I had showered and was in bed, I pulled up his number and sent him my response.

"I've considered your offer, and I know you gave me till tomorrow night to decline, but I'll be doing that now. I think it's best for me, at this time, to solely focus on my job."

I sent this without any remorse and completely full of conviction, however afterwards, and as I

shut my eyes to sleep for the night, it felt as though I had downed anxiety in a bottle. All my emotions came out - dread, unhappiness, doubt, and to add salt to the wound, I had never been so horny. I couldn't stop thinking about him, all of which was now heightened and worsened by the fact that I had completely nipped whatever this was between us in the bud.

Despite all this inner torment, I didn't change my mind, and so in no time and eventually, I was fast asleep.

Chapter Twenty-Six
Drake

Breakfast the next morning was a bit more rowdy than the previous day. My father had now arrived along with a few more guests, and breakfast was scheduled at the vineyard. The weather was gorgeous, so it was held out on the patio, with the sprawling panoramic view of the field before us, and it should have been more than enough to completely capture my attention and make the morning a good one. However, I couldn't take my eyes off the woman that had so blatantly rejected me the previous evening.

Giving her the extra day to think about my proposition had been a formality because I had been sure, and especially after our rendezvous in the garden, that she was just as drawn to me as I was to her. This was supposed to be a fun week for both of us, one possibly to be cherished for a very long time afterward, yet she had sent me that cryptic message last night and outrightly rejected it. I couldn't understand truly what had gone wrong.

I watched her now seated at a different table from us with other guests and willed her to meet my gaze; however, she refused. She continued with her work and with eating as though I didn't exist, and it tore me up even further. I was painfully hard just thinking of her. My cock, brain, and heart recalled with every passing moment what it had felt like to be sheathed inside her warm heat, and I was willing to do whatever it took to ensure that she didn't deprive us both of it.

However, it seemed that she was even more focused on ensuring that this never happened.

She refused to let us both be alone for even a second, immediately excusing herself anytime this happened at the buffet table. The first two times I'd thought it coincidence, but when the third time she purposefully avoided my gaze, I understood what she was doing. And so, I returned to my seat and my party.

A few minutes later, however, I sent her a message. There was no point in being polite anymore or beating around the bush because I was for sure going to give her a piece of my mind.

· · ·

"Are you planning on avoiding me for the rest of the week?" I sent her a text message, I watched her and waited for her to receive it, and she did. Just as she picked up a watermelon slice to put into her mouth, her face lowered to her phone. However, she was as sneaky about it.

She shut the phone off as though she hadn't seen a thing and continued on with one of the invited lawyers that Aurora's fiancé had brought along. He had been conversing with her for the better part of an hour I could see, and she had been all smiles. So, she could deign to give her attention to others and not me? I was fucking pissed off. I welcomed the challenge, and so when we eventually left the vineyard to head toward the spa that the wedding party had been scheduled for today, I made up my mind to crumble her will and have her literally foaming at the mouth, with my cum.

The spa was a huge establishment, luxurious and well-equipped, but it wasn't difficult,
    whatsoever, to find her. The women were a bit startled, though, to see me come in, but after I explained who I was asking for, they showed me to her room.

They were reluctant to let me in and wanted to ask, but I quickly shut that down.

. . .

"She's my girlfriend," I said, and they seemed to nod in understanding. I, however, was the one left startled. I hadn't called anyone my girlfriend in nearly a decade, and to so casually throw out the title all to see one extremely stubborn woman was quite something to watch. Perhaps it was because I was on vacation, but I was taking a lot of liberties than were normal. It bothered me because there was nothing I detested more than a lack of control, but when I walked into the dimly lit room and saw her lying face down on the bed, all of these reservations seemingly flowed out of my head. There was a small towel covering her body and was oiled and glistening. I stopped at the door to take her in and felt a kick in my abdomen as my cock once again stirred to life. God, she was so fucking gorgeous. I truly had never wanted any woman this much, and as I stared at the curve of her ass barely shielded by the towel, I truly wondered if I would be able to restrain myself.

I knew for sure that she was going to make things difficult, and so I didn't announce myself. She wouldn't see me anyway as she was facedown and resting, completely prepared to have a good time. I vowed to give it to her.

Shutting the door behind us, I headed over to where she lay and looked at the supplies available. All I needed was the warmed-up massage oil, and I was ready to explore every inch of her body.

.   .   .

I didn't speak since she would have been expecting a woman and thus, I didn't want her to be startled. After spreading the oil on my hands, I started from her shoulders and began her massage. I wasn't a professional by any means, but I had been in the fitness industry for too long not to have a clue about what to do, and so I began with that.

The second I began rubbing out the knots of tension down the back of her neck and in her shoulders, I was rewarded with the sweetest moans.

"Oh," she breathed. "That's good. "Thank you."

I smiled then, unable to take my eyes off her.

She was so beautiful that it made me deeply uncomfortable, but as I continued to massage her and was rewarded constantly with gorgeous moans, I decided that I quite enjoyed this time as well. She was sure to freak when she discovered it was me, but I made sure that no matter how this ended, she would at least have had a wonderful massage.

I rolled down her towel from her back, stopping it just before her ass so she wouldn't be alarmed, and then I massaged my way down. She truly was tense, and I enjoyed watching her relax with every passing second. What tortured me was the almost violent need to taste her

listening skin and bury my face between her legs. She looked so goddamn good and as I continued to touch her, my hunger grew to a fevered pitch.

Chapter Twenty-Seven
Evelyn

There was indeed a thing called 'magic hands' because, in the current moment, I was experiencing a euphoria that couldn't quite be put into words. I had been unsure of whether I would be able to relax during this spa section. In fact, I had been determined to focus only on Aurora's enjoyment of it, but after taking her some pictures, she insisted that I leave and have the chance to enjoy the relaxing afternoon as well. I was grateful for her, but this was a bit too much. Nothing too sexual was happening, but as those strong, precise hands massaged my skin, blood roared through my ears. This felt like the preamble to exquisite, slow, sensual sex, and my clit was engorged in response. I was so wet and worried that the scent emanating as a result would trouble the attendant, whoever it was; her fault, and there was nothing I could do. I needed some privacy after this, perhaps in a bathroom stall or somewhere, because I needed to come. It already disappointed me that all I could do was soothe the ache in my clit till relief was granted when what I wanted was something thick and long inside of me. Preferably Drake's cock. However, I had closed that door the previous night, and there was no way in hell that I was going to reopen it again.

I was tempted to, with all my heart, and in a way, it nearly drove me crazy, but I was determined to stick to my resolution this time around. He, however, was not making it easy for me whatsoever. I had refused to meet his gaze all throughout breakfast, but it had truly been the most uncomfortable hour of my life so far. I could feel his stare and annoyance burning through me, and then he had sent that text. I knew then that he was watching, and that I had a chance to look in his direction; however, it had taken every ounce of will not to because I knew that if I saw him, my resolution would crumble. All I would think about was being fucked until I couldn't think straight, and this was currently the source of my problems. And to think that just a little while earlier, I was worried about money. Now I was worried about sex, and it just left me exhausted. Life was too damn complicated, and so this massage session I appreciated even more.

Right then, the masseuse began to spread my legs open, needing to get between my thighs, and I was completely willing. She wouldn't go too far, but for a moment, I wished she would. That rather than just working on the external flesh, she would go further and stick a finger in or too, or perhaps a fucking toy. Damn, I really needed to be fucked, and it was all Drake's fault. Sighing, I shook my head and turned my face in the opposite direction. She kept working, and I paid attention simply because I was so soaking wet and was spilling, so she was sure to encounter that. I didn't want to have to apologize profusely and have another thing to be embarrassed about. However, she didn't seem to mind; she kept going higher every time she diverted her attention to the back of my thighs and then returned until eventually, I had to stop her.

"Maybe not too far?" I said in a light friendly tone. "This is quite relaxing, so pardon me. I didn't want to, umm—" I couldn't find the words to say what I wanted.

"Do you understand me?" I asked.

"You don't want my finger inside you?" he asked, and I started to smile, but then a couple of things immediately occurred to me. For one, that was a male voice, not a woman, and the question had been wild. What the fuck was happening? I opened my eyes and turned so I could see who had been working so freely on my body for the better part of the last half-hour.

He wasn't amused.

There was no trace of mirth on his face, so it was very clear to me that this wasn't some sort of joke. He had come in here to do exactly what he had so far, and I was shocked to my core. I stared at him and felt extremely violated. But then, one glance down at the white pants he had on, and I nearly choked. He was so hard that he was nearly bursting at the seams, while I was so wet and turned on that I was ready to ride the next surface I could find.

However, in all this, I didn't know what to say. And so, I reached forward and tried to grab my towel, but it was too far out of reach, and pretty soon, it dropped all the way to the floor, completely exposing me. I looked down at it and was so stifled, tears sprung to my eyes.

"I could sue you for this," I said, and he replied.

"For what? Giving you a massage? Didn't touch you inappropriately."

"Fucking shit." He was right; however, he had still crossed my boundary, the one I had told him I wasn't willing to cross with him.

"Please leave," I asked with my front still glued to the table and my ass out for him to see.

. . .

I could feel his stare on me, and then I felt him move; however, he didn't leave. Instead, he went over to the couch by the corner and took his seat. He was directly facing me, then; however, he wasn't looking at my body but straight at my face.

"What happened?" he asked. "Between last night and this morning? What made you decline?"

I sighed. "I thought the whole purpose of giving me time to think about it was so that I could have the chance to refuse if I wanted to."

"Sure," he said. "But I didn't expect you to refuse."

I frowned at his bold assumption.

"I understand," I nodded. "You're not used to being rejected by women, so you couldn't imagine that I wouldn't want you. Well, here's news for you, Mr. Moran. Not every woman's response to you is yes, so I would deeply appreciate it if you respected this and please gave me my peace of mind and privacy."

· · ·

He watched me quietly, and I couldn't help but feel a slight fear tickled down my spine.

"I don't care for every woman to say yes to me," he said, "I was expecting you to test me. It's been a very long while since I've been attracted to a woman the way I am to you, and it's incredibly fascinating to me. I want to explore it, and I get the feeling that you want to as well, even though you had reservations based on the work you're currently handling. So... was I wrong? You have no interest in me whatsoever?"

I was speechless. I had expected him to be offended and to basically turn into a complete jerk about the entire situation. And here he was, speaking calmly and explaining to me in a way that truly made me melt, why he respectfully wanted to fuck me. My heart skipped several beats.

I stared at him, and when nothing even remotely reasonable for me to say would come to mind, I smacked my head against the chair. At the end of the day, and to put us both out of this fucking misery, I simply told him the truth.

"Everyone right now is taking this whole event as a vacation. Everyone is after their own, and it seems most people have forgotten that this is for and about the bride and groom. And from what I've seen, while everyone is having a blast, the bride and groom seem to be the two people not having any fun at all. I don't like this, and Aurora, I like Aurora a lot. I don't want her to be upset, and I want to make my time here completely about her and not about us."

He listened, and then he nodded.

"You can do that," he said. "My question now is why does this prevent me from fucking you right now?"

My heart stopped once again, and my brain apparently as well because even though I tried to find an answer to this question, I soon found that none whatsoever wanted to come to me. I continued to stare at him, and then once again, I collapsed onto the table in complete defeat. There was no point in fighting this; I felt like I was going to lose my mind if I didn't get some relief. Just thinking about him and wanting him had made me so fucking sensitive and cranky. I would try a different approach and restrict this but still ensure that focus remained completely on Aurora. With this decided, I spread my legs and didn't say a further word.

Chapter Twenty-Eight
Drake

I could see the submission in her actions and her expressions. She was willing and ready; however, I, on the other hand, was a bit shaken by my reaction to her. There was an endless supply of women at my beck and call, so why had I allowed myself to stoop in this way just to get her attention? For the first time in a long while, I felt as though I had given my power away, like I was no longer in control, and I hated it.

No woman could make me feel this way, so I rose to my feet with my decision made. It would be a lot more difficult for her to change my mind than for her to change hers. I didn't bother responding, just as how she hadn't even bothered communicating clearly her train of thought and decision, so I headed for the door, much to her shock.

"Drake," she called out; however, I didn't respond. It was a shame because I had been looking forward to using that room with her; however, there were a lot of things that couldn't be pushed aside for the sake of my desire, and my complete lack of control over one woman was one of them. I would rather deprive myself than be at her mercy, and I wanted the both of us to know that.

I exited the room but just as I did, the door to the spa room beside us opened. I didn't bother looking to see who it was, but when I heard the door to Evelyn's room open as well, I realized that she had run out after me. I turned around to make sure that she was properly dressed and found that she was not. She did, however, have the towel around her, which was okay, but it wasn't tight.

"Get back!" I scolded her immediately, concerned for her before even turning to see the situation. I found that it was Victoria, and my worries were allayed. She wasn't important; however, when I turned and saw the look on Evelyn's face, I realized that this probably would spell trouble for her.

She seemed so angry and forlorn at the same time as she retreated back into the room and then she slammed the door shut behind her. I understood, and in a way, I felt a bit responsible, and so I turned to Victoria. Her mouth was wide open, and she as well was in a towel.

"Um," she smiled and boldly met my gaze. "I'm sorry for interrupting. I didn't know you two were—"

"It's none of your business," I told her, and her expression immediately changed. It darkened, and I could clearly see that she was incredibly upset. I didn't give a fuck.

"Do you understand what I mean?" I asked.

"If I hear this discussed beyond the three of us and amongst anyone at the party, I will know for

sure that you were the one who tattled, and I will, as a

result, ensure that you're immediately fired. Do you understand me?"

She glared at me, and then she released a deep breath.

"Yes, Sir, I do."

"Good," I said and continued on my way.

Chapter Twenty-Nine
Evelyn

oly shit. I was in a shit ton of trouble. At first, and after seeing Victoria, that had been the true source of my panic. But leaning against the door and hearing what he had said to her, how he had cared enough to protect me even though he was clearly pissed at me, my legs were currently weak. I was a mixture of anxiety and arousal, and I didn't know what to deal with myself. This was why this massage had been needed to calm me down, but now it seemed as though I was more riled up than ever.

I liked him. I liked him a lot. There was no looking away from that any longer, and so I had to figure this out. I couldn't be careless and dismissive simply because it was easier than actually trying to work around something, even if it was my obligation to Aurora.

However, I didn't know how to fathom anything concrete with him. In a way, he almost seemed larger than life, and thus I didn't know how to imagine myself with him. Not that he had been propositioning that, but with the way

I was reacting to him, I didn't just want to cut off all possibilities to it. Sure, I was still unhappy about the fact that Aurora couldn't have the exact wedding she wanted because of his interference, but their contention in this matter shouldn't have to affect me. Or should it? It annoyed me for sure, but ... but was it enough of a reason for me to stay away from him? I mean, Aurora didn't hate her brother. From what I had seen so far, and despite this, they were still quite cordial with each other or even friendly.

So, rather than assume and deprive myself, perhaps it would be better for me to actually discuss this with him and possibly even Aurora. However, I was nervous, but I was glad that I was considering it because I was at least open to more options. I looked around the massage room and couldn't help but shake my head. What a prime location it had been for a lot of great things to happen. Yet I had ended up alone in it, staring at the wall, and so unsatisfied I wanted to scream.

I couldn't possibly relax now, not after Victoria had seen as well. Sure, Drake had warned her not to be a tattle tale, but I didn't see how she was going to be able to keep this newly found info to herself. She was probably going to use it to find every which way possible to frustrate, mock, or even blackmail me, and ultimately, she might even tell Aurora.

There truly was absolutely no fucking way I could relax now, so I put my clothes on and headed out. After these spa sessions was lunch at a nearby restaurant; however, I knew that I wouldn't be able to wait till then. There would be too many eyes, so of course, it would be nearly impossible to reach him. Unless I reached out to ask for his audience?

I stopped at my locker as this idea came to mind and pulled out my phone. I wanted to call him, but I wasn't sure that I was able to sound coherent yet, so I texted him instead.

"Where are you, please?" I asked. I truly didn't want to sound so polite, but currently, I understood that there were a lot of eggshells between us, and I had to tread lightly. So, I sighed and added another line.

"I really hope we can talk. Please let me know."

I sent it off, gathered my things, and exited the spa. However, twenty minutes later, there was no response whatsoever. I had expected it would be somewhat difficult to reach him, but the reality of it was much more disheartening than I knew how to accept.

The verdict had been given. My choices now were to either accept this and move on with my life like he so obviously had, or I could instead put down my pride for a little bit and reach out this time around? So far, he had been the one to do so; perhaps it was my turn?

Sighing, I pulled out my phone once again and thought of calling Anna, but there was nothing she could say that could help me make this decision. It had to come from me completely, and so, after giving things a few more minutes of thought, I contacted him. This time around, however, I didn't text him because perhaps that was easy to ignore, but a phone call for sure would be much harder.

My heart leapt into my throat in the next moment as I placed it, and the phone started ringing. I immediately rose to my feet and found that my legs were weak. In the bid to hide my anxiety from any onlookers, including myself, I found the nearest wall and leaned against it.

It kept ringing, and I prayed he would pick up. I was never quite timid when I was with him, but the thought of this right now had completely turned me into a weakling. It was humbling and embarrassing all at once, but what could I do?

The call rang to disconnection, and this was incredibly hurtful. I told myself, though, that he was busy, and that all I needed to do was to simply try again. However, I didn't think I could.

I began to consider then that perhaps this was for the best. Perhaps by pushing him away the way I had, I had finally gotten what I wanted. But was it the right thing? After all, if he had no interest whatsoever in me and clearly exhibited this, then I would for sure not hold on to him for any reason.

Nodding, I agreed with this and put my phone away. There was no need for me to participate happily in whatever else was coming, so, as I should be, I started to head back to the spa where Aurora was busy as well with her mother. Just as I arrived, however, and before I could ask for directions to where she was, my phone began to ring. At first, I ignored it, just for a couple of seconds, but just before it disconnected, I jumped and dug into my purse to retrieve my phone.

"Hello?" I answered and couldn't believe just how eager and nervous and stunned I sounded. Fuck, I wanted him, and it frustrated me at just how much I was overthinking this. I mean, why couldn't I just give in and allow this man to do what the fuck he wanted to me? When else was I ever going to come across someone of his caliber?

"Evelyn," he called, his voice raw and raspy. He

sounded somewhat cold and perhaps even annoyed. But I didn't care. I was no longer going to live in my head, at least for the duration of this phone call.

"I sent you a message," I told him once again, so nervous my words were nearly breathless.

"I'm in the spa," he said. "I haven't checked."

"Oh," I replied, hope flickering in my chest.

"Um... "

"What did you say?" he asked.

"What?" I replied. I heard him clearly, but I needed more time to get my head screwed back on. I truly couldn't process any coherent thought because in the moment, it felt like the only words available to me were whatever I had thought of prior to this phone call.

"What did you say?" he asked, and I was forced then to think.

"Um.. I wanted to see you?" I asked. "I was wondering if you were still here or if you had left? I mean, it's just... a brief talk. I didn't know things might get even heavier, so we might not find another chance?"

He went quiet, and I did as well, my eyes tightening shut because I was now very clearly rambling and out of my mind.

"Come to the male spa," he told me. "Room 18."

"Oh," I replied. However, before I could say another word, the call disconnected. I remained in place, however, as I processed all he had just said, and then I put the phone away.

Chapter Thirty
Evelyn

He was probably being massaged as well, I imagined, and all over again, I was wound as tight as a knot. The previously built tension not yet dispelled stirred up like a storm inside of me, and before I could stop myself, I was marching back to the spa. I tried to tell myself to slow down; but I couldn't, and in no time, I was back at the spa.

"The females' section is in a separate—"

"No, it's fine, I know," I told the receptionist as soon as I got in. I just... I was told to come to room 18. She seemed a bit confused by this at first, but as she took in my nervous eyes and my now reddened hands tightening their hold on my purse, it seemed as though she understood.

"He called you?" she asked again, and I nodded.

"You a hooker?"

A very cold shock shivered through me.

"What?" I asked, and she gave me a look that clearly said she was uninterested in listening to whatever explanation I was about to give because it would clearly be a lie. I wasn't about to give one, plus I wasn't about to explain myself either, so I sighed and didn't respond.

"Which way to room 18?" I asked, and she nearly rolled her eyes.

"I'll accompany you. He's in the middle of a session now, so I have to confirm that you were actually invited and that he wants to see you."

"Fair enough," I said, and she went on her way. I followed behind her as we passed a few shut doors, my only prayer being that no one from the wedding party would suddenly come out of any of the rooms. On my uneasy feeling, I felt like a fugitive, which made absolutely no sense, but it also helped stir up a certain kind of thrill in all of this that I couldn't quite explain. I was excited and nervous, and so when she knocked on the door and opened it, I almost walked into her.

She stopped then and sent a stern look at me, and truly it took everything inside of me not to respond with a slap. She was so unnecessary and wrongfully hostile that it was fucking grating on my nerves.

"Please wait here," she said sternly, and it was time for me to roll my eyes. She headed in, and I waited as I had been asked, and then she shut the door behind her.

It took all of three seconds, and she was back out once again looking even more confused than ever.

"You can go in," she said, perhaps not understanding my connection with the man.

I didn't give a fuck because what I needed and wanted was to see him and speak to him. And so, with breath held, I headed into the dim and warm room and hoped for the best.

Chapter Thirty-One
Drake

I wasn't surprised that she had reached out to me again. I knew I wasn't insane. There was something here, and whatever the fuck it was, I knew that it haunted her the same way that it haunted me. However, where I was willing to explore it, she was terrified. I understood her reservations, as she had explained it to me. However, I truly didn't give a fuck. It kept me in a bad mood, and so when she came into the room, I wasn't particularly excited to see her. The masseuse kept on with her work, not missing even a beat while silence continued.

I waited, refusing to say a word and giving her free rein to say whatever she wanted. Eventually, though, and when the silence had gone on long enough to irritate me at her lack of a response, I turned to face her. What I met was a sworn gaze glued on the masseuse's hands and how they worked into my skin. She was massaging my shoulders down the arc toward my ass, and this sight, for some reason, completely captured Evelyn's attention.

She started then at my attention and met my gaze; however, she seemed a bit dazed and wide-eyed.

I looked at the masseuse then and issued out the instruction.

"Can you give us a bit of privacy?" I asked, and she nodded.

"Yes, Sir, I'll be waiting outside. Just let me know when you want me to come in."

"Okay," I replied, and she sent a smile as well to Evelyn before heading out. I waited until she had shut the door, and then I laid back down and shut my eyes. My face was turned away from Evelyn, but I was hoping it would give her the confidence to say whatever she wanted to without holding back. However, once again, she remained quiet.

My patience ran thin.

"Please leave if you don't have anything to say," I said, and she immediately reacted.

"I do," she said, "I mean, I'm sorry, I'm just a bit..."

She didn't completely finish the sentence, but I was immensely curious about what she had been about to say.

"You're just what?" I asked, and to my surprise, this time around she replied.

"I, uh... you... I'm incredibly interested in what you proposed."

I was almost amused at her, but instead, all I could do was sigh.

"I know I explained to you what was holding me back and why I was hesitating, so I wanted to seek your opinion on the course of action to take."

She stopped then, and I knew that it was because she wanted my full attention and focus on her. So, I turned until I was facing her. My towel, however, and off-course, fell off, exposing me, but I didn't care. We'd fucked each other mindless before, so there was no scandal. As I stared at her gorgeous and stubborn self, however, I couldn't help but be amazed at how untouchable she still felt. More like a gorgeous illusion than a really actually breathing woman that I had already thoroughly fucked and couldn't get enough of.

Once again, I understood that very little of any of this made sense.

"What opinion?" I asked. "What's your question?"

She couldn't quite meet my gaze, which was a bit amusing to me, so I rose to my feet, taking the towel along with me. I wrapped it around my waist, and then I headed over to the armchair by the corner to take my seat.

She watched me, and then she eventually spoke.

"I think it's best I tell Aurora first. To see what she thinks about this. This is the major mental block what's holding me back, and so I—" she stopped then, and it soon became apparent that it was because of the way my expression darkened at her words.

"You're," I stared at her because I couldn't believe her words. "You're asking me to take permission first from Aurora before we can fuck?" I asked. For a few seconds, she went quiet as she hopefully contemplated what she was asking, and then, to my shock, she nodded.

I couldn't believe it, but at the same time, I realized that I liked her even more. This more than anything revealed her innocence and honesty, and fuck, it did something to my heart once again. But it was also quite foolish and amateurish.

"No," I replied, "I'm not going to inform and seek approval for my sex life from my younger sister."

She stared at me, and truly I remained patient, enjoying this contention because it was almost hard to believe that it existed. It made me want to understand more about her. I wondered now how she handled other aspects of her life. She was not shrewd whatsoever, and it amazed me.

"Are you rich? By any chance?" I asked.

She seemed taken aback by the question, and then she fronted.

"I do okay," she replied.

"Well enough to not give a damn that I am incredibly wealthy and probably worth every perceived risk?"

She stared at me. However, I truly was curious because I had come across too many women who had been ready to, for this very fact, throw whatever else caution remained to the wind.

It was what I expected, what was normal, but then here this dork was, and she was only concerned about being considerate of my sister. Fuck.

"Yes," she replied, and I was a bit startled.

"Yes, you do okay enough to not give a damn about my money?" I asked, and she nodded.

"Yes."

I had a feeling as my gaze went down her body that this wasn't true, but it wasn't a point to argue about, so I continued on with my conversation.

"This shouldn't even be a topic of conversation," I told her. "I can fuck whoever I want. I want to assume you can as well and keep things a secret. I mean, this will only be a few days, so why contemplate it?"

"You and Aurora as well? Were you two friends even before this? Isn't your relationship with her a client and professional relationship?"

She was stumped at this question, and I fucking understood her. I rose to my feet then and approached her. She, however, took several steps back until eventually she connected with the table. I didn't stop. Not until my body was pressed against hers, and I was staring deep into her eyes. I was so fucking hard now, and I knew that she could feel every bit of it.

"Can you keep a secret?" I asked.

She swallowed, and then when she saw that I was going to wait till she responded, she nodded.

"Then keep this," I told her.

I leaned down then and took her lips in mine, soft, slow, and sweet. By the time we broke away, my heart was thundering against my chest. I stared into her gorgeous, huge hazel eyes and knew that this woman would be hard to get out of my mind or forget at the end of all of this.

"It's too late," she squeaked, and I cocked my head, wondering what she was referring to.

"What do you mean?" I asked.

"Victoria already knows," she said.

"She wouldn't dare speak," I replied, however, she didn't seem convinced.

I kissed her again because I didn't give a fuck about Victoria, and frankly, I didn't give a fuck either about who knew, but I did care that her worries were allayed so that she could be as free as I needed her to be. I wanted her to thoroughly enjoy this, just as I knew that I would as well.

I started to lean down once again to kiss her; however, she stopped me.

I loved the way she looked at me as though she was completely weak and, in this moment, just a bit helpless. At other times, she seemed so serious and focused on her work. But now, there was no doubt in my mind that she was completely under my thumb.

"This is your fault," she cried, and I was surprised.

"What?" I asked, amused, and couldn't help but notice just how low our voices were. I loved this, I realized. It felt more than anything that she was a lover I had known for years. There were no prying eyes; the room was warm and intimate; it smelled heavenly; she looked divine... I wanted to savor this somehow, to get used to it.

"I don't want to interfere," she began, and I immediately knew where she was going with this.

"If you don't want to interfere, then don't," I told her, and she stopped.

"You really can't just let her have the wedding she wants?" she asked, and I stared down at her.

"There's more to the story."

She watched me, her hands softly splaying to spread against my chest.

And then she nodded.

"Okay," she said. "Secret."

"Secret," I agreed and kissed her once again. The purse she had hanging over her shoulder fell to the ground, and I knew then that she was completely in my hands. She had weakened, body and mind, and I was going to enjoy every fucking moment of it.

She had on a simple and almost skimpy white tank top,

and this was incredibly easy to take off. After pulling it over her head, I flung the fabric away, allowing me the exquisite view of her full breasts. Her bra was lacy and gorgeous but most importantly her breasts lay so beautifully within that I nearly couldn't look away. I wanted to spend hours putting them in my mouth and sucking until she cried. However, today and knowing that we had limited time as always, I cupped them in my hands and began to knead. Needing more access, I resumed kissing her as my hands went behind to unhook the bra. She spilled out, and my lips moved down her neck. She smelled heavenly, courtesy of the massage she had finished as well, and I couldn't get enough. I tasted her skin all the way down her flushed chest till I got to her breasts.

Her nipples were the most beautiful shade of pink, and I wasted no time in pulling them into my mouth. I rolled the hardened peaks in my mouth and sucked, and she responded by throwing her head back. She was slightly gasping for air as she held on to my head, and I loved just how possessive it felt.

She reacted in a way that made me more turned on than ever, and it took all of my willpower to control myself. I wasn't quite sure when my towel came off, but soon enough I was lifting her onto the surface, and the cotton was falling down my hips and puddling on the ground around my feet.

She loved it. She couldn't look away from my hardened and now exposed cock as it straightened against the table. However, when she reached out to touch it, I stopped her.

"The massage from earlier," I told her. "I want to complete it."

She smiled at this, and then she nodded in excitement.

God, she was so fucking sexy. I couldn't stop looking at her. The way her gorgeous slightly damp hair framed her face, her soft pink lips, her gorgeous skin. I leaned forward once again to kiss her simply because I couldn't resist and took advantage.

I pulled away, but my cock was in her hands. She leaned forward, and in the next moment, the pulsing head was in her mouth.

It was my turn to lose my breath, and even though I didn't want to be distracted by her eyes, I immediately shut mine. I savored the heat and the pleasure that arrowed to my crotch at the feel of her heated wet mouth fluttering over. I was already leaking, and she took me deeper. Then, as if she couldn't get enough, she began to suck, her head bobbing, and I loved watching her. I wished I could take a picture to physically keep this moment forever; however, I mentally took the image and enjoyed it. When, however, I could feel my entire body beginning to prickle dangerously with the pleasure warning me that I was on the verge of losing control, I pulled away. She was so reluctant that her hands followed, nearly causing her to fall off the bed, but I quickly righted her, and then I kissed her once again.

She soon quieted down, and then she looked at me with huge, gorgeous eyes.

"Why?" she complained, and I lifted her once again onto the surface.

"I have a compulsive need to finish the things I started," I told her, and her breathing seemed to catch in her throat once again. She had on a mini leather skirt, which I unfastened the button of. In no time, I was pulling it down her legs, and before me was her dark lace underwear.

Earlier on, she had had nothing on and had been absolutely soaking wet.

I'd wanted nothing but to lean forward and taste her, but those intentions had been derailed. Now, however, as I looked at her, I could barely wait. However, I wanted to make this as torturous as possible for her, so I didn't take her underwear off just yet.

Holding her thighs apart, I licked the pad of my tongue down her cleft, loving that I could still taste her through the soaked fabric. I loved the way she shifted and churned, restless and so fucking aroused she couldn't stop moaning.

"Ahh," she breathed, her fingers pulling on the roots of my hair. It hurt, but the sting was just what I wanted. Eventually, though, and when I couldn't keep myself from her anymore, I pulled the scrap of fabric down her legs, and finally, she was completely exposed before me.

She wasn't shy this time around. Her eyes were shut as she writhed across the surface, kneading her breasts and rubbing her hands all over her body. Pleasure was sending bolts of electricity through her system, and she was trying to contain it all. She made such a gorgeous picture, and once again, I couldn't help but stop to just watch; however, she soon felt too tormented to contain this.

"Drake," she called, her hand going down the flat of her stomach and down to her sex. I watched as she touched herself and moaned, sliding her fingers in and out.

She started out slowly while moaning my name, but this was a way better show that I wanted to watch.

"Go faster," I commanded, and she complied as best as she could. Eventually, though, she pulled her hand out, and

I lowered myself between her legs, taking her clit into my mouth.

Her back completely arched off the surface in response, and I was sure then that we could once again be heard outside of the room.

Once again, I didn't care, even though her concern had been keeping things under wraps, but I was beginning to understand and accept that keeping things quiet between us at moments like this was near to impossible.

My hands moved over her heated body as the moments passed until finally, I pushed her hand away and took over. I watched her as I slid my fingers in and began to finger fuck her. She was so tight, clenching so greedily around my hands, wet and so fucking gorgeous.

I leaned down then as well and took her in my mouth. Shutting my eyes, I savored her, the wetness swirling round my tongue, her restless frame which I had to reach over to somewhat secure down across the bed. However, she couldn't remain still, especially as she was so incredibly close to the edge.

I wanted to watch, however, as she completely fell apart, so I straightened once again and held her down as best as I could. And then I rammed my fingers in and out of her as rapidly as I could.

I paused to stroke the knob of her clit, rolling it in hard rhythmic cues, and she screamed. In the next second, she was coming so hard that she once again nearly rolled off the bed. I managed to hold her, but her entire body was clenched at the sweet tension, so it was a bit difficult to keep her in place. She leaked onto my hands, completely over-taken by the intensity of the pleasure, and the mere sight brought me an element of satisfaction that I couldn't put into words.

What amazed me even further though was that she called my name. In this special moment when she couldn't even recall her name, she called out my name, over and over as the orgasms wreaked so violently through her. It was indeed a thing of beauty to see, and so I lost myself watching as she recovered.

Eventually though, she came to and stared at me as though she was still in shock. She rose on top then and threw her arms around my neck. Angling her head, she took my lips in the sweetest, deepest kiss, and I found myself unable to think for several moments afterward.

My knees became weak as she broke away; however, I tried with all of my might to remain as unaffected as possible, even when she began to trace kisses down my torso. My breath caught in my throat as her tongue flipped over my nipples, and then amused, she pulled it into her mouth.

I smiled as well, loving the tease in her gaze and actions. I felt so much like I was being used, and I didn't think I had ever allowed myself to feel vulnerable in this way, especially with a woman. But here I was with her, and it felt as though my entire heart and body were open to her. It was fucking wonderful.

She traced the kisses down my torso, and I loved the feeling and pressure of her mouth on my skin as she tasted every bit that she could reach. And then she was laying down flat again to take my cock in her mouth.

I moved even further up to make things as comfortable as possible for her, and then for the next several minutes, tried to hold on to what I could of my sanity.

The way she sucked me took me to a different plane of existence. One where I could only feel, and it was more than enough to turn me into melted wax. Even the very thought and possibility were unbelievable, but the way she bobbed her head and cradled me with both hands at the root made me understand and accept that there was something special. She blew like I was the best thing she had ever tasted, and just hearing her moans and seeing her enjoyment was more than enough to get me off.

When I reached the verge of an orgasm, my thighs bunched up, and I tried to pull out. However, she held onto me from behind, refusing to let go so, I emptied myself in her mouth.

"Fuck!" I rasped out. My head falling back as the orgasm blacked out my thoughts and mind for the next several moments afterward. When I came to, I was genuinely surprised that I was still standing because that orgasm had been completely unbelievable.

She was leaning back against me, watching me with the most satisfied look on her face. Her hand was around my cock, still stroking even as she licked my cum off her lips.

In that moment, I had so many words to say to her, however, none formed on my tongue. It was for the best anyway because I could sense feelings so strongly, and it was eerily close to me never wanting her out of my sight.

I softened slightly after cumming so hard, but as she continued to stroke me, I got on top of the surface and was soon ready to take her. I wanted, however, to feel her on top of me. To prolong this moment for as long as possible I held her and kissed her.

I would never be able to tell how long that kiss lasted, but the way our movements slowed, as

though we were in the perfect, indescribable sync, floored me. We moved together, writing passionately against each other as we licked into each other's mouths. I had dreamt slowly of fucking her till something broke. Going so hard that we both lost our minds. However, as her softness fit against the hardness of mine, I knew that this was where I wanted to be, and I never wanted to leave. Inside of her, kissing her as I fucked her, the pacing perfectly synchronized.

It didn't take long before she began to plead, and I loved just how strained her voice was. She could barely string words together, but I knew exactly what she wanted.

Unlike the previous time, I had no clue whatsoever where a condom was, and like the previous time, I didn't really care to get up and find one.

There were ways that precautions could be taken afterward from what I knew, and so nothing was going to stop me as I held my cock and positioned it at her entrance. Positioning my hips, I took my time sliding in, watching her eyes. She tried to open them to stare at me, but they were too heavy-lidded with pleasure. The sensation was exquisite as I slid into her walls, clenching hard around me, and then I was hitting the hilt. She completely collapsed onto the surface of the bed, going limp in my hands, and I kissed her.

I could barely contain my emotions as I fell back against her. I held her more tightly than I had ever held anyone or anything and fucked her until I could feel my body tremble. Her legs wrapped around me, and as she rocked her hips to match the fervency and intensity of mine.

The feelings were more intense than I had ever felt them, and yet they lasted even longer. Perhaps it was all the kissing and our hands moving across each other. Every touch was so affectionate, every moment so unreal that I couldn't speak.

Once again, I lost complete track of time, but when we both came, my heart crumbled. I wanted this to fucking last forever. The sensations as the orgasms tore through both of us made me feel as though I had just been peeled away piece by piece. This, too, seemed to last forever, and since I had no intention of moving out of her, I just laid down on her, and she held me tightly to her chest.

Once again, a plethora of things I wanted to say came to mind, but it was best not to voice any of them. Plus, I couldn't exactly think straight. I shut my eyes, and to my complete shock, we fell asleep.

Chapter Thirty-Two
Evelyn

The shrill of my ringing phone from my purse startled us both awake. At first, I tried my best to ignore it as I lived out moments of pure bliss. However, as we recalled where we were, we soon accepted that it was time to retrieve it. It was sure to attract the right attention, and the absolute last thing I wanted to be doing was trying to explain to anyone who came on curiously why Drake Moran was sprawled on top of me and still inside of me.

I didn't want him to leave, though. So badly that even if this was the price, I was sure that I was somewhat ready to pay it. However, as life goes, the good things had to come to an end, and so he moved, ready to leave. I kept my eyes tightly shut as he got off me, scared that he was going to see more than I wanted him to. So instead, I pretended to be too busy trying to catch my breath and recover, hoping that he would say something.

I was so completely exposed that I didn't know what to

do; however, he soon brought a blanket or a sheet of some sort, and just like that, I was completely protected. I was so grateful and relieved that my eyes came open.

They met his, and I could finally speak.

The minutes passed, and I became so self-conscious that I didn't know what to do with myself. We were both now covered, but it was as though we had exposed a part of ourselves to the other that neither of us could clearly explain. What had happened on that bed had not been just fucking whatsoever. We had made love. Heart-melting, soul-connecting love, and neither of us knew what to say to the other.

Eventually, though, and thankfully, he was able to speak with coherence, unlike me.

"What are you doing later today?" he asked.

My heartbeat fluttered at his words and the way he looked at me. His eyes looked glassy, almost as though he couldn't believe I existed and couldn't get enough.

My confidence rose, my happiness spiked as well, but I kept my face blank. I had to keep myself intact and checked at all times so that I wouldn't get carried away.

Looking at him, it was so easy for me to lose myself in all that he was and how he made me feel.

"Um..." I thought about the itinerary that had been given out.

"I think we have some show for later on today," I answered.

"Not we," he said, and I wondered what he meant.

"I'm going motorcycle racing in Monticello. I want you to come with me."

I heard his words, bright and clear, however, for some reason, it took me a while to comprehend what he was asking. I heard motorcycles, but this felt like a ... date.

No, it's not, Miss dreamer. It's just a chance to spend more time together so he can fuck you.

This made my stomach flutter because whatever it was labeled as, I was incredibly interested. However, this couldn't happen, right? This was what I had been concerned about? Getting carried away.

"No," I replied, and his brows shot up at the sudden rejection.

I mean, I tried to get up then, and it was an embarrassing struggle. My body was so weak that it felt as though it weighed like a ton of lead, which I couldn't quite wrap my head around.

Holding the sheet around my chest, I soon managed to stabilize myself, and then I pulled together what was left of my confidence and looked into his eyes.

"The wedding event tonight is a charity dinner."

"I know," he said. "I'll be there."

"I uh... I need to be around Aurora to capture her moments."

He looked at me, and then he went towards a wardrobe in the room. In there, he seemed to dig within his hung pants and then he returned with his phone.

"How about I tell Aurora that she is not to have any moments for the next several hours so you can come to the racetrack with me?"

"No," I refused, however, he kept tapping away at his phone.

"Drake," I called; but he didn't respond, and I panicked. Furious, I got off the bed, stumbling on the sheets. In the end, I almost fell but instead I stumbled into him, but he caught me. I glared up at him, unhappy to say the least.

"What are you doing?" I yelled. "We talked about this!"

"Yes, we did," he nodded as he stared into my eyes, making me melt; however, the anger had more to do with this now.

"I wasn't texting her," I said calmly. "I was speaking to someone else."

"I," I said, feeling absolutely ashamed. However, I reminded myself that he was the one that made me jump to this conclusion, so I held my head high.

"Please don't joke with me like that," I told him. "This might just be a casual chapter in your life, but it's the entirety of mine. My career, my fucking reputation".

"God, you're so fucking stiff," he complained. "If I didn't know how you fucked, I would have been convinced you were carved of stone."

I glared at him then and started to turn around so that I could leave; however, he held on to my waist, plastering me to his body and refused to let go.

"Stop," I complained softly. My eyes lowering.

He, however, tried to get my attention, and when he could, he leaned down and kissed me. My entire senses immediately went into hyperdrive, as though they couldn't help but be drawn to his taste, and by the time he pulled away, I was once again dazed.

He had all of my attention as he stared up at me, and so when he asked once again, all I could think about was figuring out a way for this to happen.

"I have to check in with Aurora," I told him. "I'm so sorry, but I don't see a way around it."

"I do," he said.

"What?" I asked.

"I'll tell her I need you to take photos at the racetrack."

I listened and remained quiet for the minute it took me to process what he had just said. And then I realized what he had just said.

"Wait what? Motorcycle racing?"

"Yeah," he replied, and just like that, I was ready for him to fuck me once again.

"You ride motorcycles?"

"Leisurely," he said. "At some point before my business blew up, I wanted to go pro but decided against it. It's best left as a hobby. I haven't been able to keep up with it as much as I would have liked to over the past few years, so now that I have the chance, I want to take advantage of it."

There was no way now that I could say no, even if I wanted to. However, I wanted to be the one to talk to Aurora.

"I'll tell her myself," I said. "Is that okay?"

"Are you sure?" he asked. "It'll be easier if I just handle it."

"I know, but I'll feel better, plus it's more appropriate."

"Okay," he replied, and then he leaned down to kiss me once again. Afterwards, he grabbed his clothes and exited the room, leaving me enough time to get myself together. I wished I could fall asleep truly, but the still lingering fear of what we had done got me to immediately gather my things as well and make my escape from prying ears.

As I headed out of the spa, the workers around all

stopped to look at me. I could only imagine what they were all saying, but when I recalled the way he looked at me, I decided that I didn't give a fuck.

I was forced, however, to give a fuck later in the day when we returned to the mansion. Unfortunately, Victoria was in my party despite how hard I had tried to avoid her. She made sure for me to notice that she was staring at me the whole time and talking to others. I knew she was trying to make me as nervous as possible, but with the way things were going between me and Drake, I didn't think that even if we were found out, I would be incredibly broken.

Especially not after how he had made love to me that afternoon. My only concern was Aurora, and despite Victoria's obvious gossiping, something told me that she wouldn't dare defy Drake's instruction not to run her mouth around the house and guests.

So, I focused my attention solely on Aurora, and as soon as we returned and I had refreshed myself, I headed over to her room. There was a lot to discuss besides my new illicit relations with her brother. For one, I wanted to talk about the major photoshoots that were coming up. I had found some locations so far that gave me the most gorgeous ideas, and I wanted to put them together in addition to what she had asked for. Plus, now that her fiancé was available as well, I wanted to incorporate him into the whole process, and I knew that she would love it.

She was having her manicure done when I arrived. Her face instantly lit up as she saw me, and then she called me over. Wine, sparkling grape juice and pastries had been served, and she's getting terrified because she couldn't say no.

"It's your week," I told her. "Why would you say no?"

"Well, I bought a dress which was already quite tight, but it was for my previous size. I mean, my initial size. If I eat any more, I'm going to toss the dress away and end up looking like a whale."

Nodding, I understood, but she was already so skinny that I didn't think she could look like a whale no matter what she said.

I kept that information to myself, however, since I knew that as a bride, there was no way she was going to listen to or believe what I was saying. So, I moved instead to the topic of her fiancé.

"Since I'm making a special album for you," I said, "Why don't I include him as well? I can put some focus on him when you're not doing anything interesting, so that the feeling will be inclusion."

"That's amazing, Evelyn," she said. "I didn't really think about him in relation to this since he was never really around, but sure, right. It wouldn't be complete without him."

She agreed, and so we got to talking about how to facilitate this when there was a knock on the door.

My heart jumped, even though I had managed to convince myself earlier that there was no need for that. However, only when I saw that it was Victoria did I relax. Aurora, definitely, wasn't aware yet, but I knew now that it was only a matter of time before she eventually heard what was going on.

I completely ignored Victoria but she, on the other hand, stared at me long and hard, making it quite obvious that she had some beef of some sort with me. It was completely uncomfortable. Aurora, however, wasn't too keen on her, so she didn't bother to acknowledge her presence.

Victoria, on the other hand, seemed to have taken me as her new source of entertainment because she stared at me hard, and when I darted a darkly amused look her way, there was almost a sense of disgust on her face. However, she didn't say a word, not in front of Aurora, and I knew then that she had had no choice but to keep her word to Drake.

It made me even more excited to see him, however, I couldn't ask what I wanted to with Victoria standing there, so I headed out to the balcony and shut the door behind me. More than anything, what I wanted to ask him was what time his trip was going to start. It was almost 3 pm now, and if he planned to be involved in the dinner later that night, I suspected that he would be ready to leave, so it made me a bit anxious not knowing.

Once again, the dilemma arose as to whether to call him or text him, but since I was in Aurora's room, I sent him a message. To my extreme delight, he responded nearly immediately, and I couldn't help my smile.

"4 pm okay?" he asked. I imagined that this was quite late because I didn't know of a motorcycle track that was close by, but perhaps he had other plans.

"Alright, I'll confirm with you soon," I texted back to him. I turned around to return to the room; however, just as I slid the door open, he sent another message.

"Come to my room?" he asked, and my eyes slightly widened. I couldn't keep the blush off my face even as I put the phone away, and this was my mistake because it gave Victoria the opening that she wanted.

"Is it appropriate to be having personal sexual relations where you work?" she asked me; my eyes nearly popped out of their sockets. I stared at her then and found the smug smile on her face.

"Excuse me?" I asked, even as I knew that Aurora had gone unusually quiet and was listening, probably confused.

"Am I wrong?" she asked and nodded toward my phone.

"I saw you blushing and of course I can't mistake your glow. You must have had an especially wonderful morning."

Aurora burst out laughing then.

"What the hell do you mean, of course, she's glowing? Aren't I glowing as well? We all spent the morning in the spa."

"You always look wonderful, Aurora," I said.

"However, that is absolutely not what I am talking about, and Evelyn knows it."

She looked at me then, drawing the attention of the attendants in the room, and I was forced then to look at Aurora.

She looked surprised and as though she was waiting to counter this. I was fuming, but I knew that she was trying to provoke me into being defensive. I managed to keep my calm.

"No, actually, I don't know what you're talking about," I said. "Would you care to elaborate?"

At my words, she seemed surprised.

The smile on her face faltered, and just like that, the true darkness of who she was and how she felt was completely exposed. Before she could respond, however, Aurora stepped in.

"Victoria, you two are always at each other's throats. It makes me wonder all the while what happened between you two in college."

This I absolutely didn't want to respond to, but I did want to talk to Aurora. However, now was definitely not the right time, plus I wanted to leave, so I simply made my excuse.

"I'll be back before it's time to go for dinner, but in the meantime, Mr. Moran invited me on a motorcycle riding day trip of some sort. I'm not really sure about the details."

Her eyes nearly popped out of their sockets.

"What do you mean he invited you?" She was shocked, startling everyone in the room with her heightened pitch. "He invited you and didn't invite me?"

"That's what I was saying," Victoria said in a low tone; however, Aurora was too amazed and apparently excited to pay her any attention or even hear her.

"When is he going?" She picked up her phone. "How come he didn't invite me? My fiancé loves motorcycles as well. Why the hell is he using the photographer I invited for his own purposes?"

"He wants you to capture him, doesn't he?" she asked. "I hope he's fucking paying you extra? I'm going to be extra pissed at him if he isn't."

She spoke so fast and so excitedly that I didn't really know how to respond. I stared at her and wondered if I should clarify, but then I decided that there was no need to, at least at the moment. I looked at Victoria, and she too seemed stumped. Eventually, though, and to my relief, she took her leave, mumbled something about returning on time, and left.

It was my time to head over to get ready, but I absolutely had nothing appropriate to wear to a motorcycle track. I was excited, though I had to admit, and so I excused myself and headed over to my room.

Chapter Thirty-Three

Drake

"I heard you're going motorcycle riding!" Aurora's excitement through the phone made me stop what I was doing and cock my head, wondering how she had been informed. It wasn't a secret, but I wasn't exactly willing to invite the entire wedding party. It was a special time ahead that I had been looking forward to, and the one person I recalled inviting was Evelyn.

"Evelyn told you?" I asked.

"You really want to take my photographer to work for you without even bothering to invite me along?"

"Photographer to work for me?" I looked up once again from my laptop and realized that this was how she had sold it to Aurora. Smiling, I couldn't help but shake my head. "It's private. Only she is invited."

"Absolutely motherfucking not," she cursed, and I was amused again. It was always so fun to me when she cursed in that way. "My fiancé is coming. I told you he loves motorcycles."

I considered this; however, before I could respond, she spoke.

"You've hijacked our wedding so far with everything that you wanted, so you can't say no for this. You have to agree."

I sighed. I definitely didn't want company, and Evelyn, I wanted there because I wanted her to ride with me. Plus, I was sure to want to fuck at some point, and there would be no one else I wanted. I can imagine it now. Perhaps, I would sit on the bleachers, and she would be wrapped around me... Riding made adrenaline shoot up my system in a way that I couldn't quite explain, and I just needed her to be there when I needed to fucking calm my excitement down.

Sighing, I knew I couldn't refuse now, so I agreed. Plus, it would definitely make Evelyn feel better, I supposed.

"Sure," I said. "We leave in twenty minutes."

"Oh my God. Really, that's so soon. Alright, I'll let him know. How are we going?"

"Helicopter," I replied, and she was off the phone in the next second.

I continued working; however, my mind couldn't help but go to the woman that I had announced my plans to and who I had been expecting a call from. Just then, there was a knock on my door, but I was reluctant to get it.

It came again, irritating me, until I realized that I had told Evelyn to come over to my room.

I got up then and headed over to the door, and when I pulled it open, I saw her indeed waiting.

My heart jumped in my chest as I saw her. Every time I laid my eyes on her, I was sure she couldn't look more beautiful, but in this moment, I had to lean against the door because fuck... She looked so casual, her face barely with any makeup, but by pulling her hair completely back, she looked so fucking gorgeous that it took me a while to process her outfit.

"Hi," she said, and I opened the door wider, ushering her in.

She had on a cropped top, stretchy, long-sleeved. It completely exposed her stomach, and then she had fitted jeans that shaped the curve of her ass in a way that made me want to bury my face between her cheeks. And then she had on platformed biker boots, and I couldn't look away from her.

"You got a jacket?" I asked, and she immediately turned self-conscious.

"Oh, I'm sorry," she said. "I tried to dress appropriately, but I didn't really have any biker wear. I hope this is alright."

I leaned forward then and kissed her on the cheek as my phone began to ring once again.

"You look wonderful," I said.

"I'm just worried you might get cold on the way there. I'll give you my jacket, don't worry," I said and returned to my desk.

"You're right on time," I told her. I just need to finish up with this review, and I'll be ready to leave.

"Alright," she said, and I tried to focus on my work. It was difficult since she was standing right there, and it made me realize just how excited I was to have her around. It surprised me, truly, and I couldn't help but glance back at her. I hadn't felt this way about anyone in perhaps forever, and I wondered what it was about her. Suddenly, I wanted to know everything about her. After this week, and who knew, I might never get the chance.

"Do you usually work with one client at a time?" I asked as I continued my review.

"Um, sometimes," she replied. "I'm not always so busy."

"How about right now?" I asked. "You're solely focused on Aurora?"

"Yes. And you, apparently," she said, and I paused then, unable to keep myself from turning to stare at her.

"She thinks I've asked you to take my photos."

"I have my camera gear packed," she replied. I raised my brows then, needing an explanation, but she was distracted as her eyes kept going around my room.

"Uh, that was her assumption. I'm going to correct it, but Victoria was there, and I didn't want to make it a whole thing."

"It's not a bad thing," I said as I turned fully then to watch her. "You think we can sneak off at some point to fuck in a corner?"

At the words, there was a kick of arousal in my stomach, and as her lips slightly parted, I could tell that she had a similar reaction. She stared at me so softly but shyly, and then she blushed and looked away. How fucking adorable. I loved it especially as she bit down on her bottom lip, and I found myself rising to my feet then.

I wasn't supposed to be doing this. I was supposed to be concluding my work before we left; however, I had made the mistake of inviting her over, so I had to pay for it. I didn't even know what I wanted to do. I just knew that I wanted to feel her and be close to her, so I headed over.

My arms went around her slim waist as I arrived, and

then my hands went downwards to cup her ass. I wished she had worn something a bit softer and flowy for easier access, but this too was good. I needed, however, to see what she wore underneath, and so my curious fingers slid down as I leaned down to kiss her. By the time we parted, my hands had hiked up the thin fabric that she had on.

Breathless, I pulled the strap up just over her hip, and she gasped into my mouth. I understood why.

"You're wet?" I asked, and she swallowed.

"Soaked," she replied, and my brain scrambled to a halt. "When you pull like that…"

"Grabs your clit?"

She smiled again, and I couldn't stop myself from leaning forward to nibble on her plump lower lip. I kissed her long, soft, and deep, and when we parted, we couldn't look away from each other.

"I'll get my jacket," I said, and she nodded.

"How do I look?" I asked, and she sighed. I completely understood and felt something flutter through my belly. Her gaze was full of appreciation, and I loved every moment of it.

I had contemplated between a short-sleeved fitted black shirt and a tank top, and in the end, decided to go with solely the tank, tight jeans, boots, and the jacket I was now going to hand over to her. I looked good, huge and strong, and she looked even more sexy beside me. Picture-perfect was what came to mind, and I wanted to take a picture, but this desire immediately shut down.

I knew a dangerous situation when I saw one, and slowly, this was what this was turning into.

I found the jacket in my closet, brought it out, then I

placed it over her shoulders. She held onto it and then leaned over to sniff it.

"I love the way you smell," she said, and it made me smile. Soon we got out of the room and walked side by side.

"Perhaps I should go ahead?" she asked. "I'll meet you downstairs."

"No need," I replied and caught her hand to keep her by my side.

Just then, Aurora emerged from her own room with her fiancé in tow, and I could see the smile slightly falter from her face as she noticed that Evelyn's hand was in mine. Evelyn, ever watchful, pulled her hand away, and Aurora, ever careful, ignored it and returned the smile to her face.

"Ready?" she asked and bounded over. I kissed her cheek, and we were on our way.

"Motorcycles and everything else are there?" she asked, and I gave her a look at the ridiculous question. From then onwards, I removed my attention from both women but instead focused it on my soon-to-be brother-in-law.

We were right on time because only after just a few minutes of talking, the helicopter arrived, and we were all ushered over.

Chapter Thirty-Four
Evelyn

"How long is this trip going to take?" I asked Aurora.

It was quite difficult to hear in the heli-copter, but it was also quite uncomfortable to have been seated with her for so long, and yet we hadn't spoken. She was solely focused on scrolling through her phone while the men spoke, and I didn't know how to feel about this. I hadn't missed her look of surprise, or was it displeasure, when she had seen my hand in Drake's.

However, she had quickly covered it up and continued on. It was clear now, however, that she was somewhat with-drawing from me. It wasn't surprising; it just felt a bit disheartening.

To my surprise, however, she turned right then and smiled at me.

"We have about twenty-five minutes left." she said and turned to look at her brother. I tried to avoid his eyes, but I couldn't any longer. He nodded, and then he looked at me. My eyes went down his nose, biceps, and the slabs of muscle straining against his skin, and I couldn't help but shift restlessly. The act between my thighs, coupled with his inhumane sex appeal and the tension in the air, made me want to combust from the inside out. I was so antsy and turned on that it was hard to breathe.

"Aren't you cold?" Aurora asked suddenly, and at first, I thought she was talking to me, but it was soon clear that she was referring to him.

"I'm fine," he replied, however, I was already taking off his jacket. I froze then in mid-movement, wondering if I had made another mistake. However, he reached out for it, and I handed it over.

"Is that his jacket?" she asked, and I nodded, unable to meet anyone's eyes. Instead, I stared out at the panoramic view of the city from this vantage point, even though it was now impossible for me to appreciate or even take it in.

"Yeah," I heard him reply.

"So cute," she commented, surprising me. "It's like you two are a couple."

No one responded. However, she kept pushing.

"Are you two a couple?" she asked, truly and as I turned to her, I was shocked by how direct she was. I mean, I had thought she would have wanted to bring it up when we were alone, but she had asked right there without any reservations.

I immediately replied as defensively as I could possibly be.

"We're not," I replied. "Not at all. He just thought that I would be cold and offered it to me briefly. I'm sorry for forgetting to return it."

She smiled at me almost sympathetically, and then she

turned to him. He had his eyes on her at first, and then he turned his attention to me.

"Sure you don't still need it?" he asked, and I shook my head.

A long silence followed afterward, but then Aurora, God bless her little evil heart, struck again.

"Are you two sleeping together then?" she asked, and this time around both my eyes widened in shock, as well as her fiancé's.

"Sorry!" he called out; however, she was completely amused.

"You all are acting so stiff, as though I'm going to blow up."

"That's rude," he said, but she shook her head.

"No, it's not. What it is is obvious. Evelyn, is this what Victoria was babbling about in my room earlier and trying to say?"

At her words, I immediately turned to Drake's face and saw it darken. I automatically wanted to come to Victoria's defense, but when I realized that she got whatever would be coming to her as a result, I stopped myself.

"Kind of," I replied. "I wanted to bring it up but privately."

"Ah," she said, still smiling. However, I couldn't quite tell how she truly felt about it.

"What was so obvious about it?" Drake asked, and I grew even more nervous. I mean, sure, it was good he was trying to find out so that he would tone down whatever had given us away for the sake of the rest of the ceremony. But it was also extremely uncomfortable.

Plus, I felt truly like I couldn't read anybody, and it

made me feel quite vulnerable. Like absolutely nothing was in my control, including Drake's reaction.

"Well, for starters, you gave her your jacket," she said.

"I've seen the way you are with other women, and I've never seen you be that considerate before. Plus, of course, now that as soon as I became suspicious, then all the looks you kept sneaking at her at dinner suddenly made sense. I was so nervous because I thought you didn't like her, that you didn't think she was needed at all. Who would have thought it was because you were interested in her?"

I turned away then, my entire body flushing because now Aurora was just saying too much. Her words were nice, but she was going too far. We were just involved, yet she was insinuating more than I wanted at such close proximity to him where I could barely hide anything. We both went quiet then, and I turned to look out of the window.

Her reaction truly was surprising to me, but perhaps she didn't want to sulk about it or be unpleasant, given that we were all in such close proximity to each other.

Soon, though, and thankfully, we landed on a field close to the tracks, and I was so incredibly relieved.

I tried my very best to look away from Drake, but truly, it was difficult to. Especially since he decided that there was no need whatsoever for him to put on his jacket. He was all muscle as he ushered us over to the places where the motorcycles were kept greeting the staff there.

They welcomed him happily, and I watched him, from then onwards, completely forgetting that another person was in existence.

He spoke to them about the motorcycles as well as Aurora's fiancé, while I brought out my camera and started taking pictures. Eventually, I joined Aurora on the bleachers, and she seemed to be more relaxed than ever before. She stared at me then with a smile, and I truly hoped that since we were now alone, she wouldn't try to tell me how she truly felt about it.

To my surprise, she didn't bring it up again and it just made me feel even more comfortable. Eventually, though, she spoke, and relief filled me.

"This thing between you two, it's more of a casual thing, isn't it?" she asked. I looked at her, and then I nodded.

"It is, and it isn't, as though it started from the beginning. It's just been once. Twice maybe," my voice breaking. She kept silent then, and I waited for what she would say. When she, however, didn't speak, I grew even more nervous.

"I, uh, I consider you a friend. So, I was incredibly nervous about this. I don't have any motives; it's just... he's very persuasive and attractive. I promise it won't affect my work here with you, and the second your wedding is concluded, I will be completely out of the picture."

"Can you guarantee that?" she asked.

I turned, then, shocked at her words. However, as I stared into her eyes, I nodded.

"Yeah," I replied.

She remained silent for a while, and then she smiled.

"There are so many similarities between you and Drake," she said. "You two have quite strong personalities, so in a way, I'm not surprised that he was drawn to you."

"I don't have the right to interfere," she said. "He told me that he was going to take this week as a vacation himself, as a way to rest, and I really don't mind. He works so hard constantly, and even though I'm not exactly his biggest fan, I still care about him, so I won't get in the way. Just... be careful," she told me. "I consider you a friend as well, and I don't want you to get hurt. Men like him sometimes are quite hardened and can be just as persuasive as they are ruthless."

I nodded in complete understanding, and she smiled.

"So... Victoria, huh?" she said, and I sighed.

"She wanted to use it to blackmail you or something?"

"Who knows," I replied. "She sure thought that I ought to be afraid that you would find out."

"How did she find out?" she asked.

"Today at the spa," she said. "Drake sort of intruded into my room."

"Ah," she said and kept smiling.

I wondered why, and then when she looked at me again, I noticed that her cheeks were completely red.

"What is it?" I asked, genuinely curious, and she replied.

"Let's just say Drake was not the only male that had the same idea."

It took me a second to understand, but when I did, I blinked, looking towards where her fiancé was now coming from.

"Oh," I said, and she bit down on her lower lip.

I took my camera then and took a shot. However, her hand shot out to cover the lens, but I pulled away and was able to get the most gorgeous picture of her. The sky was turning golden behind her, her hair blowing in the wind, her cheeks flushed.

"Look, look," she said just then, and I turned and watched as Drake got onto one of the motorcycles. He put the helmet on but nothing else, and I was instantly worried for him. He, however, looked so divine, and since I no longer had anything to hide, from Aurora at least, I got up and took as many pictures as I wanted.

"Take some of David too," she screamed, and I smiled and did as she asked.

We headed over to both men as Drake waved us over, and I couldn't believe how shy I was to be in his vicinity. Aurora headed over excitedly to her fiancé and kissed him while I remained a distance away from Drake.

I took a picture of him as he glanced back to look at me, and the way his eyes ran down my body made me melt.

Aurora, with her smiling face while I could only mutter a few words.

"Be careful," I said, and he sent me an even more gorgeous smile.

He revved up the engine now, and I watched him go along with two other drivers. It seemed as though they would be doing a race of some sort, so with my heart in my throat, I stood and watched.

Drake started with a bang, and in just a few seconds, he had left everyone in the dust except one of the other riders I didn't know. I watched as he moved seemingly with the wind, and I couldn't breathe. Majestic and fucking dangerous were words I no longer even thought were befitting enough to suit him.

I watched him especially bend his entire body as he took the curves on the track, and my heart went to my stomach.

"Evelyn, pictures!" Aurora called, and only then did I remember myself. Barely breathing, I kept taking as many as I could and ran ahead to catch them at the right angles, even climbing a bit higher up the bleachers and got the shots I needed.

The race didn't last long. They raced a couple of laps, and then the others began to drop in slowly; however, Drake kept going. It was a joy to watch him, but the potent mix of being horny and so fucking afraid at the same time was draining.

Eventually, he got off and stopped close to me. Aurora, however, was too busy discussing something with her fiancé. He took his helmet off, and I captured every moment of it, right until he stared straight at me and shook his hair out of his eyes.

My knees nearly gave out.

"Come here," he said, and I was like a puppy because I didn't even recall how to refuse.

His arm went around me as soon as I reached him, and then he kissed me senseless. I completely lost my ability to speak when he released me. I also lost the ability to stand, and as I stumbled, his arm was the only thing holding me up.

"You okay?" he asked, amused, and I nodded.

"What do you say?" he whispered, looking deep into my eyes.

"Still willing to fuck?"

"I'd like to take you somewhere on the motorcycle."

"How would that work?" I wondered, genuinely curious and knowing now that I had genuinely lost my mind.

"There are several ways," he said. "We could try."

"No," I said as I looked behind, but found that Aurora and her fiancé were nowhere to be found.

I shook my head then and sighed, much to his amusement.

"Kids," he said, and I smiled.

"Anywhere else," I replied. "Anywhere else but on this motorcycle."

He looked out onto the horizon. "Helicopter?" he asked, and I laughed out loud.

"Why don't we just wait until we get back," I suggested, and he nodded.

"I can work with that."

"How about a ride, though?" he asked, and I instantly stepped back. He was, however, too fast, much faster than I could have imagined because before I could go out of reach, he caught my hand and pulled me to him.

"I'll be careful," he told me. "Since I have you with me, you'll have a blast, I promise."

I already knew that I was going to say yes, so I didn't struggle much as he put the helmet on me. It was a bit big, but it was soft, of course, no excuse for me to refuse. So, I had no choice then but to set down my camera.

He guided me as I got on the motorcycle in front of him, and he glued his entire body to mine. I could feel every part of him, and coupled with the thrill of the whole situation, it felt like my heart was about to pound out of my chest. My blood was roaring in my ears as he revved the engine once again; however, I was too concerned for him.

"You need to wear an extra helmet," I told him, but he shook his head and leaned forward to kiss me again.

"I'll go much more slowly," he said.

He hit the gas then, and my face was completely shielded. I held onto the handles like he did, and pretty soon, we were zooming away. I truly wanted to scream, especially when he began to turn. He had said we would go slowly, but I understood now that he lied to me. Or perhaps because the experience was new, it just felt as though we were flying. Regardless, I prayed for my life and promised myself I would never trust him until a few minutes later when we were slowing down and returning.

Soon we came to a complete stop, and Aurora and her fiancé appeared once again. They looked fine, which made me imagine that perhaps they hadn't gone to be naughty like me and Drake. Regardless, she headed over when she saw me and was incredibly excited to see that we had gone on the ride. She supported me in getting down while Drake talked Aurora's fiancé into an additional ride.

I needed to calm down, so I went with Aurora to get some snacks, more than content to tone down the excitement and to simply watch the men for the rest of the evening.

Chapter Thirty-Five
Drake

This truly was one of the most amazing evenings I had had in a very long time. It wasn't just the motorcycle ride but the entire package. My sister suspected I loved the gorgeous woman whom I couldn't stop watching. Everything about her was so alluring that midway through the ride back, Aurora embarrassingly kicked my foot and told me to stop staring. I couldn't help but smile, while Evelyn looked away to hide her blush. I contained myself then, and soon we arrived back in the Hamptons.

Everyone got down, but before she did, I leaned down and kissed her. It's a long night with the events planned for the rest of the evening, and I doubted that we would be able to see her. It was a full bonfire situation down at the beach. Everywhere would be dim, which I guess was good. But it also meant that everyone would be paying more attention than ever, so perhaps she would want to work instead of being seen with me. Regardless, it didn't matter because eventually, we were sure to have our time with each other.

I truly wished for a time in between so I could go to her

room, but my mother instantly came to me as soon as we arrived since she had heard about the ride. She was quite upset about it and especially at the fact that I had taken Aurora with me.

Evelyn found the time after taking a few more pictures to sneak away, and thus I had no access to her until later that evening. I didn't change; there was no need since it would be a casual event. She, however, did, and from the moment I noticed her later on, I couldn't take my eyes off her.

Victoria had arranged a dinner on an incredibly long table by the beach. It was a private event, so quite intimate. However, it also meant that Evelyn couldn't stay close enough to me since she was staff. She was at the extreme end as we began the dinner, and everyone gave their toasts to the bride and groom. Several times she got up to take her pictures, and even though I didn't want to, my eyes couldn't help but follow her.

Unfortunately, however, and about halfway into the event, something quite unpleasant happened. Lindsey arrived.

I was already aware that she was coming, yet I hadn't given it a second thought until she arrived and started acting as though we were the bride and groom. From then on, even though I tried, I could barely spot Evelyn. It was as though she had completely taken herself out of my vicinity, and it made me even more annoyed with Lindsey.

Once, she hurried over with the drink she had refilled and immediately linked her arms to mine. Irritated, I pulled my arms away and walked off. I pulled my phone out of my pocket right then as I received a call and went over to the bar.

I wanted a few minutes alone to calm my annoyance, but unexpectedly, however, I wasn't granted that. My mom came over, but I was always happy to see her. I ordered a slightly sweet fruit wine for her, and she joined me as we watched the dancing going on around the humongous bonfire.

She was silent for a while, even though I knew what she had come over to talk to me about, but I didn't care to oust her. She could stay as long as she wanted.

"If I leave, she'll probably come over to bother you again, won't she?" she asked.

"Then don't leave," I replied.

"You can't accommodate her?" she asked, and I looked at my mom.

"If I could, we wouldn't have broken up in the first place."

"Yes, but she's always been like this, trying to get back with you. You just seem particularly irritated today."

I thought of Evelyn, my gaze once again going through the people present, but I still couldn't find her. Regardless, I didn't respond.

"Is it because of the photographer? The one Aurora likes?"

I turned then and looked at her. I was about to deny this and to brush her curiosity away; however, I wondered to myself what the point of doing this was?

"Yeah," I replied. "Because of her."

"There's something there?" she asked. "More than what your father mentioned?"

This made me smile.

"I don't know," I replied. "What I do know is that it is particularly irritating for Lindsey to be acting as clingy as she has thus far."

"Understood," she said.

"Want me to get rid of her?" my mom asked and smiled.

"Her father's the governor and he's giving me quite a lot of business. I can tolerate her for the rest of the evening." She placed a kiss on my cheek then and rose to her feet.

Chapter Thirty-Six
Evelyn

I was acting just as problematic as Drake would have probably assumed that I would. For all I knew, this was a test, and I was failing so woefully. This girl, whoever she was, had come out of nowhere and completely made me disappear. I was working, but it was as though I had my

eyes more trained on him than anything else. And so, whenever his face turned, and I assumed he was looking for me, I went out of sight.

I watched them, though. He was forced to accommodate her, or maybe he wanted to, but from the way others gravitated towards them, it was obvious that she was the one that most expected him to be a couple with. She was gorgeous, and her body was insane. She had on the most gorgeous dark one-piece, had her hair tied up with tendrils escaping, and the most gorgeous red lips. She looked wealthy and gorgeous, and I couldn't believe how I felt in comparison.

. . .

I needed to get my head on straight but no matter how I tried, I eventually had to accept that taking myself out of the way was the best way to do that. Plus, I had my own special private moments with him from earlier, so there was nothing to complain about. The party was going to be staying later, until past midnight probably, but by 10:00 pm, I was more than ready to call it a night.

There was a party heading home, so as soon as I said goodbye to Aurora, I joined them and headed back to the mansion. It was looking to be a quiet evening, and despite how it currently felt as though my chest was constricted, I had to admit that I was looking forward to it.

I was sure that I could brush away just how closed up I had become as soon as that girl had arrived, but as I brushed my teeth and took off my makeup, it was all I could think about. The way he looked at her seemed eerily like the way he looked at me as well. Sure, I had noted his annoyance sometimes, but how was I to know for sure? More importantly, I shouldn't care. I didn't want to care; however, just like I predicted, I did, and it was infuriating to say the least.

I was sure that I would prefer a quick shower so that I could head off to bed quickly and forget about my worries and nonsense concerns; however, before long, my phone began to ring.

I was instantly nervous, reluctant to look since I could only assume that it was him calling, but then when I realized that perhaps this was the root of all my problems because my expectations towards him were now becoming too high, I got up and retrieved the phone.

Turns out it was Anna, and she was the one person in the world that I really wanted to talk to at this moment, so I immediately picked up.

"I haven't heard from you in like two days?" she immediately started complaining. "Are you doing alright? Or are you having so much fun that you just decided to forget about me altogether?"

I smiled about this because of course she was being dramatic. As I thought about her question, however, I realized that it wasn't quite far from the truth.

I smiled and looked out through the window at the gorgeous stars beyond. This truly was a beautiful place, and for a moment, I couldn't help but wish that I could stay longer.

That yesterday, in particular, could go on for much, much longer.

"I think I have been enjoying myself a little bit too much," I replied.

"Uh oh," she said. "I smell trouble in the Hamptons. What happened?"

I sighed then and thought about him.

"We had the most fabulous day today. From the spa to riding motorcycles and then the bonfire at night."

"What? For a wedding? Wow. Maybe I should have come along. Sure, I can't get an invite?"

"You probably can," I replied. "If you really want to come over, let me know."

She sighed then.

. . .

"I definitely would, but I can't because of work. This is a very busy week and given how things are already so awkward between me and my boss, I'm trying to work so hard that it's all we can both think about."

"Sounds good," I replied, and she laughed.

"You, on the other hand, sound as though you are barely working. Are you still taking great photos?" she asked.

"I am. All of this is more fun than I had expected."

"Drake is part of that, I reckon?" she sighed and her smile faded at the use of the word.

"He is, and this is the problem. Today, and after the day we had, I felt like I was floating on clouds, but now..."

"You're back to walking on the ground like the rest of us?" she asked.

"No, I felt like I was slammed back into the ground," she replied.

. . .

"What happened?" she asked, and I told her about Lindsey.

"The thing is... I don't even know who she is, yet I was so jealous I almost retreated into the shadows completely, ensuring that no one, especially him, saw me. I mean, what was that for? The point of this was that we would both be having fun, and none of us would lay any claim of ownership on the other whatsoever, so what the fuck am I doing?"

"You're being human," she replied. "And you're being a girl. It's quite normal if you ask me."

"Well, what if I don't want to be any of those things?" I asked, and she laughed.

"You kind of don't have a choice."

"Of course, this was going to happen; he's a catch. But it's only literally the first day, so I don't think there's any cause for alarm. Plus, how many days are left before the wedding? I say enjoy yourself, ignore your jealousy, and look forward to coming home. That's it. Don't overthink shit."

"All of this is what I was trying to tell myself earlier, but here I am talking to you in the bathtub, drinking wine and eating chocolate alone after literally running from the scene."

"Sounds tough," she said dryly, and I was amused.

"Evelyn, I knew you were going to have problems with this, but I was hoping somewhat that your dislike of him for interfering with his sister's wedding so much would keep your emotions at bay. However, this doesn't seem to be the case."

"That's because she's not completely mad at him. Sometimes she is when it hits her, and at other times, she seems to be just fine."

"I understand," Anna replied. "Anyway, back to your dilemma. Stop overthinking. Enjoy yourself, and yes, you're allowed to be slightly jealous. That's who you are. You're not the type to share partners, so, of course, you're going to immediately feel some kind of way. My advice is don't respond to it. And especially do not interrogate him. You both agreed on what this should be, right?"

"Right," I nodded as I turned to stare at the stars once again. "We did, and he has the right to do whatever he wants."

. . .

"Exactly, so as long as he's being safe, and you are too, tell yourself that you'll enjoy yourself when you're in the mood within the next few days and then come back home."

"Sure," I replied, and I could hear the smile in her voice as she ended the call. Afterward, I took her advice and tried to relax. What I was soon finding, however, was that despite how hard I tried, this just seemed all-around to be an extremely difficult feat.

Eventually, I fell asleep in the bathtub. A little while later, I was awakened by the sound of a little knock from the bedroom door, and it instantly startled me awake.

Chapter Thirty-Seven
Drake

I had no clue when she had left, but I knew that after I finally noticed that she wouldn't be staying behind with the rest of the younger guests for who knew how long, my interest instantly waned as well. So, I returned home, wishing that she was with me so that I could take her on a drive. I had a jet-black McLaren that I had been wanting to have a little fun with but hadn't quite been able to work myself up to feeling excited about it until now. Now there were so many things that I wanted to do and watch her enjoy along with me. For instance, the beach. A few couples who were at the bonfire rehearsal dinner eventually went away from the crowd, and you could see them holding hands and walking by the waves.

It was a serene, beautiful sight, and even though I wasn't staying any longer I couldn't help but wish that she was available so we could do the same. There were a lot of questions I wanted to ask her, I realized.

I also realized that this desire was extremely inappropriate given the state of our relationship, but in the romance and nighttime, I didn't really give a fuck. I wanted to be speaking to her in low tones that no one else could hear between us too, and I wanted to see the fire dancing in her eyes. I already knew that it would be licking underneath her skin, and perhaps we would have even found a spot of our own where we could lie, perhaps on the sand, and be together. Whether that or we could just talk, either one would have been great.

These were what I couldn't stop thinking about, and so even though I had tried to convince myself that her leaving was for the best, I eventually had given up battling with myself and headed back to the house. It was empty as the majority of the guests were still at the beach, and it was the perfect time for us to spend together.

My only hope as I knocked on her door was that she wouldn't be asleep, but even if she was, I found that I truly didn't care. I wanted to see her, and I didn't have to be considerate about it given the nature of our current relations. It took a little while, but eventually, she answered the door, and my heart thundered in my chest as I watched the door come open.

I perused her appearance, and I was not disappointed. As I laid eyes on her, it was very clear to me that she had been asleep. Her hair was tousled, her eyes and cheeks slightly swollen, and it made me wonder then if she had simply left because of Lindsey or if she had simply just been tired.

This wasn't a question, though, despite how tired I was, that I thought appropriate to ask. It was sure to open a can filled with worms, and if we were truly going by our earlier agreement, the foundation of which was nonchalance and all of this being casual, then there was no need for me to know.

"Can I come in?" I asked. For a long moment, she stared at me as though she wasn't quite sure what she was seeing and couldn't believe that I was here, at the door.

"Uh," she started, and then eventually, when it seemed as though she heard a sudden noise from the staircase, she stepped back and ushered me in.

I was amused, the stark difference between her and Lindsey coming to mind. While the latter had tried her hardest to announce to everyone that there was some intimate connection or history between us, this one here was trying to hide ours as best as she could.

It was indeed our agreement, but I had to admit now to myself that I most certainly didn't like it one bit.

She shut the door behind me while I looked around and assessed her room. It was much smaller than mine and quite earthy, which I loved. There was a lot of white and dark green, a pop of pink here and there. It was a good room, and I wondered if it was ok with her.

"Is this place okay?" I asked. "Do you feel comfortable here?"

She smiled at this then and started moving.

"It's great. It looks better than most hotels, so I can't exactly complain, can I?"

Her words hit me in a different way from the way she had intended it.

"You can complain," I told her. "About whatever you need to."

She stopped then and turned to me. We stared at each

other, and then she continued on her way into the bathroom. I went to her window.

It was so quiet here, quite the contrast to the noisy party I had been coming from, and I found it infinitely more peaceful. Not just because it was quiet, but because it was her space. It smelled like her, I realized. The entire home had a distinct smell due to the scents used all around, but hers had taken over, and I couldn't miss it because I had inhaled it from her neck as I had kissed her, tasted it on her skin. I would never forget it; it was far beyond this, even, and our current interactions. I stared out at the sky then, not realizing that she had returned, as I wondered truly how far I wanted to take this.

"Hey," she called, and I turned around then to see her standing by the door to her bathroom.

"Did you want to speak to me about something?" she asked, and it made me smile.

"No, not really," I replied. "I noticed you left the party early, so I wanted to check up on you."

"You left way too early, then," she said. "I'm sorry. You didn't have to check up on me; it's supposed to go on until the early hours of the morning."

"I know," I replied. "And that's why I left. It's one of the reasons, at the very least. Plus... I noticed you had left as well."

I started to head towards her then, and she remained in place.

"Yeah," she said. "I was uh... quite exhausted. Busy day."

I stopped then in my tracks because I couldn't help but be sensitive towards her and her words.

"You're exhausted now as well?" I asked, and it was clear exactly what was happening. She straightened then, her eyes going towards the door, and then I watched as she swallowed.

"Um... I feel a bit better now," she replied in a much lower tone, and it was amusing, to say the least. I continued on my way to her and didn't stop until I was mere inches away.

"You don't like parties?" I asked, and she smiled.

"Generally no, I don't, but this party wasn't bad. It was quite nice. I don't really ever want to give Victoria compliments, but I have to in this case. A bonfire dinner party, as opposed to the usual at restaurants, was a pretty good idea."

I looked away then as I considered her words, but only one response came to mind.

"The water will be too cold to swim in."

"Yeah," she replied.

However, and as I recall, the one glimpse I had of her in a bathing suit, the urge to swim came over me.

" What color was the bathing suit you were wearing earlier?" I asked. "I was barely able to see you."

"Yeah," she replied shyly, her head lowering. "It's a gorgeous night too, so I was quite busy trying to get the needed shots."

"Understood," I said and waited. She finally thought about my question and then she answered.

"Hm, it was green," she replied. "With white and black straps. In case you need more details."

This made me smile.

"Definitely don't need more details, but I'm glad to know." I glanced back at the door. "I want to go for a swim,"

I told her. "To round up the night properly. Fancy joining me?"

She immediately began shaking her head to refuse without even so much as considering it.

"Um, not exactly," she replied. "I'm really tired and -"

My hand reached out to hold her chin, and it instantly made her stop. I couldn't help running the pad of my thumb then across her bottom lip, and she instantly went still. I looked into her eyes then and could feel her anticipation. I leaned forward and kissed her.

She tasted just as sweet as I remembered, perhaps even much sweeter now. I found myself wishing that the taste of wine lingered on her lips, but she had properly cleaned up before me.

"We could take a shower afterward together," I told her. "Don't worry; I'll make sure that you're properly clean and tucked in by the time we're done."

She stared at me, very clearly tempted but still battling with herself about holding back.

"Uh..."

"Say yes," I urged as I leaned forward once again to kiss her. She melted into it, her hand resting against my chest so that she could maintain her balance.

"I'd love to swim, but I'd rather we speed things up."

This made me smile.

"What do you mean?"

"Let's skip the pool and just use the shower here."

I tilted my head at her, and then she diverted her eyes.

"Alright," I replied, my hand going to the tie around her waist. I undid it, and in no time, it was falling open to reveal the skimpy but sexy nightgown she had underneath. She didn't have a bra on, so her breasts were full and perky against the fabric. It dipped low, revealing her gorgeous cleavage, and I couldn't help but reach out to cup the weight in my hands. They were gorgeous on her. Though full, they wonderfully complemented her frame, and it made me wonder if I would ever tire of looking at her. There was just something exquisite about her presence that instantly made me feel slightly awed that we had connected. Indeed, there were so many gorgeous women in the world, most of them at my beck and call, but none quite like her.

"What is this about?" I asked as my arm went around her waist.

"What do you mean?" she asked, smiling up at me. She was glorious just like pearl, and I couldn't stop staring. I cupped her ass behind, pressing her into my hardness so that she could feel the effect that she had on me.

"I'm so drawn to you," I kissed her. "I couldn't stop thinking about you earlier. I had to leave early."

Her smile grew even wider.

"That's how flames work," she said, reaching up on the tips of her toes to wrap her arms around my neck. She nibbled on my chin, pressed kisses on my cheek and up my temples, and then she finally placed one on my lips.

"So... want to?" She looked around, and I understood why she seemed a bit lost.

The moment, though sweet, wasn't as charged as earlier, and I actually liked it. I wanted to talk to her instead. To find out a bit more about her. It was unnecessary. All I needed to do was fuck and leave, but I wanted this, and so I let her go and stepped away.

"I'm a bit hungry," I said. "All the socializing made me drink more instead of actually eat. Will you accompany me down to the kitchen?"

She seemed a bit surprised at this and even a tad bit alarmed, and it was quite amusing to watch. Eventually, though, she seemed to make up her mind and then she nodded. I was somewhat starving as well. I was so busy tonight, only realized that I mostly drank after I came home. We smiled at each other then and started to head out.

I wanted to hold her hand, and the urge truly startled me because it was the first time I had felt that way. I immediately suppressed it and continued on my way, and soon she was shutting her door and coming behind me.

Chapter Thirty-Eight
Evelyn

S ometimes I truly didn't know how to feel. One minute I was confused and forlorn, and in the next, the object of my concerns and trouble was inviting me to head down to the kitchen with him to get something to eat. It was almost 1 am, which was pretty late, but I was sure that we could still be seen. Still, as I watched his strong back ahead as he guided me down the stairs, I truly didn't have the strength to care. All of a sudden, from previously forlorn and confused, I was excited and tingling all over. I absolutely did not feel hungry any longer, but I wasn't going to refuse his offer, so I submitted to however this was going to turn out, and soon we arrived at the kitchen.

They had staff all around, so anyone could whip up what he wanted for him. We could even order in; however, I knew as he pulled the fridge open and began to look through, he was doing this because he wanted to spend time with me. This unfortunately made me feel things I had no business feeling. I admonished myself not to get carried away. However, this was impossible. He was so gorgeous, so attentive, and the way he had ridden that motorcycle from earlier in the day had taken up permanent space in my mind.

"Do you want something sweet or savory?" he asked as he glanced at me. I was caught right then, completely entranced, and with not a functioning brain cell left to even process his question, not to talk of answering it.

"Uh... s-sweet," I said, knowing that this was so inaccurate. I was actually starving and had more or less been drinking all evening, so why the hell would I want something sweet?

"Pancakes?" he asked. "Waffles?" I can make those. I was about to immediately reject these until I heard his proclamation that he could make them. I was instantly curious.

"How come you can make them?" I asked, and he smiled.

"In the early days of my career, I was creating a course for the clients in one of my gyms, and one of the issues they always had with their diets was sweets. So, I set out to create low-calorie alternatives. A lot of experimenting was needed then, so I picked up some essential kitchen skills. Though now it's been so long, I wonder if I will be any good."

I was absolutely sure he would be however, I didn't really want to eat anything sweet, so I decided to be honest. I went over to him and pulled the second door of the fridge open.

"Do you want something sweet?" I asked as I looked through and found some meat. "Because I'd want something a bit more savory, like steak, and then we can have something sweet. Small portions if you will."

He looked at me, then his eyes shining, and then he leaned forward to kiss me.

"That is a wonderful idea. Fancy potatoes?" he asked. "We can have it with the steak. Fast and easy."

"Yes, and yes," I replied and helped him in retrieving the ingredients. I was so excited I had to admit, but I was equally just as scared. I knew most people were still at the party, but this was exactly what bothered me because they were sure to return soon and would possibly meet us in the humongous kitchen. We weren't naked, of course, or writhing in each other's arms, but I didn't know of any other way to announce to everyone that we were together; other-wise, why the hell would we be interacting in the middle of the night, much less cooking together? So, I made quick work of all my subsequent chores.

I helped him with slicing the potatoes, seasoning, and popping them in the air fryer, while we worked on the steak together. He claimed his was the best; I argued my own was just as good if not better, and in the end, we decided to do it together while exchanging technique and, of course, kisses. Truly, I love the way he kissed me. Five minutes didn't go by before he leaned down, eager and hungry. They were brief but oh so sweet, and each time he drew away, my grip on the edge of the counter tightened.

Still and despite how often I wanted to jump him, I managed to control myself until the steak was done. I was distracted also by his reverse seasoning method, but he convinced me with enough kisses to trust him, and by the end of it, I was excited to taste. After cutting the steak into pieces, he stabbed one with a fork, and my hand reached out to take it; however, he pushed my hand away. He instead insisted silently that I accept it the way he was presenting it, and I felt myself melt. I held his gaze as I ate and chewed, and he did the same to me. The taste was divine, and at the soft moans that emanated from me, he leaned forward and began to kiss my skin. From the underside of my jaw, he moved down my neck all the way down till his mouth covered the hardened peaks of my nipples through the shift of my sleeping shift. I was on cloud nine. I felt like I was floating, like I was in a dream, and I never wanted it to end.

The way he looked at me, the way he spoke to me... I felt like the center of his world when hours earlier it was easy to convince myself that I didn't even exist. This made me, though, understand and accept this for what it was. It was a fantasy, and even if there was something more, it surely couldn't be acknowledged or acted on until after this week was over. I nodded, watching him as he brought a piece of the steak to his lips as well and took a bite.

"Let's plate it," he said, and I retrieved the plates that we would be using. There was a huge dining room away from the kitchen, but we didn't bother going that far. He pulled out the stools by the island, and we both took a seat.

"Wine?" he asked. I didn't really think I could stomach any extra alcohol for the night, but I didn't exactly fancy water either, so I accepted the bottle he retrieved. He poured the rich red liquid into the wine glass he had brought along, and I watched it flow. He sat back down afterward, and I realized once again that not only were we sharing the same plate, we were also sharing the same wine glass. He took a long sip, and I was tempted to do the same as well, making sure to hold his gaze and sip from the exact same place that he had. He smiled then, and once again, he kissed me, and I drowned in the taste. Eventually, we both parted, and as though shaken, we continued on quietly with our meal.

Chapter Thirty-Nine
Drake

I couldn't remember having this much fun with anyone. It was intimate yet simple, and it truly felt that I could remain in her presence forever. I was well aware that this was not the preferable way to go, but I couldn't help it because I wanted to know everything that I possibly could about her. As we ate, I couldn't continually suppress the questions that I had, especially about her work.

"Is photography something you want to do forever?" I asked. "Or is it just a hobby?"

"Forever," she instantly replied, and I couldn't help but smile at her assertiveness. "I'm in love with it, so anywhere it takes me, no matter how big or small, I'm ready to go."

I completely understood her, and it made me nod.

"You are the same in a way, right?" she asked after another long silence.

I was startled at what she was saying, but she soon explained.

"You liked fitness," she said. "You quit your high paying 9-5 to pursue it."

This made my entire chest flood with warmth, but of course, I made sure to control my expression to convey the image that I was as uninvested as possible.

"Yeah," I replied. "I grew to like the business because of my dad. He had gyms; however, he didn't want me to go that route. He'd tried to grow his business using the brick-and-mortar route, but after running into severe problems about a decade or more earlier, he sort of gave up on that."

"Until you brought the licensing business model," she said, and I nodded.

"Yeah. That revolutionized everything."

Nodding, she set the fork down to take a sip of the wine, and I watched once again as she ensured to close her lips around where mine had been. Once again, it was so simple, yet I felt the effect in my chest in a way that I couldn't quite describe.

We weren't dating, so I had no claim whatsoever to her, but in that moment, I felt as though she was completely mine. She was definitely treating me like this was the case.

"Do you have any advice for me?" she asked. I was surprised to hear this.

"Pertaining to what?" I asked.

"My company, and how to increase it from personal one-on-one service related to something much bigger and scalable."

"You don't want to be involved in the personal side?" I asked, loving that we were having such a technical conversation like this because business growth was one of my favorite things to converse and strategize about all the time, with anyone.

I nodded then and thought of her question, and eventually, I came up with a suitable answer.

"You need to know where the money is," I said. "At the time, I wanted to be emotional about the business and simply wanted to keep growing the gyms, but when my father's business started dwindling, I knew that we needed to step up or be forced to step down. I was really intrigued by the challenge by then, so I started attending lots of courses, and that was when I found out that we could license out the business's marketing methods."

"Using my marketing methods, the gyms started getting filled when I implemented them. And then I quit my job when I saw how effective it was and joined fitness altogether."

At my words, she nodded, perhaps trying to decipher how she could implement these in her own work.

"Follow the hunger," I told her. "If money is your gift, find the people who are the most hungry in your field and satisfy their hunger. Your business will explode as a result."

She nodded again, and then she asked, "You prefer business to fitness now?"

He nodded. "Yeah. Fitness was a start, but that's because I wanted to get strong. Afterward, the thrill of implementing strategies to ensure business growth became the main drug. And it is one with limitless potential, so I deeply enjoy it."

She nodded again; however, I was beginning to get whiplash, so I reached out and stopped her, much to her amusement.

"What is it?" she asked, amused.

"The nodding," I told her, and she laughed even harder.

"Alright, sorry," she said and tried to nod again, but her hand went around her neck.

"Sorry."

Shaking my head, I leaned forward to kiss her and lost myself in the kiss. We were more or less already done with dinner, and with this one moment, the atmosphere had changed. We kissed for so long and so deeply that I forgot where I was. Not until I somewhat heard voices coming from the entrance to the house. Our privacy had been interrupted, but the last thing I wanted was for the night to end.

"If we were back in my apartment in the city, I would have taken you right here," I told her.

She blushed so hard that she almost couldn't meet my gaze. And then she cleared her throat.

"I understand. I would have been thrilled."

Such a dorky response, and I watched her as she took our dishes and went to drop them into the sink.

I rose up then, took the bottle of wine along and began to head up the stairs. She came with me, and neither of us said a single word to the other. There was no need to. The moment was charged, the night dark and intimate, our hearts connected. We didn't need to speak further to understand what was going to come next. I was brimming with excitement as a result, nearly unable to control it, but I had to think about where we were.

"Your room or mine?" I asked when we reached her floor.

She gave this a thought and then responded.

"Mine. If anything goes wrong, I can always claim that you came to my room and not the other way around."

Much to her alarm, I was slightly stumped by this;

however, my alarm soon turned to humor when I realized just how startled this made her.

"I mean, what could possibly go wrong?" I asked, and she spent the next five minutes listing out whatever she was able to pull out of her head and ass.

"Sudden walking baby, nosy relatives, screaming pickle, singing wind - "

I listened to all her attempts to tear a laugh out of me and felt my heart endeared to her even more. I played along though and listened; however, none were funny enough. Eventually, we arrived in her room, and I noticed the slight disappointment in her face. She pouted in protest, but that was soon gone from her face when I leaned forward and took her lips in a kiss.

Tonight, I had to have given out the most kisses I ever had, and yet it wasn't enough. I'd never even really been a big fan of it, but with her, it felt like I was connecting in a way that I couldn't explain. It was beyond just kissing, but instead the softness acts of submission and synergy, and it was more than enough to nearly force my heart out of my chest.

Eventually, though, and when we had to catch our breaths, I pulled away and looked into her eyes.

"I want to eat you out," I told her, and she blushed once again.

She didn't say a word. Instead, she glanced back at the bed behind her, but I had other ideas. Holding her hand, I took her over to the tall wall with windows on the south side of the room and sat her on one of the single chairs. The view beyond was of our manicured gardens, the pool, and the beach beyond.

It was incredibly beautiful, all lit dimly by moonlight and a scene I always wanted to remember. The windows were slightly open, and a slight breeze managed to come in that slightly blew the soft, floral lace of her curtains.

It was all like a picture, and as I turned to the woman seated before me with her legs spread, I stopped and took the moment needed to capture and store a digital image in my head.

I lowered then, my eyes fixed on hers as I approached, and she seemed to shiver with anticipation. I leaned forward, and to my delight, found that she didn't have any underwear on. She had been about to fall asleep when I headed in, so this was understandable. It gave me so many naughty ideas because from now on, I was for sure going to find a way to check if she was severely underdressed anytime she headed out of the house.

"I'm going to check from now on, you know," I said as I leaned forward to lick up her mound.

Her entire body shook in excitement, her eyes fluttering shut as she leaned even further into the chair.

"That's dangerous," she managed to rasp out, and I smiled as I savored the taste of her. She was so aroused, so sensitive...

So greedy.

My hand dug into her hips, yet it couldn't stop her from writhing and from grinding her sex into my mouth. My tongue pushed into her pulsing hole, and at the stroking of my thumb against her swollen clit, I was rewarded with a fresh dose of her release.

She moaned and called out my name over and over again, like a prayer, desperate, affectionate... infatuated.

I couldn't get enough of her movements. They were so electric, so sensual... it drove me crazy to see how I could bring her completely under control. Without this, she was a tough cookie, stern, focused, reserved. But, here, in the intimacy of this moment and in my mind, she had completely submitted to me, and I adored her for it.

"Drake," her hand reached for my head as she moaned, needing something solid to hold on to. Grabbing hold of her legs, I parted them even wider and slung them over my shoulders. My head lowered once again, my hand and finger working in tandem, and she fell apart.

She came with a scream that she tried to control. Her hand slapped over her mouth, while the other dug into the chair's handle. She tried her best to pull away, beyond sensitive, and I allowed her to but only after sucking on her clit one more time. I was ravenous now and needed to be inside of her and soon grabbed her as though she weighed nothing and took her to bed.

Chapter Forty
Evelyn

I didn't know how I would ever be able to move again, but as he fucked me from behind, his hands wrapped around my hips and my ass hitting his abdomen, I knew that it was going to be an ordeal. The previous time he had been civil. He had been thorough, and the pleasure had been exquisite, but this time around, I knew that he had been holding back prior. He fucked me with abandon, as though something had come over him. He couldn't be satiated, couldn't be asked to slow down. He chased his pleasure with my body like a madman, and I fell in love with him with every passing second.

By the time I was flung onto my back and my legs were caught once again so he could ravage me from the front, I had lost count of how many times I had come. He was so rough yet so attentive at the same time, and the combined mix was potent. Eventually, though, as he collapsed on the side of the bed beside me, I could barely string a coherent thought together.

I hoped with all my heart that he would stay a little

longer with me but didn't exactly expect it to happen. To my surprise, he cradled me in his arms, held me tightly to his body, and I melted into him like wax. For a few seconds, I was a bit concerned about his silence, but then he leaned forward in the dimness of the room and kissed me. My neck, the base at the back of my head, my lips. I was so overwhelmed with emotion for him, and it exhausted me to my very bones.

It only took a few seconds as I shut my eyes, and the next moment, I woke up, and to my surprise, I met him still fast asleep, and that I was still in his arms. With any other man, it would have felt directly suffocating and uncomfortable, but with him, I never wanted to leave.

We were facing the window, and the sun was just rising. The scene beyond was breaking as I watched the daylight slowly filter in. He shifted a couple of times behind me, and through it all, I couldn't believe how intimate this felt, how close he was to me. Every part of his naked body was pressed against mine, and to say it was magical was an understatement.

Sighing, I knew that it would soon come to an end. From what I can remember, this day, just like the others, would be packed with activity, but the good news was the wedding would be in two days, and I was looking forward to that. It also meant that the time for my separation from Drake would be coming soon, and suddenly the world seemed bleak. I could feel my body tense up with worry, but then once again, I admonished myself that this had been the agreement. Therefore, I should try my very best to enjoy myself to the fullest today.

I sighed and shifted even closer, feeling his erection

begin to prod against my lower back. He was awake now, I was sure of it, and despite concluding earlier that it would be best to remain still until he was ready to leave, I decided now to be a little bit audacious. Hopefully, he would be in an excited mood as well and fuck me before he left. It was the exquisite start to the day that I so desperately needed.

I waited a few seconds, and true to the expectation, he leaned forward and kissed my cheek.

"Keep moving like that and we might not get out of bed today," he said in the raspiest voice ever. It was deeper than usual yet so silky smooth that I felt myself begin to leak between my thighs.

"I would love that," I said, and for a moment he went still, quite surprised at my words, and then he held me even tighter.

I loved the way he squished me so close as though I weighed absolutely nothing, and as a result, I couldn't help but reach behind to take a hold of his cock. It truly was hardening, so I lifted my leg just a little, and he was soon situated exactly where I needed him to be. I was slick, and so having him rub through my wet folds made my eyes shut closed and my breathing ragged.

"Do you know what the plan is today?" he asked. "Any activities we have to be present for?"

I could barely think as I writhed my hips, riding his cock with my sex, making him harder, slicking him up. He released a groan as well and buried his face in the crook of my neck. I loved the way he breathed me in, and then he kissed my skin, and I shivered all over.

This was an elite way to wake up, and I stored every passing moment of it to memory.

"We have a..." I tried to think of his earlier question as I stroked the head of his cock in my opening. I teased him by pushing him slightly in and then pulling out, and his arm tightened around me.

"You're fucking killing me," he breathed, and I smiled.

"We have a golf tournament today. That vogue photographer is coming over... it's going to be like a magazine shoot, I think. At least, that's what I heard Victoria has planned."

He, however, didn't respond because by now, I was taking him all the way in. I pushed my ass against him, relishing the sweet fucking fill of him stretching me to the brim all the way to the hilt. At the end, I was gasping for breath, and my entire frame arched.

"Fuck," he cursed, and I nodded in understanding. No one filled me up like him. Nothing else fucking felt like his cock. He grabbed my breast then, his hold so rough that my sex trembled around him. I was weak, couldn't think straight anymore, so my attempt at having a conversation in the midst of it completely failed.

I urged him to move despite the fact that he wanted to take his time. He obliged, but pretty soon and once again, he was out of control. Perhaps I could hold my moans the previous night somewhat, but this morning all of my self-control seemed to have broken into pieces.

Eventually, in panic, I buried my face into the pillow, but there was something about this angle and the way he held me that made me want to lose my mind. Or perhaps it was because I was so rested from the previous night and so at peace that all that flooded my head was extreme lust. The illicit sounds of our ragged breathing and the wet movements of our most intimate parts filled the room. Everything smelled and sounded like sex, primal, unbridled, desperate sex, and my brain emulated from the intensity.

"I'm coming," he told me, his hand reaching down to stroke my clit.

He went so fast that I could no longer muffle my sounds in my pillow. Instead, I found his lips and sealed mine over his. Needing some form of coherence, however, the added stimulation from his heated tongue did me in.

My body clenched as the tension reached its peak, and along with him, I fell apart. His moan was tortured and guttural, and the sound reverberated through me like a spell. A kind of joy I didn't think could possibly be explained in words filled and nearly overwhelmed me. He whispered things into my ear that I couldn't clearly decipher but somehow only seemed to heighten this feeling, and by the end of it all, we were so intimately intertwined that I didn't know where he stopped, and I began. I knew then that we couldn't leave this bed, at least not for the foreseeable hours. As though I had not just spent the entire night in what had to be the most restful night I had had in years, he held me hostage, refusing to let go, and in no time, we were once again falling into a deep sleep.

Chapter Forty-One
Drake

The intrusive and loud knock on the door pulled me awake. At first, I had been determined to ignore it, but when eventually it was accompanied by quite rude and harsh words, Evelyn got up.

"What the fuck," she started to curse as she reached for her phone, and then I watched as her eyes widened.

"Holy shit!" she cursed. "It's 10 am."

This still seemed pretty early to me, given that this was a vacation week, so when she tried to jump out of bed, I held her back.

"Just a little while longer," I said; however, she refused and continued to fight. She giggled, however, since I still refused to let her budge even while she tickled me, and suddenly, as though in response to her amusement, we definitely heard from the outside someone kick the door open and barge in.

From my waist down I was covered underneath the blanket, so there was no cause for alarm, but Evelyn, on the other hand, had to quickly grab the sheets to cover her breasts.

At her alarm, I turned around then in bloody annoyance to see whom had the audacity and unsurprisingly saw that it was Victoria. She seemed incredibly startled though as though this was not a scene she had been expecting in any way. She stared at both of us, and then I, immediately began to get up, her eyes widened in shock.

"Um… I'm sorry, Sir," she said with a strained smile. "I-I just wanted to tell her about the planned photoshoot. The photographer has arrived, and Aurora has been calling for you for the past hour. We're already running behind schedule."

"You're still talking?" I asked, and it took her a moment to process my words. Afterward, she turned around and sped from the bedroom. Thankfully, she closed the door behind her, which gave me some more alone time with Evelyn.

"I need to go," she said as she hurriedly stood up and then headed toward the lounge area from the previous night to retrieve her clothes.

"Fuck, so late."

She started hurrying toward the bathroom; however, just before she could go too far, I reached forward and caught her.

"I'm late, Drake," she said. "We overslept. I'm in huge fucking trouble."

"I'm the boss," I told her. "You're not in any trouble. You're fine."

"Actually, Aurora is my boss, and right now she needs

me and I'm not there. This was one of the things I was scared of. I have to go, now."

I listened to her words, and even though I didn't necessarily agree with her haste, I understood where her loyalty was. It was one of the things that had immensely drawn her to me, but now it was keeping me from her.

"Alright," I replied. "I need to get ready as well, plus I left my phone in my room. I can only imagine the fires waiting for me to put them out."

She smiled then, and I tilted my head as I watched her.

"We don't have any time to take a shower together?" I asked, wanting to milk every moment with her as much as I could.

"No," she immediately refused. "This will lead to more sex, and guess who Aurora will be furious at?"

"The both of us?" I replied, and she gave me a dry look.

"I'm serious."

"She's already furious at you. I didn't want to be labeled an enemy as well," she said and tried to pull her hand free. I let her go, but not before placing a kiss on her hand.

I was startled though, just as she was when I did this because it was unnecessary. For what had to be the past twelve hours, I had kissed her on and in nearly every single part of her body, and yet I couldn't just let her go now to get ready for her day without this little one?

She felt just how special and intimate it was because she looked at me then and a long silence passed between us. Without a word, she continued on to the bathroom, and I really began to wonder if I was as unaffected as I thought I was.

I had had more casual relationships with women than I

could count, and I had never been this way. For one, I had never spent a night with them and remained reluctant to leave till the morning.

If we weren't being interrupted now, if I could, I would spend the entire day in bed with her. Talking and eating and fucking. Sleeping and then waiting to do it all over again.

Currently, as I thought about this, excitement filled me, and I wanted to burst but I felt some dread as well. This was far from normal, and I truly didn't want to restrict myself from enjoying it all.

Plus, I wondered as I found my clothes and began to put them on. What was so bad about being with her even after this week was over? She was breathtaking, loyal, hardworking, driven. What would be wrong in taking this even further?

I couldn't see a problem whatsoever, and so with one last look at the bathroom, I decided to open my mind toward it. I was in the best of moods, even after I returned to my room and found my phone still blowing up with missed calls and messages, I patiently sat down to eat my breakfast and started responding to them. Only a few seconds in, however, and my heart lurched.

Most of them I realized now had been from my father and mother, and I wondered why. They had called, sent urgent messages asking where I was. Surely, they weren't worried about my location, so all I could think of as to why they would have urgently needed me was one thing.

Immediately, I put the coffee I had been sipping aside and rushed out of the room. In no time, I was knocking on their door, however, it took a while for them to answer. I was so terrified I found myself shaking. If anything had happened, I knew that they would remain silent until I came over for Aurora's sake so that we could calmly decide on what to do. So, as I grew impatient with the locked door and barged in, I prepared myself for the worst.

It was just as expected. I headed in and found my mom in bed covered with the blanket. My dad was by her side, and he had her hand in his. She looked so weak and ill. During the day and with color and her outfits, she had managed so far to not look so different, at least to those not looking too closely.

But now she seems so pale, lifeless, and weak. At this moment, I could truly see the illness eating away at her.

"What happened?" I asked as I headed over to her side.

"Where the hell were you?" my dad asked, and I could tell just how upset he was from the tone of his voice and sternness in his tone. I knew that he was scared, worried, and possibly helpless.

"We wanted to call a helicopter last night, but we couldn't. We couldn't reach you, and we didn't want to alert Aurora either."

I looked at my mother, and she shook her head.

"Unnecessary," she said. "I just started having difficulties breathing earlier this morning. Not last night. He was worried and wanted to raise the alarm, but I stopped him. I wouldn't have waited this long before contacting you, and if we had overreacted, Aurora would have found out."

"Overreacted?" he asked, his tone rising.

"Darryl," she called softly, trying to calm him, but he grew even angrier.

"I understand that we're trying to be considerate of

Aurora. That we want her to be happy during this period, but that's not all that's important. We also have to take care of your mother as well."

My mother sighed, while I stared between the two of them. I headed to the couch to take my seat. Truly, at times like this, I wish I could rewind time. Currently, I'd take the past few hours over this. From feeling so relaxed and happy, I was tense and scared all over again. I kept a straight face and began to corral my thoughts, but my insides were in turmoil.

"Can you hold on for the next hour?" I asked. "I'll send for Dr. Harold immediately."

"We've already spoken to him," my father replied. "He's on his way."

"So no need for a helicopter?"

"Absolutely not. I'm fine," my mother replied. "But what I need you to do is to ensure that Aurora is occupied with her shoot on the golf course. The other guests as well. In this way, she won't notice we're gone or that we've not arrived yet until later."

I stared at them, understanding, and then I nodded.

"I'll do my best to keep her busy."

Chapter Forty-Two
Evelyn

I received the call just as I was putting on the last of my makeup for the day. Aurora hadn't contacted me, which was very unlike her, but it just proved all the more that she wasn't quite happy with the fact that I was absent as she got ready. And so, to put even more pressure on me to get ready, as I was applying my lipstick while I was slipping into my shoes.

I had known ahead of time that we would have such an event like this, so I had prepared. I had packed on as much sunscreen as my skin could take and had the cutest little ensemble with a pleated skirt and a white shirt.

I didn't understand golf, but I expected anyway for the shoot to be quite fun. A lot more guests had arrived, most of them quite elderly and middle-aged and wealthier than could be fathomed, so I knew that for sure they were going to feel right at home at the golf course and have a blast with their day.

All in all, in the morning, I was plenty excited and looking forward to the day. The only slight dent and dread was dealing with Aurora, but I was in the wrong, plus it wasn't something I could avoid, so I geared myself up with courage and was soon on my way.

My phone began to ring then, and I ignored it. But when it called again, just as I was heading down the staircase to Aurora's room, I had no choice but to pick up in case it was her. What I saw, however, was that it wasn't her. Instead it was Drake, and although butterflies instantly fluttered in my stomach at seeing him, I was already nervous because whatever he was going to say was for sure going to make me lose my head, and I couldn't, not anymore, at least for the rest of the day. I had to make up for disappearing and give my whole attention to Aurora.

Still, I picked up just as I arrived in the hallway leading to her bedroom, and he replied.

"Are you with Aurora?" he asked.

I couldn't quite keep the smile off my face, but after noting the coldness in his, it immediately started to falter. He wasn't the most bubbly person when he spoke, but he usually didn't sound so stern and gloomy, at least when he spoke to me. Or perhaps it was in my head, and this was how he always sounded? Whatever it was, I was quite startled and a tad bit worried.

"No, I'm not," I replied. "I'm just heading up to her room now."

"Alright," he said, but then he went quiet again. He seemed so distracted and distant that I wondered what was wrong. Had I done something?

"Um," I eventually spoke. "I'm at her door now. I'll have to end the call."

"I'll call you back," he said, and I wondered why.

"A-alright, sure," I replied.

The call disconnected then, and I stared at the phone quite strangely. Then I knocked on Aurora's door and headed in. I had to admit that I was nervous because obviously I wasn't exactly on her good side currently. However, I didn't feel quite nervous about it. Not till I got into the room and saw the three women that were present.

I didn't even recall that Victoria had barged in on us until I saw the scowl on their faces, and then I sighed.

I didn't even have a confident leg to stand on because I felt in the wrong, but I wasn't going to be made to regret my night with Drake either, so I readied myself to accept the criticism, whatever it may be.

"Do you know how much preparation has gone into today?" Victoria asked.

I glared at her in response, and then I turned to look at Aurora. She lowered her eyes from me and returned them to her phone. She had a hair stylist working on her hair and a few others sorting through some clothes on a rack.

"I'm sorry I'm late, Aurora," I apologized and picked up my camera.

"Why exactly are you late?" The girl Lindsey from the previous night asked, and at first, I ignored her. I picked up my camera and started tinkering with the settings, getting ready for my day, but she soon got pissed off by my attitude.

"You're going to ignore me and act like you're in the right here?" she asked.

I looked up then. I stared at Aurora, but she was acting for all the world like she was deaf, so I ignored her.

"Please let me do my job. It's nothing to you if I was late."

"It's something to me if you were late because you were with my boyfriend," she said.

I stopped then and sighed because she was that girl. She'd acted like it, she definitely looked like it, and I was in no way going to participate. The only unfortunate thing was that Aurora was present, and her ears were no doubt going to be soiled as a result.

"Please take it up with him, not me," I replied. "I really don't have anything to add to this conversation."

"Even if you told me not to do it again, I would. All so that you can stop this conversation right now and allow me to do my job."

"You're a fuckin-" Victoria started, but at the harsh look I sent her, the rest of the insult quickly died on her lips.

"Be careful," I told her. "I can be tolerant of the guest but not you. Be very careful with how you speak to me. I haven't dealt with you yet on how you barged into my room. What kind of disrespect is that?"

She scoffed.

"Do you deserve any respect? Your client is right here and getting re-"

"Oh, please shut the fuck up," Aurora suddenly spoke.

At first, I was startled, but when her words registered, my head lowered as I tried to hide my smile.

I knew she wasn't happy with me either, but she wasn't about to tolerate whatever nonsense they were starting. I couldn't even stand it and would have preferred to just leave. Whatever they wanted to say about me within themselves, I really didn't mind. I just truly didn't want to be in the vicinity.

"Evelyn," Aurora called, and I lifted my head, ready to respond.

"Yeah?"

"I'm not really happy," she said, and I nodded.

"I understand."

"I know that I showed that I didn't really have a problem with it yesterday, but I wouldn't be completely honest if I said that I wasn't a tad bit displeased. I really want your focus during this period. You were kind of like the outsider in all of this, someone that could make it bearable. Now I feel like you're a part of it and you're a part of them."

I couldn't argue with this because even though she wasn't exactly fighting with Drake, I still knew that things weren't exactly the way she had imagined, and for that, there would be some hidden resentment that would be difficult to shake off.

"I know," I replied. "I'm really sorry."

"It's alright," she said. "Please focus for the rest of the day."

"I am here," I told her. "I'm all yours."

Just then, however, and unfortunately, my phone began to ring. The room was so quiet prior that it immediately drew the attention of everyone present. I tried to ignore it, especially when I saw who it was from; however, when he called again, I had no choice but to answer it. I wanted to go out to the balcony for some privacy; however, when I knew that this would do nothing but raise more suspicion as to whom I was talking to and possibly stir a bit more anger from Aurora, I picked up the phone right there, determined instead to control what I said.

"Why aren't you answering?" he asked, and I was both startled and annoyed.

I really didn't want to be harassed for the tense setup today, but it seemed as though it was destined to be my fate from all angles.

"Was a bit occupied," I replied.

"I'm going to need your assistance," he went straight to the point, and I wondered what he was talking about.

"Sure,"

"Are you with Aurora right now?" he asked.

"Yeah," I replied.

"Can you go somewhere where she can't hear you?"

This was a bit difficult because even though everyone seemed busy, I knew they were intently listening. I really didn't want to move, so I just remained in place.

"Sure," I replied. I waited; however, and a few seconds later, he spoke.

"I have to take my mother to the hospital. My absence will be incredibly noticed, as well as my mom's, since we have quite a lot of guests arriving. This will bother Aurora, I'm sure, and I can't really think of a suitable explanation right now, so this is why I'm calling you."

"Oh," I said, wishing now that I had truly gone some-where more private. There was no way that I would be able to control my expression and knowing that so many eyes and ears were on me made it even more uncomfortable.

"Any ideas?" he asked. "The helicopter will be arriving soon, so I need this sorted before we leave."

This was serious and urgent. I wondered if whatever the problem was, was it something to be alarmed about. I no longer cared what any of them thought, so I hurried immediately to the bathroom. In there, I shut the door, thankful that it, as well as the step, seemed pretty solid, and thick, and then I continued speaking.

"Um... will you both be gone all day, or will you only need a few hours?"

"Probably all day," he said. "I want her to be monitored for a little while so she can go through the rest of the ceremony as strong as possible."

"Oh," I replied, a gnawing suspicion beginning to tug at a corner of my heart. However, I couldn't quite connect the dots just yet.

"You could tell Aurora that it's some business meeting?" I suggested.

"My mom isn't involved with the business."

"A birthday?" I asked. "Of one of her friends' kids or grandkids?"

"If so, then it should have been planned, and Aurora should have been informed. This would only just upset her even further."

"Um..." I wondered then why they didn't just tell Aurora that her mother was ill. Perhaps they didn't want to disturb her at all? I understood that bit, but I also knew that if I was in her shoes right now, it would kill me not to know.

"Funeral, then," I replied, "It was sudden, you have to hurry over, but you'll be back before nightfall.."

"This sounds plausible," he said. "Alright, I'll go with this, and I'll keep in touch. Try to stay with her and distract her from the absence. I know she'll feel bad a bit; it is a pretty important photoshoot today, isn't it?"

"Yeah, since her fiancé is around they were really

looking forward to it. And I heard she suggested it as well because he likes golf."

"Yeah," Drake replied. "It can't be helped. Anyway, be reachable at all times. I'll talk to you later."

"Alright," I replied. I wanted to head out immediately; however, I also needed a few minutes alone to calm my heart, so I stayed in place. About five minutes later, I walked out, and it unfortunately seemed that Aurora had her phone to her ears and a very deep brow. A frown was forming on her face. I assumed then that she was talking to Drake; however, for some reason, and as her eyes settled on me, she seemed to frown even more, if that's even possible. She didn't say a word, even though I knew that she was listening attentively to whatever Drake was saying.

Eventually, and still without saying a further word, she ended the call, and then she turned to look out the window.

I understood how upset she felt, and so when she stood up from her chair and went out to the balcony, I truly wondered what to do. I wanted to go with her, but I wasn't sure now if she felt as safe and comfortable with me as she used to be, and this made me quite unhappy. Eventually, though, and when I saw that she wasn't coming back into the room, I looked out to the balcony and took a few steps towards it.

"What have you found out to worry you?" Victoria asked, but I ignored her. Lindsey got up from her seat then, clearly irritated, and then she stormed out of the room.

I hesitated but eventually I opened the glass balcony doors and headed out. I didn't go directly up to her, but I did stand behind her in case she needed me or had any questions.

"He's already called you and informed you, hasn't he?" she asked, and I nodded before realizing she couldn't see me.

"Yes," I spoke up, and she sighed.

"A friend's grandchild's funeral. For businesspersons, they had to be there. It's sudden."

She turned to me. "Does that make any fucking sense?"

I stared at her and without thinking instantly shook my head.

She seemed to become even more upset and truly I wanted to hit myself. But what else could I have said. The business always seems to come first, even today. She couldn't tell the partner that her daughter had a photoshoot today? That her wedding is tomorrow? And that she couldn't step away. Why is—"

I paused in my tracks, that gnawing feeling once again coming to my heart. I was cautious, so I simply put my hand on her back and rubbed. I knew that I couldn't say anything because whatever I did would sound like I was defending Drake, and I wasn't exactly wanting to make her even more annoyed.

"Let's just fucking cancel the whole day," she said, and shrugged my touch away. I instantly panicked because this was definitely not what Drake wanted. However, for a moment, I did push him aside and considered if this was something that Aurora needed. I eventually decided that it was necessary. They wanted out of love not to bother her, and all parties involved would feel extremely unhappy if this misunderstanding interrupted the wedding festivities in this way.

It made me wonder once again why Drake was complicating this? I mean, it was normal for someone to fall sick during events like this, right? He could have just told her, and even though she was worried, she would be consoled by the fact that she would at least see her mother later that night. But the way he made it sound was as though it was—

I paused then in my tracks, that gnawing feeling once again coming to my heart. He hadn't sounded worried at all about the illness. It was as though it was something old that had flared up, and they were going to the hospital to manage it.

"Oh," I said underneath my breath, and Aurora turned around.

"Oh what?" she said, and I managed to form a smile at her.

"Nothing. Also, I know you might want to take a break, and I support whatever you want to do to make you feel better, but your fiancé is around, and I think he might deeply appreciate the activities continuing. Plus, today is Victoria's day. She brought in the photographers and flowers and all. It will really cause a dent in the entire ceremony if it's just simply cancelled."

She considered my words quietly for a moment and then she pulled out her phone.

"I'll call David," she said, and I nodded in response.

Chapter Forty-Three
Drake

This was indeed more intense than I thought it had been flying on the helicopter this week. I was glad that I had it prepared and had it on standby for emergencies such as this. For one, I was happy that she seemed a bit more relaxed and had her eyes shut, but I knew she was in pain and knew her well enough to know that as usual, she was trying to bear it all and hide it for our sake. It hurt me. I really wished she wouldn't do that. Right from the very beginning, she had been nothing but calm, gracious, and it always annoyed me. I wished she would have a furious reaction because what was happening to her was the absolute worst. However, I had to be even stronger as well, and so I kept my expression as calm as possible and headed toward the helicopter with her.

"I want to come along," my dad said for the umpteenth time, and I stopped momentarily to speak to him.

"Aurora needs you today. I know this is important, but we made a decision to keep her mind worry-free until the wedding. There's just a day left. Please stay with her today; we will return. She'll be reassured as well seeing you."

He considered this, and then he nodded.

"Keep me updated every half hour. If not, I'll call, and you better pick up."

"I will," I replied and patted his shoulder. Then I went on my way.

I remained quiet all through the ride. I watched her and couldn't believe how frail she had gotten, how weak and vulnerable she looked even in this very moment, and it broke my heart all over again. Just as it had, from the very first moment we found out that she had less than six months left to live. We were in the tenth month now, and every day that passed, I could feel my heart deflate a little bit more. I had tried to distract myself from everything, but now I was faced with it, and it was difficult to say the least.

Looking away, I stared out at the city below as we flew and tried my best to shut off my brain until we arrived. The view, however, did absolutely nothing for me, so I shut my eyes. What came to mind was the woman I had spent the entire night and early this morning with.

She had been so calm on the phone when I called her. I imagined, especially after Victoria's impolite intrusion earlier this morning, that she received both a mouthful and earful, yet she had sounded as though she had simply brushed it over her shoulder. Given how nervous she had been about how this would affect Aurora, I was quite happy. I could see now that she wouldn't crumble easily, and I especially loved how she had suggested the explanation for Aurora. I had been unwilling and unable to think in that moment, and she had come through, and I was immensely grateful for it.

There were more than enough memories in my mind of her from the previous time for me to sift through, and the longer I spent on them, the warmer my heart became. Ever since I had received the call from my father, it had been chilled, but now I could feel the warmth coming to it, and I welcomed it with all my heart. The warmth of her body, her scent, the soft way she breathed when she slept, how she kept shifting until every inch of her body was glued to mine, and yet it wasn't enough.

I loved especially how her legs intertwined with mine when we fucked. I could feel the extent of her pleasure from the way she rubbed and stretched against me. She had gone mindless with pleasure several times the previous night and I was immensely happy about this.

Sighing, I opened my eyes, and to my surprise, I found my mother looking at me.

"Everything alright," I asked, my heart instantly warmer as I watched her. A little bit of color seemed to be coming to her cheeks. So, I straightened then and went closer to her. She lifted her arm, frail and a bit shaky, and then she placed it against the side of my cheek.

"Caught you smiling to yourself," she said. "You aren't happy that I'm in this bed, are you?" she asked.

I didn't want to laugh, truly, but as soon as she said this, my entire body began to rumble. I leaned forward then and kissed her because she was such a wonderful woman and mother that it hurt to even breathe.

It was meant to be a brief kiss, but as I was so close to her, I didn't want to leave, and so we remained like that for a few more minutes before I eventually had to pull away. I smiled at her, and she smiled back. I pretended not to notice the slight wince as well as the pain once again hit her abdomen.

"You've been so stoic these past few years," she said. "Almost unapproachable. These last few days, though, you've been a bit lighter. I'm really happy that you didn't lose that softer side of you even with how busy you've been so far."

I nodded as I listened to her, knowing she was doing her best to make conversation to distract us both.

"Rest, Mom," I told her. "We can talk more after you've been treated."

"It's fine," she said. "This helps."

I nodded then and held her hand. She continued to watch me, and it was so endearing how overbearing she could be. When I was younger, this definitely was a point of annoyance, but now, I never wanted it to end.

"Have you spoken to Aurora?" she asked, and I nodded.

"How did she take it?"

I thought back to my sister's response earlier and sighed.

"Silently," I replied, and she nodded.

"She'll be fine by tomorrow. She has no choice but to be anyway, she'll be married."

I nodded and continued to watch her.

"The person I think we have to be worried about is the photographer," she said. "Will she be able to handle Aurora and your dad?"

"She doesn't need to handle them," I said, "She just needs to observe calmly and let me know if there's anything going wrong."

My response was simple enough, and my only hope was that we would move on to another topic, but my mom refused to budge.

"You like her?" she asked.

Normally, I would have ignored the question altogether, but these moments with her were more precious than I could explain, and so I gave it serious consideration.

"Yeah," I replied. I was a bit surprised by my response because I was expecting that it would take a little while for me to admit this, but time, I realized now more than ever, was so brief that there was no point in denying what I knew and felt all because of the fear that it could change.

"Right now, at this moment... I really like her," I told my mom. "I know that it might be too soon, but I think for once, I'd like to explore where this could lead between us even after this week's festivities are over."

She nodded quietly; however, she didn't seem very excited.

"You sure?" she asked, and this made me amused.

"Yeah. Why?"

"I mean, she's only known you a few days, and you know I've heard rumors."

I smiled again.

"That was our agreement. She's not acting out of the ordinary. Our intention was never to date."

"Ah," she said, "Is that how you kids do it these days?"

"Somewhat," I replied, and she nodded. We remained silent afterward, and finally, we arrived at the hospital in Manhattan. The helicopter landed on the roof, and soon enough, she was being brought down and transported into the hospital. She was here now, so no matter what happened, there would be people to immediately attend to her, so I calmed down a little bit.

She grew completely silent as she was admitted, and then her tests were conducted. It was just as Doctor Harold had mentioned in the Hamptons, and it scared the hell out of me.

"Variceal bleeding," he said. "She was at risk for it, but luckily she came in time so there is no rupturing."

Shutting my eyes, I released a deep breath, and he came over to squeeze my shoulder. Over the past several months, we have had one too many of these meetings.

"We're going to go with Sclerotherapy now and beta-blockers. Hopefully, and afterward, she won't have to spend too much time here and can leave in a couple of hours. "

"A couple of hours?" I asked and breathed easy.

"My sister's wedding is tomorrow. I truly won't be able to explain things if my mom can't make it."

"Don't worry, Mr. Moran. I'll try my best," he said, and I nodded in gratitude. I leaned back then and watched as they started work on her and couldn't help but check in with Evelyn.

"How's Aurora?" I texted. "How are things with the guests?"

I knew that rather than asking Evelyn, who was just the photographer, I was supposed to be instead asking Victoria, who was fully in charge as the wedding planner, but not hearing correct details or just generally being barraged for whatever reason stopped me. Whatever Evelyn had to say would be good enough, so I waited with anticipation until she responded.

Chapter Forty-Four
Evelyn

I had truly thought all these days that Aurora had been upset. However, watching her now in comparison to earlier, the difference was very clear to me that she had been holding back. Without her mother and brother being present, and her being very upset about this, she had basically turned into her brother—doing the barest minimum and holding a scowl when anyone took too long and got too enthusiastic over anything.

It was like watching him, so I couldn't complain, plus I could see that Victoria, as a result, was having the worst possible time along with the photographer that, surprise, surprise, was too much of a force for her to control. He had been expecting a blushing, over-the-moon bride; instead, he got a grumpy, done-with-all-this-shit bride, and he was not amused.

The guests, though, seemed to have taken the day as their own party and were participating heartily in the tournament, going to the shoot when asked and basically enjoying it as well. All except Aurora's dad. He tried to hide it with his sweet nature. He tried to be as friendly as possible, but multiple times, eventually, he was nowhere to be found. Even more this convinced me that whatever was wrong with their mother was not something new. It was an illness they had already been aware of and were clearly managing and had told Aurora nothing about.

It began to dawn on me then that this actually might be the underlying reason behind Aurora not getting the wedding she wants and, instead, her mom getting the wedding she wanted for Aurora. It made absolute sense to me. And so, eventually, especially when, by the look of things, it felt as though the salsa club dancing event planned for later that evening would not be happening, I called Drake and hoped that he would respond.

"Hey," he greeted, still sounding forlorn and exhausted to the bone.

My heart instantly softened as well as my tone.

"How's it going?"

"Okay," he replied. "We should be back later tonight or tomorrow morning. Thankfully the wedding's later tomorrow."

"Yeah, thankfully," I said.

"Why are you calling?" he asked. "Is anything wrong?"

"No," I replied, reconsidering if I should mention this to him. It would be tough to pull off, but I couldn't see why this couldn't be acceptable to placate Aurora as well. Otherwise, and with possibly no forthcoming explanations on her mother, the wedding day itself was bound to be quite sour.

Currently, she was clinging and mostly only talking to her fiancé, refusing to let anyone close by and treating us all like the enemy. Yes, especially me. Ever since I had left her room, we had not even exchanged a single word, and it was all just so sad, to say the least.

"I'm sorry if this puts any additional stress on you, but I'm just going to suggest this and if it's something you don't have much of an interest in, then please let me know."

"Alright," he said. "Let's hear it."

"Aurora's been having a really bad day," I said; however, he didn't respond. I sigh. "I'm thinking that why don't we give her the wedding she wants ultimately. I mean, she doesn't quite have to cancel the big one already planned, but I've heard what she wants for the church, how she wants it to look, the location, what she wants to wear."

"Tonight's free, I think. The salsa dancing thing is not really making anyone excited, so maybe we can blow it off, or even handle this late and surprise her with the wedding. I've checked, and the church location is not too far from the house. I mean, it is far, but that can't be helped. Plus, we can blindfold her, though she might be a little upset and refuse to cooperate given the state she's currently in."

I kept talking, not realizing that I was rambling until eventually, I realized just how quiet the line was. I immediately apologized.

"I'm sorry," I told him. "I said I was going to state my case with only one sentence." To my surprise, his response was positive.

"It's okay," he said. "I like your idea. In fact, I love it a lot. I've just not had the time to think about it, plus Victoria, none of us imagined, would make such a detour with her wedding planning."

"Yeah," I replied.

"So, can you handle it?" he asked. I was shocked. For a

few seconds, I couldn't say a single word, and then I got ready to reject him.

"Um..." I began; however, he didn't even give me the chance to respond.

"You can work with my assistant," he said. "Just tell him whatever you need, and he'll get it done."

"Oh!" I said, realizing now that I just possibly might be able to pull this off. "Shit."

His breath released harshly then, as though he had heard me come to the realization that maybe, just maybe, this very needed thing to calm the waters was quite necessary.

"Alright, then," he said. "I'll get him to call you. His name is Scott."

"Sure," I asked, but before he left, I stopped him once again.

"Just one more question," I said. "I'm sorry."

"It's fine," he replied. "What is it?"

"Will you... the guest list," I asked. "She would really love if you and her parents were there. Is it possible? I'm so sorry to ask."

"Don't be," he said. "And if you're right. I know she'd love us there. I'll see what I can do. Mom is already feeling better, so I'll ask the doctor to gauge her condition by then, and I'll do everything possible to see if we can make it. I'll keep in touch with you."

"Alright," I said, and the call came to an end.

I was so happy, especially as I gazed across the field then and found Aurora very unwillingly posing against one of the golf carts alone. Her fiancé was by the side, trying to speak to her, but she ignored everyone and barely gave a smile. I wasn't too worried; this was part of the ceremony, and her pictures for the magazines could present her as a model rather than a blushing bride due to the lack of blushing involved. As for the pictures where she would be absolutely filled with joy, I planned to do my very best work tonight.

The first thing I needed was to head down to the church, as described by Aurora, so that I could see what I would be working with. It was among the very first things she had mentioned to me at the beginning, so I knew that she would absolutely love it. Plus, I needed to get her fiancé in on this. Unfortunately, I hadn't known her for too long, but he, I imagined, would know all of her preferences.

I would have liked to use this as an avenue to contact her brother, probably more often than was necessary, but I knew that the last thing he would want was to be disturbed. And so, I intended, like he had suggested, to focus on her fiancé and Scott. Scott informed me before I had even said a word that he was on the way to the Hamptons, but I stopped him and quickly headed over to her fiancé.

Aurora took one of her endless breaks, relaxing and sipping on what I suspected was one too many non-alcoholic cocktails, but she wasn't listening to anyone today, so no one stepped in.

He had a smile for me as soon as I approached, and I was immediately relieved by it.

"I need some information about Aurora," I said, and his brows lifted in surprise.

I explained to him about the plans we had, and immediately his face brightened up even further.

"She would love that," he said. "She's been having the worst day."

"Yeah," I replied and looked towards her direction once again. I could see, unfortunately, though, that Lindsey and Victoria were flocking around her and looking my direction, and it made me wonder if they were crazy enough to suggest that I was making a move on her fiancé because the more they talked and looked towards me, the darker Aurora's expression became.

I sighed and continued with my phone, taking all the information needed for her favorites. Victoria started to head over to me then, and I concluded my inquiry and went in the opposite direction before she could reach me.

On my way, I called Scott once again and informed him that I would be coming to the city.

"Get the driver in the compound to take you," he said, and the said driver found me as soon as I returned to the house. A few minutes later, we were headed out to run all the errands needed for later that evening.

Chapter Forty-Five
Drake

I was startled awake by people walking down the hallway. My eyes came open in the quiet of the hospital room, and instantly, my attention went to my mother. She was sleeping peacefully, I hoped, and recovering, and I couldn't help but pull out my phone to take her picture. She hated being photographed in these moments, so whenever I could, and whenever she wouldn't give me hell over it, I took pictures for my own memory and to show Aurora when she eventually found out.

We had agreed that we would tell her after she and her husband returned from their honeymoon. We didn't want anything whatsoever to ruin their enjoyment of this special time together, so we were willing to bear all the inconveniences arising as a result.

Speaking of inconveniences, I went over to my messages and found that besides some work situations, no updates had been sent to me. From my father even, and especially not from Evelyn. So, I called Scott, and he immediately picked up.

Not wanting to disturb my mother, I headed out and spoke freely to him.

"Where are you both now?" I asked. "Everything going well?"

"I think so, Sir," he replied. "We're at the wedding dress shop now, but they seem to be having a problem finding Miss Moran's dress. The one she preferred."

"There's a dress she preferred?" I asked, wondering why she hadn't gone with that after all. What difference would it have made?

"Turn on your video," I said, and he did as instructed. I looked then, and it wasn't hard to spot the gorgeous woman in khaki shorts and a white polo shirt, digging through wedding dresses.

Her hair was in a high ponytail, and just like that, I recalled just how much I had missed her. For the next minute, all I could do was watch her as she conversed with the attendant and inspected several dresses until, curiously, Scott's face appeared on the screen once again and obstructed my view.

"Sir," he called, and I groaned.

"Yeah?"

"Is there any way we can help?" I considered his question, and just as I was about to say no, an idea occurred to me. I turned then, glanced back at my mother's room, and told him to hold on.

When I got in, I could see her eyelashes slightly move, and I was convinced then that she was awake or perhaps just lightly sleeping. So, I headed over and placed a soft kiss on her cheek.

It took a few seconds, but eventually, she stirred, and then her beautiful, gentle eyes opened.

"Hey, baby," she said, and I smiled. It had been so long since she called me that, but it was endearing all the more to hear.

"I might need a little help from you," I said, and she nodded.

"Sure."

"Don't task yourself too hard with remembering, but do you know anything about an alternative wedding dress that Rory wanted?"

She pondered on this for a moment, and then she nodded.

"Yeah. It was the first one she agreed on when we went searching, but it was too hippie. A lot of rough-cut lace, the weirdest bows."

This amused me as I understood now why it wasn't selected.

"Well, we have a surprise wedding that we're planning for her tonight, which hopefully you'll be attending, so we want her to have the dress that she wants."

"Oh," she said, slightly surprised by this. "Really? I'll be able to get out of here that soon?"

According to the doctor, in a couple of hours, but you have to take it extremely easy for the next couple of days.

"Of course," she said. "For Aurora's sake, if not for anything else. Your father was just watching me too closely last night and this morning."

This made me extremely sad and unhappy, and she could immediately tell, as my expression turned cold.

"If you had waited and hadn't spoken out, you would be dead by now. You understand this, right?"

At my words, she stared at me, and then she sighed.

"Yes, I do. I'm just trying to not be a bother."

"You're our mom," I told her.

"Really?" She smiled again and stroked my cheek.

"I'll help out with the wedding planning as much as I can. I heard a lot of her preferences back at the beginning."

I picked up my phone once again and called Scott back, but at the last moment, I ended the call altogether and called Evelyn instead.

It took a little while since she was clearly distracted, but eventually, she answered.

"Hey," she greeted, her eyes a bit wide in surprise.

She seemed a bit confused as she peered at me, almost like the elderly, and it made me smile.

"I heard you're looking for the dress Aurora wanted in the beginning?"

"Yes," she replied, startled. And then she turned sideways to look at Scott. "Yes, I am. I think we'll find it soon, though. I didn't really remember it, but the attendant here seems to. I'm just hoping it hasn't been sold yet."

"My mom can help you," I said. "She was there on the day, right? I'll hand her the phone."

"What?" she asked, but before she could ask any further questions, I handed the phone over to my mom.

She couldn't quite hold it because she still felt too weak, so I held it at just the right angle, watching as Evelyn greeted her sweetly. She smiled in response, and then they proceeded on, coordinating the dresses.

I watched my mom's face through the process as she

spoke to her, and then eventually, they found the dress. It took another half an hour, and by then, I was gearing up to tell them to give up.

"She's pregnant, though," my mom said. "Will it fit her anymore? She's grown a bit more from earlier."

I shut my eyes at this, not wanting to imagine what I didn't want to, and pretty soon, my mom nudged me back to the present.

"We're done; next is flowers and decoration."

"Yes, right," I said and turned the phone back to look at Evelyn.

She couldn't quite meet my eyes, and I wondered if this was how she had been with my mom as well. So shy.

"Things seem to be going well," I said, and she made a face.

"I don't know; there's still so much to do, and we need to prepare the location as well. I just hope we'll be able to make it by nighttime."

"We can have the wedding late," I told her. "So don't be unnecessarily stressed and don't be in a rush. Let me know if you need any extra hands or contacts. There are a lot of staff in my company that can handle this stuff easily, you'll be able to work with them."

"Okay," she replied, and then she stared at me, her eyes glistening. My heart skipped several beats. She was so beautiful that it hurt, however, I was well aware of my mother's presence close by, so I didn't linger.

"Alright, keep me updated," I said, and the call came to an end.

Chapter Forty-Six
Evelyn

I needed a few minutes after that call to catch my breath because what the hell had that been. Every time I saw him, it was as though time seemed to stop. Suddenly, I couldn't breathe so well; I was so shy that I wanted to pee my pants, and so horny I wanted to hump the nearest surface I could find. So completely ridiculous and weak, yet as I put the phone away and returned to packaging up Aurora's wedding dress, it felt like I was floating on air. I stayed near surfaces, grabbing onto whatever I found until soon enough, we were out of the store.

We didn't need any catering of any sort, but there was this one vintage cake I had seen at a store in Brooklyn a few months earlier. I had gone looking for croissants for a believe-it-or-not croissants themed pre-wedding photo shoot and had come across the bakery. The cake was a gorgeous, small cake with pearls and the most elegant vintage swirls. It would go so perfectly with Aurora's aesthetic, I was sure.

Afterwards, we went to the florist. I was no stranger to these and had my go to vendor. It was last minute, but thankfully, I was able to order the flowers needed; a wide assortment of white roses, vines to hang off the altar and drape along the pews, dahlias, tulips, lilac orchids, and ranunculus.

I debated about red roses for a while until eventually, his assistant Scott reminded me that the budget was without limit and that I could get whatever I wanted in whatever quantity, even if it didn't work out. I was impressed and flustered at the same time but regardless I wasn't prone to waste, so I solidified my vision of how I wanted the photos to look and included it. Then I ordered candles in all sizes and in the hundreds because this had to be a magical moment. This made me also realize that I would need temporary workers, and instantly I called Anna. As a recruiter, she knew how to get these, and of course, she also, as a result, earned her invitation as well. She was so excited, especially as we headed over to her apartment to pick her up, and then it was time to head back to the Hamptons.

To my tiny bit of surprise, Scott told us that Drake had ordered us to take the helicopter. This way we could get to the church on time to get started while the rest of the supplies came over. Anna couldn't believe her eyes and was too scared to get in, so that delayed us. When she eventually gathered her nerves, though, we all boarded, and her mouth remained wide open amusingly for the length of the trip.

Midway through, she leaned forward and whispered into my ear.

"You're going to propose to him, right?" she asked, and I was startled.

"What?"

"You're not?" she asked, horrified and flabbergasted all

in one. "You're going to just walk away from all of this in two days. Thanks for the nice time. Are you insane? You really have no ambition at all? Or no vile bone in your body because I can put it there?"

"Shut the hell up," I gritted through my teeth at her, and thankfully Scott didn't hear. Or perhaps he did because he not only wasn't hiding the fact that he was watching us, he also wasn't hiding just how amused he was by how we hit and treated each other. Eventually, we arrived, and my entire plan was to avoid Aurora. It was too sad that within the next few hours, she was going to think I had abandoned her altogether and hate me even more, but I couldn't feel bad because of this. Hopefully, later on, she would understand and forgive me. Anna took her dress to my room, and then I busied myself with heading over to the church with Scott to get started. It was indeed an old church and a bit unclean, so we immediately got to work in polishing surfaces.

Soon the supplies began to arrive as well as the temporary workers for everything, and I completely lost interest in all else beyond completing this and getting it ready for the very small wedding party. This was indeed the original party that Aurora wanted, and I was so glad to be able to give it to her.

Chapter Forty-Seven
Drake

"Do you have anything special you want to wear?" I asked my mom as I took hold of her wheelchair and began to push.

She thought about this for a moment, and then she nodded.

"This might be a bit tacky but..." she turned broody to look at me and I wondered why.

"But what?"

"I still have my old wedding dress."

"You can't wear your wedding dress to Aurora's wedding, Mom," I said, and she laughed.

"No, it doesn't look like the flowing wedding dresses of today. It's more of a formal evening dress now. Off white, puffy sleeves, buttoned up. Absolutely gorgeous. I saw it the other day when I was packing for Aurora's wedding and wished that I would be able to wear it one more time."

This was all she had to say because, in the next second, I was making arrangements for us to head over to their townhouse first. She found the vintage dress in no time, and it was gorgeous, but as I watched her try it on, I couldn't help but feel sad because I knew that if it weren't for how much weight she had lost over the last few months, she probably wouldn't have been able to fit in it.

"I want to get dressed in here before we head over," she said, and I nodded. We called her stylist and makeup artist, and after taking a shower, she started on getting dressed and bringing life back to her face. I couldn't recall the last time I had seen her do this, and so I sat at the back watching. Time seemed to have completely slowed down, and I truly enjoyed the slow pace. It also once again gave me the time to think about another excited woman who had been running around the city trying to organize a last-minute wedding. I called Scott then, not wanting to interrupt her and pick up in a video call like he now knew to do.

He gave me a quick update and then turned the camera, and the first thing I noticed was what a complete mess her hair had now turned into from what it had been earlier. She was busy arranging the flowers that started all the way from the altar to the entrance. Everywhere I looked, there were flowers and candles, and it was breathtaking. The wood of the church was dark, so it made the atmosphere intimate, and the intricate drawings on the ceilings made me feel as though I was in some ancient city in Rome. All in all, I loved every bit of it and couldn't help but sigh. Because as grand as the wedding we had planned for Aurora was, this one took the cake. It was what I also imagined weddings would be. A few loved ones, rustic, intimate, unique. This scene was practically impossible to replicate, and I couldn't wait for Aurora to see it. That was if she would agree to speak to any one of us.

Afterwards, I ended the call, rejecting Scott's offer to call Evelyn over so I could talk to her, and instead, I called my dad.

"She's with her fiancé," he announced to me. He was on the patio in the golf club, enjoying the sunset with a few friends, and was in a significantly better mood than earlier. "They're not even here," he said. "I think she got too upset and just returned home. Where the hell is her temper from?"

"Be patient with her," I said. "This entire thing wasn't what she wanted. But we're about to fix that."

"David is aware, right? He'll be able to get her out on time. But what about you? Will you be there? I won't miss it for the world. I'm wearing a burgundy suit."

"Oh," I said with a smile, and he gave me an amused look.

"You?"

"Blazer... patterned."

"Just the way Rory likes it," he nodded, and I smiled.

I ended that call and returned my attention to my mom and saw her staring at me. All the life had come back to her face, and she looked so stunning.

"Was that your dad?" she asked, and I nodded as I rose to my feet.

"Did you want him to see you?"

"No," she responded. "I told him not to ask; it would be a surprise."

"No wonder," I said and pressed a kiss to her cheek. A little while after, we decided to drive over to the Hamptons rather than flying, and so we got in the car and started on our way.

Just before we arrived, I got word that they were wrapping up at the chapel, so I went with my mom to the church. I had wanted to drop her off at home, but she was expected to be barraged by Aurora upon her return, especially since she wasn't wearing funeral black but was instead in her gorgeous wedding dress.

Hence, we went straight to the church and met Evelyn in her finishing stage. She was taking photographs now as the hired workers cleaned up, and the entire place had been lit up by candles.

My mom gasped from beside me as we took it in, and my heart filled with pride. I spotted her then from the top rung of a ladder at an angle, taking what I guessed were sample shots with her camera. It was impossible for her to notice me, and so I simply informed my mom and went over. I tried to go as carefully as I could to surprise her but still ensure not to startle her.

I arrived, just as she was about to get down, and held on to the ladder to support her.

"Careful," I said, and she nodded.

"Thank you."

It took her a few seconds to realize the voice she had just heard, and then she froze.

I had to say that I loved that she wore shorts because, and since I was looking hard enough, I could see the creamy curve of her ass peeking out. She turned then, and I had a soft smile waiting for her. I could see the shock in her eyes even though she tried to play it cool, and then she returned to carefully descending.

I caught her the moment my arms could reach her sides,

and just like that, she was pulled down to slide down my body before her feet finally touched the ground.

"Hi," I greeted, and she nodded.

"Hi."

She seemed a bit unsettled and not quite standing right, so I held onto her. My arms wrapped around her, my heart so warm it was hard to breathe, and then, unable to hold back, I leaned forward and kissed her. I kissed her like I hadn't seen her in centuries when it was only a few hours, and from the corners of the space, I could hear very loud murmurs and even a cat call. She seemed startled then and tried to pull away, but when I wouldn't let her, she simply melted into the kiss.

Eventually, we pulled apart, and she stared into my eyes, and I knew then that I couldn't hold back.

"You've done a great job here," I said. And she nodded once again, breathless, unable to speak.

"Sure you don't want to go into event planning as well?" I teased her, and she smiled at this.

"No, they have to bend to their clients' every will. Here I am, bending to only how I want my photos to come out, and I love it that way."

"True," I said and kept staring at her, unable to look away. She grew shy as usual, and then she briefly turned away. She was so self-conscious about our audience that I let her go. There was plenty of time afterward to speak.

"Time to change, I guess?" I asked, and she nodded.

"Yes. I'll be going back to the house as well to change."

"I'll take you," I offered. "But I'll leave my mom here. My dad is on his way over. Granted, we should all be back with Aurora in about an hour. Mom wants to spend some time alone with him here with the candles."

"Oh," she said, concern on her face. "I think I'll stay a little while, then, to take some photos of that."

"No," I refused. "You can do that afterward. Right now, I'll say we've both had a difficult day and we both need a shower."

She nodded in agreement but didn't quite get my meaning until we were seated together in the back of my car. Suddenly she turned then and looked at me, and I could tell that she had realized what I had said.

"By shower, you meant?" I leaned forward to whisper in her ear.

"I'm going to fuck you against the glass."

Her chest heaved then as she tried to catch her breath, and I couldn't help but press a kiss to her cheek. I truly loved teasing her in this way, but I had meant what I said, and it was apparent that she believed me because when we arrived, her knees were quite wobbly as she got out of the car. Only holding onto the handle and later holding onto me saved her as I hurried around to her side.

She held onto me then as she walked upstairs, and I walked with her to my room.

When we got to the bottom of the staircase, however, Aurora, who seemed to have just been informed of my return, hurried over to the top of the stairs and stared in shock at the both of us. It was obvious that she was confused and furious, especially when she saw the way I held on to Evelyn after ignoring her. Evelyn immediately moved away from me, and despite my resolution to prevent this, I eventually had to let go so she wouldn't feel too uncomfortable.

"Really?" Aurora asked. "You blew off an entire day of the wedding you arranged for to go frolicking with your new girlfriend?"

I was immediately irritated with her complaints. Evelyn, on the other hand, lowered her head, and I could tell she felt bad. I was glad, though, that Aurora wasn't attacking her directly and understood that she wasn't doing so and was instead trying to pin all of the blame on me because she still really liked Evelyn. This confused me, but I could tell that Evelyn was still quite upset. It made me feel bad because I knew just how hard she had been working for Aurora, and I also knew that all of this was my fault.

"Where's David?" I asked; however, she didn't respond. She glared at the both of us, and I could see the sheen of moisture in her eyes as she turned around and stormed off.

Chapter Forty-Eight
Evelyn

The past couple of days felt as though a lifetime had passed. All at once, it was as though it had gone quickly yet too slowly at the same time. This moment, especially, was slow. As I stood at the bottom of the staircase with Drake by my side, I was torn between wanting to go after Aurora to give her a hug and wanting to slap some sense into her. All in all, I was so exhausted and generally too affected by Drake's presence to even correctly ascertain how I felt. So, all I could do was sigh and focus on putting one foot in front of the other. I needed lights and a quick charge of my current batteries before the next hour elapsed, so I turned toward him to excuse myself.

"I'll go get ready," I said, completely forgetting about what he had insinuated earlier.

He let me go, though, and it was only when I was nearly halfway up that I remembered. I turned to him then, my cheeks flushing, and he smiled as though he could completely read my mind.

"After," he said. "We'll have all the time we need then."

He was absolutely right. I didn't want to seem too eager, but it was extremely difficult to do when there was a man like that standing at the base of the stairs and looking at me in that way. All of a sudden, I was heady once again, and had to hold on to the railing. Soon, I arrived back in my room and received a call about updates from the current preparations being made.

"Almost done," her text read. "We're cleaning up now."

I sighed happily and lightheartedly but still nervous as hell because what if Aurora hated this as well. I truly hoped it would cheer her up, but unless they fully explained to her the health challenge her mom was facing, a corner of her heart would continue to hold this resentment toward them for their seemingly disregard for everything she wants for the ceremony, and this couldn't be farther from the truth.

I had been sweaty and gross all day, yet I had very limited time, so I quickly took a shower and wondered how Aurora's fiancé was going to get her to come down to the church. Perhaps it would be easy to ask her to elope, kind of, with him as a surprise? I wondered if Drake had already handled it because I'd been so busy getting the place ready, I'd basically ignored this very basic need.

I sped through my shower, and as soon as I got out, wrapped myself in a towel and called him.

"Hello," I greeted politely as he answered. I sounded kind of distant and stiff, but I didn't yet know how to be casual with him.

"Hello," he replied back, and I was sure he was mocking me.

I smiled, albeit weakly, and proceeded to ask my question.

"Is it planned out how David would get Aurora to the church? They should be headed over now."

"I was just thinking about it," he replied. "She is in an extremely sour mood right now, so the only person she will listen to is him."

"I'll call him now and arrange it. She should have already had the dress on, right?"

"Preferably," I replied.

"Alright, I'll keep it simple and tell him to dress up in a suit, go to her, and tell her that he got the dress she liked. That he wanted to at least give her the wedding of her dreams, so they should ride together to the church and do it secretly, without anyone else knowing."

"She'll agree to this?" I asked, seeing no problem with this but enjoying the banter between us. My entire body and mind felt stimulated, and I just wanted it to go on.

"Hopefully she'll agree to it, but he's our best shot. I'm not going to bother about it anyway because we've all done the hard work. This is his only task, and if he's a damn good lawyer, as everyone says, then he should be able to handle this."

Shaking my head, I couldn't help but smile. He was so sassy and cute, and I just adored it.

"Alright," I said then and tried to hang up the call, but he stopped me with more conversation.

"Are you ready?" he asked just as I stood before the mirror and pulled the towels from my hair and body.

I couldn't believe he had touched me so intimately in every single place.

"You?" I asked as I grabbed my breast and shut my eyes, imagining it was him. I truly couldn't wait till tonight because he had promised me that he'd take me apart in the shower, and I honestly couldn't wait.

"Almost. Would have been faster but I kept thinking about you in there."

"Maybe we should have just fucked then. Would have definitely sped me up."

This made me smile. I should have just shied away, but I wanted to start cranking up the heat for our later evening plans.

"What exactly did you do? A-as you thought of me, I mean."

The stuttering ruined it, so it couldn't be sexy. I sighed then and shook my head at just how unnecessarily fidgeting I was.

"I rubbed it out," he replied matter of factly. "Twice. The glass in my stall is fucking stained."

My heart stuttered.

"That much?"

"It would have flooded your mouth."

"Fuck," I cursed, startling us both. We both went quiet for a while, and then I started to apologize.

"Uh- sorry about that." I said, and then burst out laughing.

"Meet me downstairs soon," he said. "I'll be waiting with a car. Thirty minutes, okay?"

I nodded immediately and reluctantly ended the call.

Chapter Forty-Nine
Drake

She was running a bit late, but it was okay since I knew she would be heading out anytime soon. I wanted to call her just to hear her voice, but I didn't want to put unnecessary pressure on her, so I waited. I was soon rewarded because barely thirty seconds later, she was bounding down the stairs. She had a pair of heels on, but they weren't too high, so I guess this was how she could head over so speedily. She slowed down, though, when she finally noticed me and then began to walk normally. I was almost amused. I would have been, but I couldn't account for how breathtaking she looked.

I was standing, waiting for her at the base of the stairs, conversing with Scott. There had been no reason for me to wait but I did. In a way, tonight seemed like our first date. Even though it was going to be Aurora's wedding, but as I perused my outfit – a gleaming white shirt and polished shoes. I wasn't going to let this magical evening go to waste.

She had on a silk waistcoat along with matching shirt, and then a string of pearls draped around her slim neck.

Her hair was pulled back and ordered accordingly, and although her makeup was light, her lips were so red and gorgeous that I nearly swore to myself. Kissing them was the first thing I'd do after she came within reach. But because there were people passing all about and coming to say hello, I kept my hands to myself and controlled my impulse. She arrived, and I gave her a look before giving attention to the man who had just approached me. He was a guest staying in the mansion, but there was a little catering out back that they were hoping the main family could come join soon.

Aurora still hadn't left, but in a few minutes, and according to David, he would be able to get her to leave. As soon as I got the text message from him, I turned to Scott to give him the signal. He headed back to the car he had driven over with and retrieved her dress. One of the housekeepers showed him to her room where he would hand it over to David.

"I'll be back soon," I told the man after confirming that I had been absent because there had been urgent business matters in the city to attend to. I turned around then and, without thinking, extended my hand. I realized at that moment what I had just done, but before I could retract it, a warm, slender hand took hold of it and brought herself along to my side. My heart pitter-pattered in my chest, but I managed to keep myself calm. I stared briefly at her and together we walked out of the house. While Scott drove, we sat together in the back quietly. She had a huge camera bag with her, and midway through, she started to bring out her equipment, checking it, changing memory cards, cleaning the screen.

I watched her work, and although there was nothing

inherently fascinating about cameras to me, watching her be so technical about it drew me to her even closer in a way that I couldn't explain.

"Maybe you could take some of us later on," I leaned forward to say before I could stop myself.

"What do you mean?" she asked softly as she looked up at me.

"I'd love to have one of you sprawled out on my sheets."

She gawked at me just as I knew she would, wide-eyed and blushing so hard it was almost comical. And then she returned her attention to her devices and eventually put them away.

A few minutes afterward, however, she leaned over and whispered to me.

"Maybe, but my services aren't free. We can discuss payment afterward."

I laughed aloud then, and it startled Scott. However, I ignored him, and I leaned over to kiss her.

Chapter Fifty
Evelyn

I needed to avoid him. Because if I didn't, then at some point, I was bound to completely lose strength in my legs and crash to the floor like a pile of dropped dishes. I was carrying equipment with me, and this entire ceremony banked on my ability to capture the magic of it, and I could not mess up.

As soon as he broke the kiss, because I didn't have the good sense or discipline to do so, I moved away and found my way over to Anna. She had been watching as well as the few workers that remained, and I was torn between feeling extremely special for being so intimate with him and yet embarrassed at the same time, especially when I recalled that his family was here.

I immediately started to look around, but she shook her head and allayed my worries.

"They're not in here. They're outside talking and waiting while you're in here mouth-fucking their son."

"Hey!" I smacked her, and she bore the attack against her.

"We've been waiting forever," she groaned ever impatient. "Where's our bratty bride?"

"She's not bratty," I immediately came to her defense. "She's pregnant and she's stressed, and she knows her family is hiding things from her, but she has no way to find out. I'd be constantly in a bad mood too if I were her."

"Plus, there's the fact that the personal photographer she hired has now shifted alliances and is more focused on frolicking with her brother between the sheets than her wedding."

I sighed then and moved away from her, needing to avoid the taunting and negativity.

"Just stay out of the way and hold my step ladders for me," I groaned, and she blushed.

"How can I hold the ladders if you want me to stay away?"

I shook my head then and began to set up the lights I had brought in earlier. I wanted the entire space to be fully lit by the candles, but some of the bulbs of the church were indeed dead, so it completely depended on the light in certain places I wanted illuminated. This is why I had brought in some warm lights and had to ensure that it was all ready. We had twenty minutes now or even less, and I was excited.

I couldn't wait for her to see it. Eventually, I ushered all the workers out, and Scott directed them over to the house to get some dinner. And it was at that last crucial moment that we realized that we had missed possibly the most important and fundamental aspect of a wedding ceremony. We had no fucking priest or minister.

The second I realized this, my face dropped, and then I

turned to Anna in shock. She was stuffing some pastries into her mouth but immediately hurried over when she saw the worry on my face.

"What is it?" she asked, and I nearly cried.

"We don't have a minister."

"Oh shit. You need that, don't you? What about the rings as well?"

"Shit, I need to tell David to bring those as well."

I handed my camera over to her then and hurried over to Drake's side. He, I realized, was speaking with his father, so even though I quickly wanted to tell him these issues, I had to take a few seconds first to properly greet his dad.

"You've done a wonderful job here," he said, and I nodded in gratitude.

"Thank you."

"No, thank you," he held my hand and kissed it. I was a bit flustered also because of how much they looked alike. It was almost uncanny but wonderful to see in the best of ways. Afterwards, I turned to Drake, and it was a few seconds later before I could remember what I had come over for. He did that to me with his eyes and the slight smile curving the corners of his lips. I always felt so welcome and special in his gaze, and it almost made me sad because I knew that sooner or later, this was bound to come to an end.

"We need the rings from David," I told him.

"What rings?" he asked.

"Their wedding rings. The ones she planned to use on her wedding day. They can take them off after tonight if they want to, but they for sure need them for tonight."

"Alright," he replied and pulled out his phone. "I'm sure he's already bringing them along, but just in case he forgot."

"Yes," I replied and watched him for a moment as he sent the message. Afterwards, as he looked down to gaze at me, I couldn't help but be startled because finally, I noticed the slight smudge of red on the corner of his lips.

"Oh shit."

My eyes slightly widened as I stared at it, and to my surprise, his father by my side didn't hide his amusement.

"You see it as well?" he asked, and I turned to him.

"What?"

His eyes pointed to his lips.

"You, I see are the source. That's why I didn't bother asking because I knew that sooner or later the truth would come out."

Drake looked at the both of us, wondering what we were yapping on about, and then he sent the message. Afterwards, he turned to look at me once again, and I so badly wanted to reach out and wipe the red lipstick stain off his mouth, but this, of course, would be much too obvious and frankly embarrassing. I needed his father to leave immediately, and since I didn't want to drag him away to take care of this, I decided to just completely resolve the issue of the missing minister.

For once, and as I mentioned it, he didn't have a solution for me. His father, however, seemed to perk up even then.

"A minister?" he asked, "Ordained to officiate weddings? My son needs to know we have one right here."

"Who?" I asked, feeling my heart swell up with hope.

"You're looking at him," he said, and it still took me a few more seconds to comprehend. Afterwards, though, I realized that he was talking about himself.

"Oh!" I exclaimed. "Oh, that's awesome."

"Indeed it is," he replied. "I'll also be officiating for them in main wedding as well."

"No, Dad," Drake corrected. "This is the main wedding," he said, "The wedding tomorrow, will just be some giant reception."

"Oh really?" He laughed, and Drake nodded.

"You'll see the difference with Aurora. She can never hide her feelings and expressions."

We shared a little laugh in unison, and just then, his mother came over to join us. She looked so beautiful; it was almost scary, making it even harder to believe that she had been so seriously ill all day, or for that matter, that she possibly had a terminal illness. Maybe I was wrong, and all of this was just my nonsensical assumption, so I did my best to lock my curiosity away. A corner of my mind had been itching to ask all day long, but now I was certain that it would be utterly inappropriate. It also felt, as they conversed as a family, that it was inappropriate to just stand in their midst, so I quickly excused myself and returned back to Anna and my camera.

"You fit right in," she said. "Guess all the money spent on your wardrobe wasn't wasted."

"Are you kidding me?" I asked as I retrieved my camera. "If I had known I would be this involved with them, I would have spent even more. I feel like a peasant every time I'm in their presence".

"That's because you know how little you spent on your outfit. The trick is to understand that they don't know. In my eyes now, for instance, you look sophisticated and chic and very expensive."

"Well, these pearls were my mom's and they weren't cheap, so…"

"Exactly. It draws all the attention. Anyways, where's the blushing bride? Or, as I have heard, the bratty bride."

"She's not a brat," I defended her. "Leave her alone."

"Of course you'd say that," she said as I rose to my feet and turned around to watch the little family conversing with smiles on their faces.

"Of course you'd say that," Anna said. "She basically introduced you to your fiancé."

I sighed, then gave her a harsh look, and continued on my way.

"Please don't spout off nonsense when more people are there. You're going to fucking get me in trouble."

"I'll be careful," she said, but I wasn't relieved.

"Can you just not say anything at all?" I asked, and she cackled.

"Impossible. I'm here to torment you; it's my way of blowing off steam from my own complicated and extremely disappointing life."

Shaking my head, I moved away and caught the shot I wanted. I noticed through it how both men looked at their wife and mother. Their gaze on her was also affectionate, and they huddled so closely to her as though scared that she would fall but ready to catch her either way. It was so endearing and made my heart go soft. I took a few more shots of them from different angles and then went ahead to the top pew on the top stairs to take some of the entire location. I decided then that I would just stay there until Aurora arrived.

Chapter Fifty-One
Drake

I loved listening to my parents' recollections of their own wedding ceremony and everything that had gone wrong. I had heard it multiple times over the past few years since I was a kid, but they loved to repeat it, and I had to listen. I had minimal complaints now anyway because I was just so grateful that rather than mourning at her bedside this evening, she was back on her feet and talking to us. They had given her a few months left to live, but I was praying to extend that out for as long as possible and determined to cherish every moment, regardless of how it could possibly be the last. If she didn't live with my dad, and he didn't need her more than anyone else for companionship, then I would have moved her in with me.

This was why I had been so looking forward to this trip. The time away from work, and from being constantly called on or stuck in meetings, and the time to spend with her and family. What I hadn't expected whatsoever to gain was one more especially intimate interest. I tried to ignore it for the time being so that she wouldn't feel uncomfortable. My parents were watching my every move, I was aware, curious out of their minds as usual, but of course, I couldn't control myself. I watched as she took our pictures from time to time and as she went around the small church taking pictures. Then eventually, she disappeared up the wooden steps to the small space above. There were only a few pews there, but I could see who it was for, what she was doing. It was to give her the view of the entire hall that she wanted. It was all truly heart-wrenchingly beautiful. The candles were all flickering; the space was warm and cool, and the flowers were just divine. They had truly spared no expense on it, and I was in a moment I wanted to remember.

"Anyone we want to invite over?" I asked as I pulled out my phone to check up with our bride and groom of the hour, who were now severely late and making us all wait unnecessarily long.

"Nope, this is just as Aurora wanted: immediate family and friends."

"Her friends have arrived," I informed them as I placed the call to my ears. I didn't want to text him any longer in case Aurora just happened to be in the vicinity of his phone. She was sure to see perhaps what she shouldn't and mess up the whole thing. It was the last thing I wanted, so I wasn't taking any chances.

David picked up, and at the sigh he sent me, rather than a hello, I was sure there were already problems. Before it slipped my mind, I asked about additional guests.

"Are Rory's friends in now?" I asked.

"A few arrived today, but they're not very close. The closest ones will be here tomorrow."

"Oh, I guess they'll miss tonight's festivities then,"

"It's okay," he replied, and I nodded.

"Where are you both now? The candles are dying out. They've been burning for the last half an hour."

"They are endless?" he asked and I nodded.

"Hundreds. Please hurry up."

"She's in the bathroom. She doesn't feel very well. I think she might have eaten something that made her nauseous or it's the baby. I really don't know, and if I rush her too much, she knows me too much. She'll suspect that something is wrong."

I sighed.

"At this point, I really don't mind if she suspects that something is wrong. I just really need you to get cleaned up. Say you're running late for a special date or something and that you have reservations."

"We'll be there," he said. "I'll get her there now."

"Please do," I replied, and the call came to an end.

I kept covering then, waiting for his message and wishing that I could also take the time to converse with Evelyn. But she was in work mode now, and I knew that she wouldn't allow any distractions whatsoever. My parents, however, I had something to discuss with.

I eyed them for a little while, wondering if this was even necessary to say at all. But we had time to kill, and since Evelyn was here as well, I really didn't want to hold back.

"What do you both think about me finally getting a girl-friend?" I asked.

They had been conversing heartily about a few friends from the past that they had met again because of this event, but as soon as the words left my mouth, they both turned to give me peculiar looks.

"Just a girlfriend?" my mom asked, and I was truly perplexed by her words. "What do you mean by just a girlfriend? It better be more than just a girlfriend this time around," she said, and I smiled.

"Girlfriend is always a safe start, Mom, trust me."

"I approve," my dad said. "She seems lovely."

"She is," I replied and tried to search for said lovely woman, but once again she was nowhere to be found.

"Have you told her yet?" my mom asked. "That you'd like to take this little fling of yours further?"

"No, not yet," I replied. "Hopefully, she doesn't reject me."

"Why would she?" my mom asked, genuinely confused. "Did you misbehave?"

"Oh, come on, Mom."

"A man of your caliber," she said. "I know women don't expect much from you lots."

"I haven't dated anyone in years. Trust me, if I was that out of control, I would have."

"You're right," she said. "Alright, I look forward to seeing more of her around then."

"Hopefully," I said as my gaze lowered to the message that had just arrived on my phone. "If she rejects me, I'll send her to you for some winning over, so don't let me down, alright?"

"Jesus, you must really like her if you're even willing for me to talk her into it if she does reject you."

I smiled at this but didn't respond. My whole heart, however, radiated in its agreement to this statement because she was right. I was somewhat nervous because I deeply liked her a lot.

"Aurora's here," I announced, and my parents' faces instantly lit up.

"Thank God," my father said. 'Finally. The candles are dying out. It took forever to light them up."

"Uh oh," I said after I read the rest of the messages. "She's angry. She refused to wear the dress."

"Classic," my mother smiled.

"Luckily, David brought it along, though."

"Well, nothing in life is perfect. She'll hurry to change. It's her fault."

I shrugged and then I called Evelyn.

"She's here," I replied.

"I know," she smiled. "She's in jeans. I'll get some shots from the top, and then I'll hurry down."

"Alright," I said and put the phone away.

I started out of the way, and a few seconds later, just as we had discussed, at my signal the huge double doors opened to reveal the ceremony. I watched as Aurora appeared with David's hands over her eyes and then eventually, after whining, she stopped and doubled back.

"I'm not in the mood," she said softly. "And this place smells funny."

He removed his hands, and it took a while for her eyes to stop adjusting to all the light. And then the moment she realized what this was, she screamed.

We were meant to remain silent for a while longer, but we were all so startled that we froze in place for a while. And then we erupted into laughter. She was even more startled at the additional voices and screamed again as she turned to take us all in, hiding in the shadows.

"Oh my God!" Her hand slapped against her mouth.

Slowly, and as my mom headed over to hug her, she began to understand what was going on, and just like that, tears fell down her eyes.

"Oh my God! Was this what you were planning all day?"

"Not exactly," I thought to myself, but she didn't need to know that.

"Evelyn put it all together," I told her, and she turned to the opposite direction then to see the photographer clicking away.

"Oh my God!" she screamed and headed over to her. Evelyn, poor girl, took as many pictures of her approaching, coming for a hug, before she was ambushed and nearly sent to the floor.

"I'm sorry," she said, and Evelyn shook her head, holding her tight.

"It's alright."

"Thank you so much!"

"For nothing."

"Oh my God," she stopped then and looked around, and the light in her eyes was like a thousand lights.

She turned toward her fiancé then and jumped into his arms.

They were like this, seemingly forever until he pulled away and said something to her.

She screamed once again, and together they hurried out. She was obviously going to change into her wedding dress, and at this, we all heaved a sigh of relief.

"She sure does scream a lot," my dad's finger went to his ears to scratch it, and we all shared a laugh.

Evelyn hurried out then to get more pictures, but just

before she went past, my hand curved around her waist and stopped her. I kissed her once again, needing the taste of her tongue on mine and the camera nearly dropped from her hands. Thankfully, I caught it in time, much to the amusement of everyone else. She seemed so betrayed that I had made her so weak again, but then she seemed to realize something, and so she reached out and with her fingers, cleaned my lips.

"You've had red lipstick on them all evening," she said, and my eyes widened in shock.

It was the perfect revenge after which she hurried away before I could hold her accountable for that crime.

I did, however, return to my parents then, who were equally responsible and unrepentant.

Sighing, I shook my head and joined them in waiting for Aurora's arrival.

Chapter Fifty-Two
Evelyn

I almost couldn't sleep that night. From the second we'd returned to back to the house, I'd been so struck by how the ceremony had turned out that everything had seemed as though it had been planned for months. From the smiles to the people. I was in awe, and so enchanted, and it filled me up with an excitement that I could not quite contain.

Therefore, I wasn't quite ready to go to bed, which was why when Anna instantly took over the bathroom and the bathtub, I didn't throw a fit. Rather, I went straight to my laptop, needing to see the photos that I took. There were so many of them. Still, I was just too excited to see how they would turn out, so I sat at the desk and began to scroll through.

Yes, I did, in fact, take them myself. However, there was no contest here that I had outdone myself. This had to be my best work thus far, and yes, I had always put love and whole dedication into every project I had handled so far, but this one was personal. Somewhere along the line,

Aurora had become the little sister I cared immensely about, even though we were roughly around the same age, and Drake...

I sighed.

The one person that made me feel like I was walking on clouds. Their parents had more or less become friends, and Aurora's fiancé, a very close acquaintance. The ceremony tonight had been solely for immediate family, and I had been there. The only person who had felt like an outsider to me was Anna, and that was because she had insisted on helping out. Still, no one minded because the atmosphere was filled with the kind of magic that you only really felt when you were with the people that you knew loved you the most.

I looked at pictures of her mom smiling and watching as the couple exchanged their vows, at Aurora's eyes glistening with tears and looking absolutely divine in her wedding dress, of her father nearly choking up as he watched the couple, and of Drake looking as calm as ever but constantly looking toward my direction.

In short, he had been the major risk to my inability to perform properly tonight because every time he watched Aurora and her fiancé in their special moment, he turned around to me, and my camera caught his expression. It was still as serious as usual, but the smile curving the corners of his lips and the affection in his eyes for me was impossible not to note.

After a while, I avoided direct shots with him altogether until eventually, I had had shots farther away, adapting the entire space. Everything was so magical, and if it wouldn't look so tacky, I was almost tempted to include photoshopped butterflies in the scenes. I decided then that I was going to do this for some of them. I really didn't care, truly, because this was my ultimate work, and I was so proud of it I wanted to cry.

And suddenly, it made me understand and accept the importance of budget. With prior wedding photoshoots, we had more or less had to scrimp and save most of the time since very few were comfortable enough to organize it the exact way they wanted. But this time around, the location had been perfect, the candles and flowers ethereal... it almost in some ways felt like a painting from three hundred years earlier.

Sighing, I kept scrolling, and not until a drop of water fell on the table next to me did I realize that something was wrong and someone was intruding. I looked up then, and my head nearly bumped into Anna. She had just come out of the bathroom and was looking so clean and flushed. Her hair, however, was still somewhat dripping wet because it had almost destroyed my motherboard.

"Please stay away," I told her.

At first, she seemed as though she wanted to argue with me, probably thinking I was hiding the photos from her or something, but ultimately, she finally noticed the water and profusely apologized.

"Sorry," she said and stepped backward to prevent the incident from recurring. I smiled then and returned my attention to the screen.

"Wonderful night," she said, and I nodded.

"Absolutely perfect. I can't wait to work on these photos."

She went silent for a little while and then she spoke. It

should have been easy to ignore her, but the words that came out of her mouth were quite disconcerting indeed.

"Drake really couldn't take his eyes off you."

I had already noted this, thank her very much. I tried to ignore her, but then she spoke again.

"Do you think if you asked, he would tell you what is wrong with his mother?"

This made me stop because, although I had been quietly plagued with suspicions earlier about what was wrong with her, I still did not quite have the courage to pry. It was information that I had decided I would only get if he told me, not by me asking. I sighed deeply as I stared at the gorgeous woman and hoped with all my heart that she would get better.

Now, as for Drake... and as the excitement was beginning to calm down, it also brought a lot of memories made for later that night. We were both exhausted, him especially. I was certain from the emotional turmoil of the day, so the last thing I wanted to do was bother him.

But then, as I looked behind and saw Anna getting ready for bed, I had to admit that it was a waste to spend the night with her and not him. I could imagine it just like it had been the previous evening. Even if we didn't have sex, I wouldn't care. Just wrapped in the warmth of his arms, feeling every inch of his body, under the dim light, the tall blinds open before us, and allowing in the picturesque view of the grounds. My mouth hung open in breathlessness.

"What's wrong?" Anna suddenly asked, and I snapped out of my reverie.

"What?" I asked, straightening up, though I most definitely didn't forget to change the gorgeous portrait of Drake on my computer screen.

"Oh... I see it," she smiled, and I got up, blushing.

"How have things been between you two?"

I wondered how to answer this, but when my reluctance to go to the shower alone grew as I picked up my towel, I decided that somehow, I needed a push. Hopefully, Anna would catch the hint because I wasn't about to outrightly say it.

"I slept in his room last night."

She went briefly silent. However, just before I disappeared into the bathroom, she stopped me.

"Hold it right there, Miss," she said. "That's quite a thing to announce and then leave."

This amused me.

"It's not an announcement; it just happened."

"Till when?" she asked, and I was taken aback.

"What do you mean, 'till when'?"

"Till what time?"

"Does it matter?"

"Yes, it does. Before the crack of dawn, and he really didn't want you there. At dawn, he fell asleep; you tired him out. But now it's time to go; after that, honey... he never wants you to leave."

Once again, my chest was heating up dangerously.

"Which was it?" she asked impatiently.

"Well, we didn't leave till he got the call about his mother."

"And what time was that?"

"About 10 am," I replied, and her mouth fell open. I tried my very best not to show how I was affected by this, but in the end, I couldn't fight off the smile on my face. And then she said exactly what I wanted to hear.

"What the heck are you doing here now?"

I wanted to deny it but stopped myself and sighed.

"He must be tired," I said, but she brushed that away.

"And so are you. What the heck? Go to him, sleep together. You can wake up in the middle of the night refreshed and get busy. But now it's a really vulnerable and emotional time for you both given all that happened this morning and the subsequent exhaustion. Girl, please get the hell out of here."

She returned her attention to drying her hair with a towel while I narrowed my gaze at her.

"Sure you're not just trying to get rid of me so you can have the room to yourself?"

"Maybe I am," she said, and my face fell.

"Evelyn," she called. "I know you, so I know you wouldn't bring that up and stare at his picture so thirstily through the screen if you didn't want to go."

"Wait, what? Go? I'm going there?"

She seemed genuinely confused.

"How else are you expected to get to him?"

"Well, I was going to send him a text to see if he was up for it. And if he didn't see it? Maybe he is exhausted and passed out on his couch in his dress clothes?"

"If that's the case, then why go to him at all?"

I turned then and went to grab my phone.

"A text will do."

"No, it absolutely will not," she replied. "Go get something from the kitchen. Some tea? A snack. You're obviously not a stranger to his bedroom, so knock quietly on the door.

Ask if he wants something. You were thinking of him and made him a beverage to calm down his nerves from all the stress and excitement of the day. Wonderful reason. By the way, if he doesn't want you to come in, he'll thank you and accept the tea either way to be polite."

"Hopefully," I added, and she paused.

"Hopefully? Is he an asshole? Because this won't work on assholes."

"No, he's not," I replied, and she nodded.

"So worst comes to worst, as I was saying, he accepts the tea and tells you goodnight. But then because you brought something that was reviving, no foul would have been made. And you can come right here and inconvenience me, but what's new? I guess."

I gave her a look but had to admit that I agreed with her. I also knew that if I delayed any further, I would definitely change my mind. So, I turned; however, before I could reach for the table, she had already sprinted over and grabbed my phone.

"Anna!"

"No phones," she replied. "Tell him you forgot it or else you would have texted."

"That's so inauthentic. Who forgets their phone? He's not an idiot; he'll see right through that."

"My point is for you to be a tad bit spontaneous."

I sighed again as I considered her words one more time, and then eventually, I made my decision. I hurried out of the room and didn't turn back lest I turn to salt. When I, however, got into the very quiet hallway, giving the indicator that the whole house had gone to sleep like people with common sense, I found myself wandering about. I did an about-face and returned back to the room. I knocked, and then jerked the door open, but suddenly, my door was shut as well, and Anna wasn't responding.

I had several insults come to mind of how I wanted to threaten her, but at the moment, I knew her enough to know that it would be no use. She was not afraid of offending anyone, especially not me; she was practically a family member. So, she was going to banish me to sleeping right there in this hallway if I didn't do as we had discussed.

Filled with dread, I found my way down the stairs to the kitchen and found an assortment of teas in the corner. There, I quickly grabbed some chamomile and brewed him some tea. I brewed myself a cup as well, put them both on a small tray, and started to carefully head back up the stairs.

Eventually, I arrived, and it felt as though my heart was about to leave my chest. I considered knocking, staring at that door for five minutes straight, and with every passing moment, my resolve was weakening. Eventually, and when I couldn't take it anymore nor muster up the courage, I turned around to leave.

There was no need to be imposing right now. We'd see each other again the next day and then at the wedding. There was plenty of time, and I truly didn't have to rush things. I had barely taken four steps to leave; however, when the door was suddenly pulled open. I instantly froze, wondering how Drake knew that I had been standing in front of his door.

"Evelyn," he called.

I couldn't avoid him any longer. What was the point when I truly wanted to see him? The only issue was the fact that I liked him so much that I became quite nervous around him, which was frankly just annoyingly embarrassing. But now there was no point in being embarrassed. I was there and I had chamomile tea, and I wanted to be invited in.

"How did you know I was out here?" I managed to muster up a smile.

He returned it; however, I could see the exhaustion crinkling the corners of his eyes.

"I have the surveillance footage on my screen," he said, and my eyebrows raised.

"I'm more or less in charge of the family, so I have to ensure that everything is as it should be."

God, could he get more competent and attractive? I was close to hyperventilating.

"Well, I brought you some tea, and I'm... it's been a very hectic day, so as I got one for myself, I had to bring you one as—oh, I've already said that."

He was amused at this and opened the door even wider so that I could come in. At this, I was so relieved that my hands slightly shook, and instead, he took the tray of tea from me.

"Have you showered?" he asked, and my heart rate picked up. This man was seriously dangerous, and so was my memory.

"Not yet," I replied. "I was going over the photos from tonight. They're breathtaking."

"They must be," he said. "You did a fabulous job."

I blushed once again, and then he came up to me, and without hesitation, he kissed me. I sighed into his mouth and melted into the kiss. It seemed too fast and yet too soon when he eventually leaned away.

"So, how about my earlier proposition?" he asked.

I knew exactly what he was talking about, but for some reason, I needed him to talk a bit more, perhaps so that I could gain my bearings.

He had no problems whatsoever repeating himself. This time, however, there was a little twist.

"Earlier, I just... the only thing I've been able to think about was fucking you in that stall. But after this evening, after everything, what I want... I want to do more than that. So... we start in the shower and go right to the bed. I want to make love to you. I hope you'll spend the night."

I was shaken, and I knew then that I had to say what was needed before things got too far, before I was pulled in so deep that I lost myself.

"This is... this is more intimate than I could have ever imagined, than I would have expected. I like you a lot more than I would have expected."

He stared at me, and then he nodded.

"I understand. I feel the same way. Afterwards, after this ceremony is over, I want to keep seeing you. Like this."

Well, this I absolutely didn't expect. If the terms of this agreement stretched on, I was going to be in deep shit sooner or later. But the end of it, I was sure I was going to be left completely in pieces, and I couldn't take that risk. Better to cut it off now and somewhat recover since I could see the end.

"No," I replied, and his face was overcome with worry.

"Why no?" he frowned.

"I... I'm going to get hurt when this thing ends later on. If we extend it, I mean. I... it's too easy to fall in love with you. It's not something I wanted to consider earlier, but now... I think it's already happening so—"

I sped through that admission and looked away.

"I'm not asking for anything; I just... I'm trying to protect myself."

He headed closer to me then and held me in his arms.

"What if I tell you..." he asked. "That I feel the same way."

My heart came to a dead halt in my chest.

"What?"

He nodded.

"It might be too soon to say, but I know that I'm in love with you. I'm not asking for us to go beyond this week just so that we can keep sleeping together. I want to know even more about you. Everything about you. I want our lives to melt into one, and I want to see with all my heart where this will take the both of us."

I remained shocked, and then I said a prayer of thanks to Anna. And then, because this had been a damn emotional day, tears filled my eyes and rolled down my cheeks. It's so embarrassing, yet he didn't mind. He kissed me slow and deep, and then with my hand in his, he led me over to the bathroom. In there, I watched him, unable to believe what was happening, unable to believe the point we had come to. It felt like I had just jumped off a cliff together with him, and I was never so assured. A bed of roses was sure waiting for us, and if this was not the case, then I knew as he took me in his arms once again, that I would never have any regrets.

The end

Epilogue
Evelyn

Three months later

The funeral was a somber affair, the air thick with grief as we gathered around Drake's mother's grave. Raindrops mingled with tears on the faces of the mourners. Drake stood beside me, his eyes reflecting the pain of loss, and I couldn't help but reach for his hand, offering silent support.

I had more or less become a part of their family over the past three months, and they had all welcomed me so dearly, especially Aurora, who was now truly like a sister. I can recall now the Sunday lunches, laughter in the air, Aurora's pregnancy tantrums, and their mother teasing us all. It had seemed as though it was all a fairytale that would go on forever, but now it was over. So suddenly.

It still felt unreal to me. I could still remember Drake getting the call in the middle of the night from his father. I'd never seen him so flustered and out of control. We had driven straight to the hospital, and there it had been confirmed. She had finally passed away from cirrhosis. Aurora had completely broken down. After she found out when she returned from her honeymoon, the cause of her wedding being hijacked, she had been irate, sad, and then happy, vowing to spend every single day with her mom until the end. She had done it, forcing her mother to move into her new apartment with her and David and to accompany her in her studio.

Her mother's birthday was the next week. Aurora was due the week after. We had planned it to be a celebration. This was supposed to be yet another magical month, and then this had happened. Aurora was clinging to her husband, unable to look. She had stopped crying, and so had her father. They had had ample time to expect it, but still, it had come as a cold and terrifying shock.

Drake, my love, had broken down silently in my arms, in the quiet of the night where no one could see. I had fallen more in love with him then, needing to take his pain away, but there was nothing I could do. So, I held his hand tightly reminding him that I was here and that we would be alright eventually.

Soon enough, her coffin was lowered into the grave, and we walked away. We headed back silently to their town-house for the reception. There was food, light conversation, and a few smiles here and there. Aurora was nowhere to be found, but I knew she was in her mother's room. Drake mingled with a few guests and then disappeared up the stairs as well. I gave them all the space they needed, but then eventually, when I couldn't stand it anymore, I went up to find my love.

I found him in his mother's room alone, but he seemed a

bit lighter. He didn't look up when I came in, but eventually, he did and smiled. He held out his hand, and I went over to him. Then I sat by his side, and we gazed at her memorial photo together.

"She was really looking forward to her birthday," he said, and I nodded.

"Yeah."

"It was going to be your event planning debut, well, after Aurora's wedding,"

I smiled again. "I'm only event planning for this family. I cannot handle the stress. And it's for my photos."

"I know, I know," he said and squeezed my arm just a bit tighter.

I felt inexplicably sad then as I stared into his mother's gorgeous eyes because I knew I had to hold on to my secret just a little while longer. I had been so confused and uncertain, wondering whether to tell, but now... I had to wait. It was the wrong time. But by then... it might be too unexpected? Maybe after Aurora had given birth. There would be joy once again. I could wait till then.

Just then, Drake reached into his pocket, and I shifted slightly to let him retrieve his phone.

"During her birthday dinner, we had planned something together," he said, and I was intrigued.

"Really? How come I wasn't told?" I smiled then, shaking my head as I looked at her because I knew this was just the kind of mischief that they both frequently got into against the rest of us.

I was going to miss her so dearly, but for Drake's sake, I kept my emotions at bay. He moved then, and I got up. It was time to return to the guests downstairs. However, to my surprise, he began to lower, and I turned in shock. At first, I was confused, wondering why he was on one knee, but then he produced the box, and my heart stopped. It was gorgeous and emerald and velvet, and I couldn't move.

He smiled.

"I wanted to do this in her presence," he said. "We talked about it... I really wish she had waited a bit longer."

"Oh my God," I gasped, the tears I had been doing my hardest to hold back then filling my eyes

.

"I love you, Evelyn," he told me in his soft kind voice. My gorgeous and capable man. There were no words suitable enough for me to reply with. "These three months with you have illuminated my life in a way that I cannot explain. I'll propose to you again, forgive me, but I need it to be in her presence because she loved you as well. Everyone came to truly love you, and that's who you are. You are the most gorgeous, kind, smart woman I've ever met, and I just... I don't want to wait a single moment longer. Please marry me?"

I stared at him, and the floodgates opened. The tears poured down my cheeks, and he was slightly alarmed as well as amused and sad all at once. The emotions were just too much to take in.

"Is this a no?" he asked, and I lowered to him as well. But it took a while, and I was eventually able to get myself together, and the moment I did, I told him what I needed to say because I truly couldn't wait another minute longer.

"Drake," I called, and he nodded.

"Please don't say no," he said, and I laughed out loud.

"I could. I, uh... I just have something else to say first."

He frowned immensely worried, and I couldn't torture him any longer. Holding his hand, I placed it on my still flat stomach, and although it took him a little while, it soon dawned on him what I was trying to say.

"Are you?" He went white as a sheet. "Are you fucking serious?"

"Yeah," I nodded, hoping that this would go the way I hoped.

It did. To my shock, this man whom I loved with my whole heart couldn't hold his tears back. They rolled down his face, and as I watched, I hated to see them go to waste. They were so precious, so I leaned forward and kissed them.

"Don't cry, I'm sorry."

"When were you planning to tell me?" he asked, "Why did you keep it? How long?"

"Just over two months," I replied, and he gasped.

"In the Hamptons?"

"I think so, yes."

"Oh my God!" he exclaimed. "That long..."

"I wanted to wait until Aurora had given birth."

"Jesus fucking Christ, I am tired of all the waiting we've been doing in this family. No offense, Mom," he said, and I couldn't help but smile.

"I apologize on his behalf, Mom," I said to her image, and by the time I turned, he had grabbed me and kissed me. I melted completely in his arms, and by the time we broke apart, he asked me the question once again.

"I need a very clear and resounding yes," he said. "It's a moment I want to recall over and over for the rest of my life."

I nodded and did him one better. I gave him a sentence from the very depths of my soul.

"Yes, my love, Drake Moran, I will marry you."

"I love you, Evelyn," he said.

I choked on the words but still thankfully managed to say it out. "I love you more."

The End

Coming Soon...

THE BET

Chapter 1

Guy

"You are, as always, a creature of habit."

I looked up from the steak and potatoes dinner I had been enjoying in silence and couldn't help but sigh at the woman standing over my table. Without even bothering to ask or wait for an invitation, she pulled out the chair opposite me and plopped down on it.

"I knew I'd find you here."

I kept eating as I watched her. She knew I wasn't pleased by the interruption, but she was also one of the few people at the firm who wasn't fazed by my temper or irritation.

"How is that?" she asked, referring to my plate as she set her purse down. "I've only ever had their carbonara here, and it was underwhelming, to say the least. I came here with Paul, and he complained for two weeks afterward about how overpriced food always tastes so bad."

I continued eating, and at my silence, she eventually cocked her head and looked at me.

"How mad are you that I interrupted your dinner and reflection time, which everyone knows never to interrupt you at?"

I reached for my glass of wine and took a drink. "Remind me again why I can't fire you?"

She laughed out loud, her gentle voice ringing out across the room. There was a low constant buzz of others eating and making merry as well, so no one else paid her any mind.

"Because I'm your Human Resources Officer and your former teacher. I do my job wonderfully well, but you also can't be disrespectful or dismissive of me like others because I was your favorite teacher."

Sighing because she was absolutely right, I picked up the menu and handed it over to her.

"Order the seafood pasta. It's much better than the carbonara."

"Alright," she said excitedly and slipped down her glasses. A few minutes later, the waiter was waved over, and she placed her order.

"This dinner is on you, right? You pay me well, but surely not enough to pay for this sort of place. I mean, I can, but what a waste. No plate of pasta should cost anything more than thirty dollars."

This immensely amused me, and seeing this, she and gave me a soft look.

"Alright, let's talk about it," she invited, leaning back against the chair. "Four secretaries in two months? That's problematic, and people are beginning to ask questions."

"You're making it seem like I assaulted them or something," I replied. "All I did was fire them for being so monumentally incompetent."

"Yes right, so you say, yet they all deny they made the mistakes you claim they did."

I raised an enquiring eyebrow. "So, you're saying I'm lying?"

"I'm saying you preferred Mr. Connerty, and now that he's retired and moved back to Poland, you're not even trying to give anyone else a chance to replace him. I know he's been your secretary and a paralegal for you for the last eight years, but you need to find someone else that you like, or at least learn to like. You're the biggest talent in the firm, and you need someone to manage your affairs for you; otherwise, you'll be spending your valuable time doing tasks than should be done by less qualified staff."

"Thank you for repeating all the things that I wasn't aware of," I said sarcastically, but she smiled back.

"The girl today," she said. "The one you fired. She said that she proofread the contract several times before sending it two days ago. As to why there was an extra zero missing, she has no idea how that could be possible, especially since you checked the document as well."

"So, I'm at fault?" I asked.

She sighed. "I'm just saying that I know these mistakes are monumental, but rather than fire the staff, why don't you scold them or something and give them another chance?"

"And you were told I hadn't given them other chances?" I asked. "If I didn't want to give her a chance, she would have been fired from the first day," I said. "She didn't tell you about the services bill she sent to the wrong client? We had to reduce Alchai Motor's charge when they saw how much of a discount we gave to Maxwell House."

"Yikes, you still remember that? It must have monumentally pissed you off."

"I'm guessing she didn't mention this when she came crying to you, did she? Tell me, how much incompetence should I bear before I kick them out? Should I wait till they make an error that costs the company millions? Just so that I can earn the reputation of being magnanimous and friendly?"

At this, she went quiet, and a waiter came over with her food. After smiling up at him and saying thank you, she picked up her cutlery and dove in. We both ate silently, and it was comfortable. Things were always comfortable between us, and I had always trusted her judgment of character; after all, it had been that astute judgment of character that had seen the potential in me and pushed for me not to be ignored and written off as a grad who was going absolutely nowhere apart from jail for all my blowups and the troubles I had caused in school. So far, as the firm had grown, she had also been able to recruit the best talent, but so far, all the secretaries sent over to replace the now-empty seat in front of my office had been a catastrophe.

"I'm here because we have to send someone over tomorrow, but I really don't want you to also send this person away. Can you be a little more lenient if they do make a few little mistakes?"

"I'll forever be lenient if the mistakes they make are small mistakes," I replied. "If there are huge ones that could potentially harm the firm and my business, I will indeed lose my shit."

She smiled again, shaking her head, and returned to her meal. It was then I looked out through the window at the busy Manhattan late evening sidewalk and saw her. She was just getting out of the taxi, and the first thing that caught my eye was the glistening skin of her legs. Coupled with the heels she had on, they were so long my attention was arrested long enough to see the face that those slender pair of limbs belonged to. And unsurprisingly, she was just as gorgeous as I had expected. Her hair was a dark gorgeous blonde and bouncy. The loose tendrils framed her face in a way that made me unable to look away, and when she smiled at the suited man who came up to her, then I found my breath catching in my throat. She was dressed gorgeously in a red skirt suit, and although it was as elegant as could be, especially now that she was standing straight and tall and the skirt shaped her hips and legs all the way past her knees, it was impossible to hide the gorgeous curve and appeal of her body.

The man who had come up to them held out his arms as though to embrace her, but instead, she stiffened her spine and offered her hand instead. He boldly brushed it away and instead pressed her into his chest. I saw the deep unhappiness and disgust on her face as a result. She didn't like him immediately. True to form, she tried to pull away, and after she succeeded, she was tense. I watched as she moved toward the man in a pin-striped suit, and then they both watched the one who had forced the embrace as he spoke to them both.

I'd had enough business dealings to understand the situation, especially the man in the striped suit gesturing ahead with his hand. This was a business meeting, and she was either a partner or an employee, and the man in the striped suit was her boss. This was definitely not the first time they had met, judging by how she shifted closer to her boss; she was expecting him to protect her. However, he didn't seem to even notice. As they walked, she tried her best to stay by her boss's side on the extreme end, but the client soon mentioned something, no doubt complaining about this, and to her visible shock and annoyance, the boss moved and kept her right next to the client. He smiled at her like he was looking at a piece of meat that he was ready to devour, and then they all walked into the restaurant.

"Let me know exactly what you are looking for," Gloria said just then. "Would you prefer a male secretary? But the second candidate was male, and he seemed to last even less than the other females."

"That's because women are emotionally intelligent enough to know when not to monumentally fuck up. Unlike that lanky moron."

She smiled, and then she shook her head. "Alright, well, you need a replacement, and I'll be looking externally now rather than internally. We've been sending people over from the temporary secretaries' pool I had, but we'll have to go back to the agency tonight to get someone that will suit you best, so give me your requirements now, and I can use it as a strict guide."

"For one, I know they should, of course, not be an eyesore, like you have previously stated, but now I am beginning to think you want someone that somehow looks like those heiresses you dated, and when this expectation is not met, you eventually miraculously find a way to fire them in the weeks following."

At her accusation, a very blatant one at that, I looked up and couldn't help but feel wrongly accused.

"That's not accurate," I said. "I didn't care what they looked like. I only cared how they performed."

"I believe you, but in order for everyone else to believe it, at least pick someone with experience from this file and commit to trying to be patient with them for at least the next three months."

"Gloria, I'm not committing to shit," I told her. "Pick someone capable and send them to occupy that desk. They should be the ones vigilant and afraid of messing up, not me."

At my words, she sighed and continued eating. "Will you at least look at the file? I came all the way here."

"It's fine, minutes from the office. I'm sure you needed the exercise."

I rose to my feet then, and she laughed. "I can't believe you're still the same little boy from twenty years ago."

"Creature of habit," I said as I grabbed my phone and headed over to the bathroom with it in my hand.

Chapter 2

Hannah

I truly wondered just how much more of this shit I could take. It had been three freaking months now since I had been working for this a-hole, and he hadn't hesitated at every point in time to throw me to his clients in one way or the other. At first, I was sure I was mistaken, and he just hadn't seen how some of them, especially the old geezers, tried to flirt with me, get close to me, or touch me inappropriately. In fact, he had almost encouraged it, almost as though I was some prize that they had access to taste and could get a full feel later on after whatever business deal was concluded.

I truly would have quit a long time ago, but there was something he always did, which was look the other way right until the contract was won over or the deal was concluded, and only then would he even put up a fight whatsoever for me. And since I was his only secretary, I had no choice but to be in on all these freaking meetings. It was upsetting every single day, but in all other areas, he was pretty kind and fair, except in this. And the salary, so far, was the highest I had ever gotten through the agency, and I wanted to move out of my trashy Brooklyn apartment to get a much better one with views and floors that weren't being devoured by ants and termites. Also, hallways that didn't smell like rat piss or Chinese food that didn't waft up to my bedroom at 1 am. All these were the dreams I held in mind, and so far, only the salary that this man paid me was enough to even allow me the hope to entertain any of these. It didn't mean that I wasn't still furious and growing even more miserable by the day, but I couldn't quit, not yet.

After a particularly discouraging encounter, I had a talk with myself, questioning if I could go on. I ultimately made the agreement to endure and save up for a year. Just one year, and with the experience on my resume from this top marketing agency, I could move on to the next stage. Just one year, I admonished myself, even as we were shown to our table, and I immediately hurried to try to get a seat next to the boss. However, he noted this and went immediately to the bathroom, leaving me to fend off the old shit by myself. So even when I tried to sit opposite him, he caught my hand and pulled me into the seat beside him in the booth. As soon as my butt connected to the seat, I couldn't get up, and right at that moment, I wanted to shoot him. However, all I could do was smile and pretend not to notice his arm brushing against me, and basically his entire side rubbing against me. There was more than enough space on the booth, but here he was, glued to me like Velcro, smiling and bathing me with his disgusting breath that stunk of garlic.

His lunch was still stuck in his teeth, his hair thinning, and his supposed-to-be white eyes so dull that it all made me physically sick. I brought out my phone and pretended to be busy as I replied very seriously to the text messages I was receiving from the other secretaries at the agency; there was a plan to meet up later on. Something about a fired squad, all from the same boss, and hence it was supposed to be juicy. I usually didn't attend these gatherings, but at that moment, I would have given anything whatsoever to be out of this freaking overpriced restaurant and be on my way over, or perhaps on my way home. Sighing, I replied and confirmed my attendance, and then I put the phone aside and picked up the menu again.

"What do you usually like to eat?" the man said, reaching out to brush my hair over my shoulders, and at that moment, I had truly had enough.

"Please don't touch me," I said, and the bite to my tone was unmistakable.

He seemed startled, the smile on his face immediately dissipating, and then he slightly moved away. I had gotten what I wanted, but I couldn't help but feel as though it would cost me my job instead. So, before my boss returned, I added, "It's been so hot lately, and I am yet to cool down from all the heat outside. Don't you feel hot as well?"

"I need to go to the bathroom," I said. "I'll be right back."

"Keep me company till your boss returns," he said, reaching out to catch my hand. "I'd like to hear some of your ideas on the strategy we presented back at your office. You look like someone who would have a lot of wonderful and fresh ideas."

He wasn't wrong because currently I truly had some red-hot ideas, like pouring a pot of boiling water over his head and watching him melt like a candle as a result. Instead, I smiled, wrenching my arm from his.

It took him a little while to warm back up to me but eventually, he did, and thankfully, it was just as my boss returned.

"Let's order some refreshing cold cocktails for you," he said.

"Mocktail," I replied. "I can't drink alcohol."

"You can't? Why?" he asked, and I was tempted to say that I was pregnant. I didn't, however, see how this could possibly end well for me, so I simply smiled and used that excuse to rise to my feet.

On the way, I looked at my boss and couldn't help the look of hatred I gave him. He wasn't even the least bit startled and tried to talk to me, but I ignored him without any remorse and continued on my way. As usual, I knew that he wouldn't care because when I had brought up my dissatisfaction in the past with how he handled this matter, one of his many useless, disappointing, and downright aggravating answers *was that it didn't just hurt me to be a secretary and that my looks played a big part of it. I was like honey, and I had to do my own part in catching the flies for the rest of the company.*

"You understand what I mean, right?" he'd ask then. "I won't let them into the pot; that's crossing the line. But at least let them hover. You have to be a team player."

What the fuck could I have possibly said after that?

Sighing, I looked at my reflection in the mirror and wondered what they saw in me. I usually dressed femininely before I came to work for this bastard, but lately, I found myself covering up more and more. The only thing left for me now was to constantly wear a necktie to cover up my chest completely, and even that didn't seem useful.

"Fucking dogs," I cursed as I turned on the faucet, and the woman beside me gave me a sympathetic look through our reflection in the mirror. I smiled back, and somehow this seemed to calm me down. I didn't want to use the toilet, so I particularly took my time washing my hands until I had no choice but to shut the tap off and take another ten or so minutes to dry my hands.

I had purposely left my phone on the table so there was no urgency to return, even though I knew the boss needed me there, but that was the price I had to pay for being fed to the wolves. I regretted it, though, as I got out of the bathroom and stood in a corner, dreading returning. This was the perfect time now to call Mandy to catch up on some chatting. We had been so busy the past week preparing this proposal that I had all but ignored all my personal contacts, and so now was the perfect time to hit her up to while away time.

Since there was no way, I leaned against a console containing the most gorgeous bouquet of flowers and lost myself gazing at it. Therefore, when my distracted self was finally able to note the presence looming over me, my heart nearly stopped in my chest. I was so startled and scared I had to crouch down to endure the blow of fear, and by the time I straightened once again to see who had suddenly approached, I was ready to scream their freaking ears off.

But when I saw just how handsome the man standing by my side was, my tongue was instantly tied. It was almost embarrassing, to be honest, but after I took in his gorgeous face and tousled dark hair, I wasn't too hard on myself for the way I had reacted. Now if this was the geezer that was trying to touch and feel me up at every point in time during the meetings, I didn't think I would have any problem with it whatsoever.

"Did I startle you?" he asked.

I had a very long and nasty response to this question because how would it feel to suddenly be walked up on and startled to within an inch of your life?

However, I reminded myself of just how attractive he was, and it didn't take long for me to lose my annoyance just from staring up into his gorgeous blue eyes and slightly tinted pink lips. It had to be from the wine, I was sure because there was no way in hell those were their natural flush. I mean, he would just be too freaking unreal.

"No," I shook my head, barely audible, and he glanced back toward the restaurant; that move made his scent all of a sudden even more pronounced, and after smelling nothing but tobacco and garlic for the past several hours, he almost damn near brought tears to my eyes. He smelled like vanilla and lime, and sweetness, and sex, and cleanliness, and sex, and I wanted to sniff him in like drugs.

"I couldn't help but notice your distress," he said, and my fantasizing brain came to a screeching halt.

"What?" I asked, and he smiled slightly compassionately.

"Do you want me to take a recording?" he asked. "I'm witnessing a good distance from your table, or maybe my partner could do it? This way, you'll have evidence if you ever want to file a lawsuit?"

There was a lot of information coming at me all at once, and I truly did not know how to process it.

"Uh... " I began as he reached into his wallet and produced a business card. I looked at it but couldn't really process anything beyond the fact that it said law firm. I looked up once again at him, and he smiled.

"Should I go ahead? Then you can bring it to the office whenever you want, and I'll get someone to work on it for you."

"No," I immediately refused and handed the card back to him. However, he didn't accept it.

"Why?" he asked, and the truth almost spilled out. *This was New York, and I could barely afford food and rent already, not to mention a freaking law firm. I wasn't about to bankrupt myself and get blacklisted from ever being able to work as a secretary or personal assistant of any kind, thank you very much.*

"No," I smiled, bringing out the most sweetest and polite smile I could muster. "No thank you. Everything is fine. Thanks. Thank you."

He stared at me, and for the first time in so long, I felt such shame that I was denying my pain. However, as I noted the wealth he radiated, that pain and shame instantly disappeared because I understood that someone like him could never understand the pain of being born by someone like me. He probably came here to eat every day and thought nothing of it. He was physically allergic to suits that cost less than five thousand dollars in his closet, and he had a personal driver, while I had to constantly endure the dangers and disgust of the train.

"No," I replied, even more firmly, straightening my back and lifting my chin. "I'm fine."

To my surprise, he didn't push or even argue.

"Okay," he said. "Do you want to keep the card, regardless?"

Simply because he wanted to see some sort of further reaction from me, I rejected the offer again.

"No thank you."

"Alright," he said and continued on his way.

He didn't try to convince me; he didn't try to use this as a segue into asking me out. He offered his help simply, and when rejected, continued on with his life as though absolutely nothing out of the ordinary had happened. I didn't quite know how to feel, so all I could do was watch him as he returned to his seat, and then I met the gaze of the woman seated by him. She gave me a sympathetic look that definitely made me feel ashamed from all the way across the room, and so I lowered my head and, for no reason whatsoever, returned to the bathroom.

Chapter 3

Guy

"Poor girl," Gloria said as I returned to my seat after such a fruitless endeavor. "It's not her fault she's such a looker. Absolutely gorgeous."

I didn't respond, and that was because I knew she would see in my eyes just how much I agreed with her, and I wasn't about to give her this reason to further tease me into favoring secretaries because of their looks.

I had noticed her from the moment she appeared outside the restaurant until she got in. That gorgeous face, pouty lips, and gray eyes were etched into my memory like nothing else, and for the first time in a very long while, the plate before me didn't satisfy me. Though I was almost done with it, I suddenly felt famished all over again, but this time around it was absolutely not for food. Instead, it was for hard, sheet-clawing fucking, and the woman behind me was who I wanted to let off steam with.

This was incredibly amusing to me, given that I had just approached her to help her escape from that predator of a man, but here I was picturing her legs wrapped around my back and my cock in her mouth.

"It is her fault," I said offhandedly, and Gloria gave me a look.

"I have to go meet Al," she said quickly, brushing off her meal. "You'll be ready to give serious consideration to these candidates tomorrow, right? I'm going to leave the folder with you."

I was silent for a little while as I polished off the glass of wine, and then I nodded.

"I'll try to make your job even easier," I said, and she laughed. She rose to her feet, pressed a kiss to my cheek, and went on her way. I was ready to leave as well, but I found myself lingering in the restaurant. My back was to her table, so I couldn't exactly turn around to watch her, but I waited for her to return from the bathroom. She was no doubt going to pass by my table, and I just wanted to ensure that she was okay.

Perhaps she was reluctant to take my extended hand of help because she needed the job. I was once like her, and so I could understand her reluctance.

I sat there until eventually, she emerged from the bathroom. She was quite decently dressed, no doubt forced to over-hype perhaps more than the average New York woman because of all of these nonsense advances that she had to fend off from clients.

She was dressed in a blood-red skirt suit that fit her body in a way that I couldn't look away from. It wasn't her fault that she was just the way she was, curved to absolute perfection, and I didn't even think it could be hidden unless she wore a massive, oversized coat of some sort.

She avoided my eyes pointedly as she walked past, however, I caught the whiff of her scent. It smelled sweet but a bit bitter at the same time, and it etched the memory of her in my mind.

There was nothing more I could do here, and it seemed as though she could handle herself, so I rose to my feet and considered heading back to the office. However, due to the erection I was now sporting, I finally gave my attention to Charles as he opened the door for me to get into the back of the town car, I decided to call it a day.

I wanted to fuck so badly, but there was no one I wanted but that woman, of course. Given the stress of the day, I truly didn't have the energy to deal with another human being, so I simply headed back home and hopped into the shower. I tried to make it cold to cool me down, but somehow that made my body temperature spike even further, so I simply stood under the cool water and decided to stop torturing myself.

I was still hard, so I held my cock in my hand and began to stroke. It had been forever since I had done this since I had needed this kind of cheap relief, and so it was a bit uncomfortable to be jacking off in my bathroom. It made me feel weak and silly, but I needed to get a good night's rest, so I went as hard as I could with her in mind until my breath shortened. It didn't take long. Thirty seconds, and I was coming hard and strong. My hands were full, and as I stared down at the release, I couldn't help but shake my head.

Turning in order to rinse off the stain, I thought of the woman once more and wondered if I would ever see her again. I regretted the fact that I hadn't even considered trying to keep in touch with her, but ultimately, I blamed the bastards she was with because if I didn't think of that, the last thing I wanted was to harass her even further with male attention. She was so fucking attractive, and it should have been a blessing, but I understood as well how that could bring more troubles than opportunities. Shaking my head and now immensely relieved, I got out of the shower, toweled myself dry, and headed straight to bed.

Enjoyed the sample?
Please pre-order here:
THE BET

About the Author

Thank you so much for reading!
If you have enjoyed the book and would like to leave a
precious review for me, please kindly do so here:

The Bride's Brother

Please click on the link below to receive info about my latest
releases and giveaways.
NEVER MISS A THING

Or
come say 'hello' here:

Also by Iona Rose